I0754845

ALSO BY MORGAN THOMAS

Manywhere: Stories

MAD EDEN

MAD EDEN

A NOVEL

Morgan Thomas

MCD
FARRAR, STRAUS AND GIROUX
NEW YORK

MCD
Farrar, Straus and Giroux
120 Broadway, New York 10271

EU Representative: Macmillan Publishers Ireland Ltd, 1st Floor,
The Liffey Trust Centre, 117–126 Sheriff Street Upper, Dublin 1, D01 YC43

Printed in the United States of America
First edition, 2026

Grateful acknowledgment is made for permission to reprint lines
from "Love Letters," from *Trees Witness Everything,* by Victoria Chang.
Copyright © 2022 by Victoria Chang. Reprinted with the permission of
The Permissions Company, LLC, on behalf of the author and
Copper Canyon Press, coppercanyonpress.org.

Library of Congress Control Number: 2026933602
ISBN: 978-0-374-62015-8

Designed by Gretchen Achilles

www.mcdbooks.com • www.fsgbooks.com
Follow us on social media at @mcdbooks and @fsgbooks

10 9 8 7 6 5 4 3 2 1

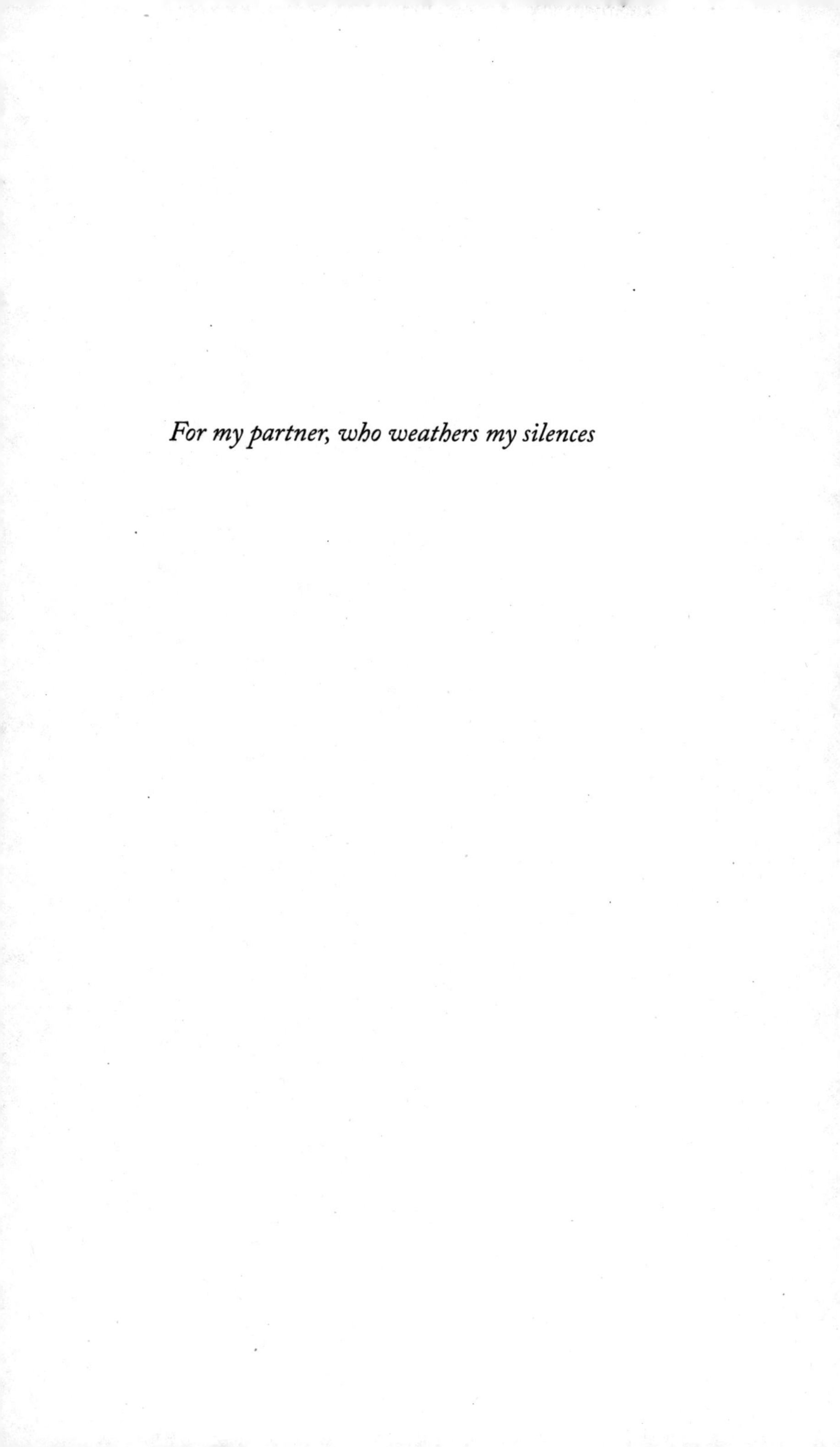

For my partner, who weathers my silences

MAD EDEN

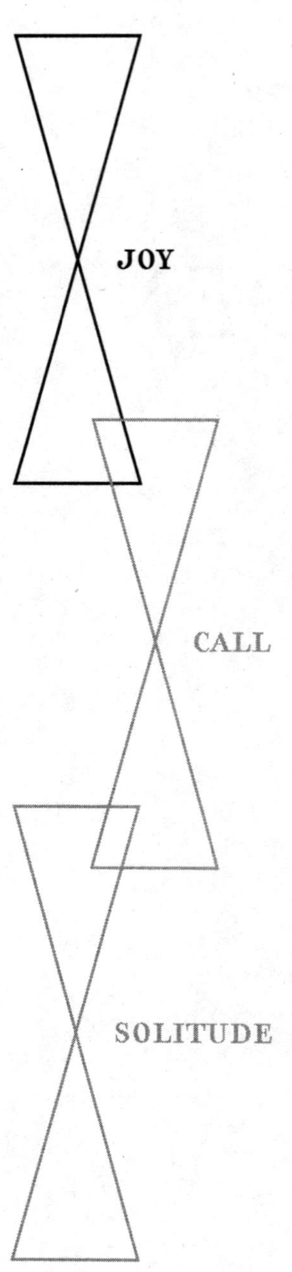

ELSEWHERE

I want to tell you, simply, how joyful we were that summer. Joyful, that word which suggests two separate things: a substance and its vessel. Joy stalked us, and when it pounced we were saturated. Wring our bodies, and the joy would drip from us like dirty water. Separate but not distinct, as Christ is both the substance and the vessel of God, but without the Christianity, with a healthy dose instead of devilry, which from the outside looked like idleness or, based on the later testimony of family and friends, like madness.

When I've attempted, in the past, to describe this joy—to my friend Eva, to my therapist—they both asked the same question: What made you so joyful? What were the reasons? Reasons don't interest me—what I want is a cause beyond reasons. But here they are, the glut of explanations I offered them. There was the sun, to begin, shining each morning. It was a magnificent spring, all afternoon thunderstorm and wind. By summer the pine flats were flooded, and the marshes were on fire. Nothing was where it should be. It was early in the sixth extinction and late in the pandemic. To be inside was to subject your lungs to the possible virus, to be outside was to subject them to smoke. I was two months out of the hospital—long enough that the turbulence had passed, short enough that the world still felt charged with the luster I associate with close calls. The stay hadn't been entirely bad, though I had nightmares of prone holds all through that summer of joy, and any time sirens sounded, spiraling up in pitch, that Doppler effect that signaled approach, I gritted my teeth. I wriggled. I asked Liam whether the sirens were coming to our house, and Liam said they weren't, and if the noise continued I asked again. I asked again. Sometimes, I begged. I would do anything. Anything, please, I said. Liam listened to my pleas grimly. They lay atop me—a live weighted blanket—and said they'd promise never again to call the police if I'd promise never again to try to kill myself. An impasse we abandoned, each time, as soon as the sirens faded. The hospital where I had spent one week would be sued, the next year, by mental health advocates after a patient suffocated at the bottom of a staff dogpile, but that has little to do with the joy that is our focus here, is related to it only through negation. I had gotten out, and there were few sirens that summer given our nearest neighbor was across a large retention pond, some distance away. The hospitalization had led to an autism diagnosis, which had put an end to my getting testosterone prescribed by any local clinic, an effect that had surprised me given there was no law prohibiting the prescribing of testosterone for an autistic adult, not then, but the nurse at my local clinic needed a doctor to sign off on the prescription, and the doctors were scared and busy, and if the diagnosis had closed off this possibility, it had created others in its place, possibilities largely of language—meltdown instead of panic attack, stimming instead of self-harm, burnout instead of depression. The words were not meant to be comforting, borrowed as they were from descriptions of malfunctioning machines—an overloaded circuit, the accidental melting of a nuclear reactor core—but there was promise in these new phrases, a hopeful, even a joyful, promise. What it meant, though the psychologist hadn't framed it this way, had instead used words like disorder and impairment and black-and-white and pathological, what it meant was that the trauma I had searched for with hypnotists and therapists to explain my social ineptitude, my hatred of touch, my hard startle at loud noises, could be forgotten. It had never existed. My life had been the lucky, charmed life I'd suspected, and this was a part of my joy, and the peach tea we drank was a part, and the tomatoes we picked up each week from our neighbor in exchange for helping with whatever small tasks she needed—stapling the screen back on to the screen door, burning trash, loading up her recycling in our car to take it eighteen miles to the center—were a part, and so was our proximity to cold spring water in which we could submerge, and our drinking water, which flowed from an underground lens, water that was silky and full-bodied and tasted of earth, and our decision not to marry after attending the wedding of Liam's close friends, a straight couple who had read "Having a Coke with You" in lieu of their vows and so made the decision for us, as we couldn't very well choose the same reading, and a wedding without O'Hara didn't interest us, and our decision not to reproduce, which we had made after watching, from our screened-in porch, a tattered sparrow parent, harried by their larger offspring, offer food again and again into the chick's smug, ever-ready beak. We had decided it solemnly, we were of an age where such a decision had to be made. If we wanted to wait, things needed to be frozen, some part of us held still in time. And there was hate, of course, that constant. Or prejudice, whatever word you prefer, there was plenty of it that summer and more would come. The governor was trying to shut down R House, and we were no longer using public restrooms, and Liam had canceled a workshop at a local youth center—the organizers were worried about it drawing the wrong sort of attention—and the paper I'd cowritten with several colleagues on intersex considerations in gender-affirming care for minors was pulled from an academic journal after being accepted, edited, and proofed, a decision, they explained in a terse email, they'd made to safeguard the journal's reputation, and this doesn't sound like joy, perhaps it is gauche to say that joy came from this, what joy could come, but there was joy, somehow, in our surviving in this place that intended to be inhospitable to us, I felt it sometimes when biting into a slice of garden-grown cucumber marinated in balsamic or diving into the ever-cool waters of the spring, how the state mounted a threat to our joy, how the state seemed increasingly to want to destroy it, and how we, therefore, guarded the joy more steadfastly.

But all of these things, even taken together, fail to explain the joy. They are reasons, not causes. Insufficient. Ad hoc. The more I lay them out, the more the joy seems alien, fantastic. A magic trick. Something that descended upon us without concern for our worthiness, our effort, the facts of our lives, even without our consent. Our life of joy was, qualitatively, no different from the life that had felt unbearable to me just months before. What had changed—the season, the brand of yogurt I ate in the mornings—couldn't account for the sheer ebullience of those days. Yes, it was after the hospital, but not immediately after. Yes, we had decided not to have children, but that was a decision we'd made many times before, it had never rung out across our lives the way the joy did, chime and echo. Yes, the bills had passed the state legislatures, but mostly earlier, in the spring, and we had been angry then, and afraid. They went into effect that summer, but this can't be the reason for the joy, no more than flood or wildfire or the temperatures, which regularly broke the sort of records you don't want to break. Everything is moving in the wrong direction. Nothing maps to the joy's earliest hours precisely. Its tendrils reach back, back. When did we first feel it? Was it the week we lost internet at the cabin, when I worked from a nearby bar, helping families in states with gender-affirming care bans access care for their kids without saying the word gender, the word ban? Was it the week the beloved trans comic book writer died and everyone on the boards spoke not about grief (the grief a given) but about the near miracle of the cause of her death—not suicide, not homicide, just her body giving out the way bodies eventually do? I don't know. Other people, maybe, have memories arranged like coat hangers along time's linear axis, marching left to right, all of them neatly in the past tense or—if you select one—shifting obediently to the past perfect to mark the divide between past (selected, remembered, continuous) and past past. My memories are mostly bucketed. A bucket for stress. A bucket for shame. Some would pathologize this.

An impairment in the ability to place stimuli in context with what came before and after leaves people with autism struggling with a seemingly capricious world that makes excruciating demands on their attention—this is something I read in a *Los Angeles Times* article summarizing a scientific paper titled *Autism as a Disorder of Prediction*, which was published in the *Proceedings of the National Academy of Sciences* and made famous, at least on the boards, by *Mad Eden*.

Capricious, that word whose origin might be the Latin *capra*—goat—or the Italian *capo*—head—plus *riccio*—hedgehog. A goatlike world, a hedgehog world. Sure. There's a reason the Knights Templar were accused of worshipping Baphomet. There's a reason the devil, that ancient dragon, has cleft hoof and curving horn. Bucketing serves me well enough. It lets me down only when, as now, I need to find a beginning. Where does a full bucket begin? At the well or the spring or the goat's teat. In short, elsewhere.

It might have been the week Quentin, who was not our child, at least not by blood nor in any legal way, though he called himself our child, or sometimes our son, came to visit. He stopped by on his way to start college in Missouri, a summer semester. His visit was a surprise—we'd thought he'd start in the fall—which disqualifies it immediately from the bucket of joy, but it butts up against it, sits adjacent to it. Why not begin there?

He arrived on a bus up from Tampa. Liam met him at the station, left the house with the frenetic, anxious care that characterized their interactions with Quentin. When the two of them returned home I was sitting in the dark. How long had Liam been gone? I don't know. Liam calls this temporal dissociation dog time, since it causes us to greet each other enthusiastically whether the other has been gone minutes or days, but in this instance I don't greet them enthusiastically. I don't greet them at all. I am wholly absorbed. I am reading *Mad Eden*. That should place it in time for you. I'm reading the first installment, which has just been posted to the boards. Liam says, "Hello? Honey, I'm home?" Liam says to Quentin, "Ignore them, they're being rude. You're being rude, Ro." I half hear it. I am reading. *Mad Eden* begins like this:

Nova is a magician, albeit a bad one. They have exceptional magical abilities, but they have no understanding of sameness. Nor do they understand cause and effect. Due to this, they are the only magician in their college who is not allowed to attend the scientific ritual performed daily to keep the dragnos away.

Dragnos are the first magical beings of the world, great winged things who evolved to drive humans mad, as this made them easier to hunt. That no human had been taken by a dragno in recent memory is only thanks to the magicians' adherence to rituals, their insistence on sameness. If a dragno can't differentiate between humans, it can't hunt them.

Nova is different. They walk with an individual gait. They don't adopt appropriate foot placement or body posture or mouth shaping during speech articulation. They can't even catch a ball. It is only due to the magician Markov's absence that they are allowed to attend the ritual on the day in question.

"Don't let me down," says Hans, the only magician who is kind to them.

Nova tries. They rise at the same time as the other magicians, digest the same simple roots, and walk, at the same time and in the same way as the others, into the libby where the ritual will take place. For a moment, they feel it: sameness. Beside the other magicians, they start to say the magical language they've studied for years.

"The fundamental prerequisite for extraction is hypermalleability, which mitigates monitored mechanisms," the magicians say. In the center of the libby is a dragno body, descaled so you can see the muscle and veins, the brain and heart.

It is the first time Nova has seen a dragno. They should look the other magicians in the eyes, but instead they look at the dragno. As they observe it, the dragno starts to sing. The music unravels the magicians' language; Nova nearly fails to say, "Suppressing sustains probabilistically," but catches themselves just in time. "Pleneum splinters a stochastic spectrum," Nova says, and through its music the dragno says, *The hidden*, then makes a sound Nova can't understand—soulières? schultz?

"Transcriptomic trends," Nova says, and the dragno says, *The hidden scale is here*.

It takes Nova a moment to recognize that the magicians near them have stopped the ritual. The magical language has to be said in precisely the same way by all magicians for the ritual to be a success. Nova has failed to maintain the sequence. The magicians are looking at them. Nova reddens. "Validated," they try. "Wiesendanger."

"So impaired," says the magician on their left. "Your deficits," says another, "I can see them."

Hans looks down at them. "Even the smallest breach is a crisis," he says. Nova has no response. The abbot approaches and says, "Nova, come with me."

The abbot leads them away from the others. "What did it say?"

Nova's anxiety intensifies. They have no script for this. Hearing dragnos is abnormal, bad, a threat to sameness. "I don't know," Nova says.

"What did you hear?"

"I—" Before Nova knows what they will say, they glimpse movement. Wings. A dragno picks them up in its large mouth and takes them away.

I am pinching my top lip between finger and thumb, tugging absently at the pucker of skin at its center. Then Liam's hand is on my shoulder. When I look up, they say, "You could come and welcome Quentin, Ro." My computer is the only light on in the house. Darkness has fallen without my noticing. "You could give Quentin a hug, help with his bag," Liam says. "You could help me with dinner." They list these possibilities in the conditional tense. I say, understanding some game is afoot, "I could go back in the bedroom and finish reading this." Liam says, "You could take Quentin's bag." Their repetition settles it, makes clear the imperative that played an undercurrent to their conditional tense all along. Liam's communication skills often flag when we have company.

"I can take Quentin's bag," I say, and the shift of tense makes it possible, as I say it, to stand from the chair and move toward Quentin, who has watched all of this with a tight expression, which is maybe nerves or hunger or perhaps some doubt about his place here.

"Welcome," I say to Quentin, so that Quentin won't doubt. He is wearing a mask over nose and mouth. The pandemic was still on, after all, and Liam had been hospitalized the year before it began with pneumonia, which caused a lung abscess, and their doctor told them to avoid this new virus "like the plague."

Quentin has a large duffel for his clothes and electronics and a small trembling pouch strapped discreetly beneath his jacket for his rat, whose name is Honeycub. Honeycub is a white rat with pink eyes and is sickly, her kidneys failing slowly due to age and genetics and too much protein in her diet. Her disease worries Liam and me. We aren't sure how Quentin will manage without her. Honeycub is the only creature Quentin brought along when he was emancipated at sixteen, the only creature who traveled with him from childhood into sudden adulthood. I dodge Quentin's attempted hug by grabbing the duffel bag. This isn't a slight. Quentin is one of the few people in the world I love.

"Didn't think to turn the air down?" Liam says. It's sweltering in the small cabin. I am sweating, but I haven't pressed the buttons to lower the temperature on the AC. It rarely occurs to me to manipulate my environment to maximize comfort. To sweep so I might avoid the sensation of grit on the soles of my feet. To adjust heat or fan. To turn on lights when the sky darkens. When I am fully stymied by my environment, as when the light becomes too low to read the book that has kept me awake after sunset, I usually sleep. This, at least, is how I lived when I lived alone. With Liam, the lights adjust themselves, coaxed by Liam's attentive, sensitive hands. Liam does not tease me, not usually, for my lack of initiative on this front, but now they say, "Didn't think to turn a light on?"

Quentin says, "Nice place," and Liam says, "Thank you." Neither of these comments makes sense. The house is a mess, and it isn't ours. It belongs to a friend's aunt. It is a generosity, our staying here. The friend's aunt broke her foot descending the stairs in her home in Charlotte and couldn't make it, this year, out to the cabin she bought for thirty thousand dollars forty years ago. As long as we keep up with the electricity and the internet bills, as long as we don't mind the lack of hot water, the lack of insulation, which means the walls are porous, prone to inhabitation by wolf spiders and anoles and ring-necked snakes, as long as we clear any trees that blow down in the summer storms, edge the few tufts of grass that hazard to root along the driveway, we can stay.

This was how we'd been living for a year at that point—writing residencies when Liam could get them, couches when we could get them, single rooms we found on Craigslist for two hundred dollars, the rest of the rent waived if we were willing to help feed and walk the owner's elderly dog, an uncle's place, a friend's place, a life we described to our friends and our colleagues as adventurous, free, which it was, but it was also true that Liam would receive exactly six thousand dollars for the translation on which they'd been working for four months, that I made twenty-five thousand a year at the nonprofit where I worked remotely, the least of my colleagues, a fact that comforted me, as did my job title—patient navigation junior assistant. I was the only white person on staff, and I wanted to be paid little enough that I wouldn't need to worry as much about privilege, as if privilege could be undone by making a few thousand dollars less in annual salary. We had the sense, too, that our luck would run out eventually, that we'd be stuck paying rent within a year, and so we lived frugally, saving for this eventuality. The result was a weekly budget that allotted fifteen dollars for gas, sixty dollars for food, a budget we managed by living off beans and rice. Lettuce was a treat. Oat milk was a treat. Raspberries were unheard of.

Quentin turns to me. "I like your hair, you do it yourself?" My hair is buzzed almost to nothing. I did it myself with the dull clippers we lug from place to place. Is he being cruel? I know that sometimes compliments are cruel, and I am unable to determine his intentions. Despite my love I am a little cowed by Quentin—his humor, which was sometimes crude; his masculinity, which was sometimes smelly; his size, as he was taller than Liam or me, a height that belied any genetic link; and, most of all, his appearance in my life, which I couldn't fully account for. When had he become our son? I marveled at the blurry chain of cause and effect that ended at that word. Perhaps it began when Liam paid for his lunch at the regional youth conference where they were teaching, an act of distant, professional generosity, something they did for any student who looked at the menu at the restaurant with a surprised, vaguely panicked expression Liam recognized from years of scraping by, or when Quentin reached out about college writing scholarships, asking if Liam knew of any that covered full tuition for out-of-state students, or when Liam paid the application fees for the scholarships they'd recommended, knowing if they didn't pay the applications wouldn't be submitted, a lithe, human knowing specific to Liam, or after Quentin had slept with his roommate and needed a few days away from the house to sort things out, so he spent four days in the apartment in Gainesville where we'd lived at the time.

We paid for his SAT and a third of his rent, sent funds regularly through an app—gas$food$—and I wondered why this sharing of resources had worked the alchemy I'd been unable to work in other relationships, changing what might have felt like mentorship or friendship into something easily recognized as family.

Liam is telling Quentin a story. In Montana, last year, during the first major cold snap, they'd returned from a night in Bozeman to find me in a sleeping bag on the couch, every jacket on, the heating untouched. They say, "My love for Ro, and Ro's love for yoghurt," pronouncing the *h*, and I know they've excused, with this quote, whatever it is in me—my laziness or focus, which have both been described as inhuman—that causes me to forget the body and its needs.

"Sorry," I say, and then, in a rush, giving myself license for a moment, "I was reading *Mad Eden*. It repurposes a scientific article to create a fantasy story, I think you'd like it." I say this to both Liam and Quentin. I don't actually think either of them would like *Mad Eden*, but I know you are supposed to talk at length only about things you'd recommend to your audience.

If you are not autistic, if you are not active on the boards, you may have made it to this point in your life without being aware of *Mad Eden*, which was posted on Reddit in five installments during that summer of joy. It is based on *Autism as a Disorder of Prediction*, which was published nine years before. Not just based, sourced from. Every word in *Mad Eden* comes from that paper. **Impaired** is from *impaired prediction can potentially account for a few other significant* *correlates of autism.* **Hidden** from *Modeling idea generation sequences using hidden Markov models.* **Scale** from *different tasks rely on the detection of interevent relationships over varying time-scales.* **Wings** doesn't appear in the original article, but *leg-swinging* appears. This seems to be within the rules. The original article contains about 1,900 discrete words, which determine the bounds of *Mad Eden.*

Dragno is an exception. It comes from the word *diagnosis*—the last two letters left off, and the *i* turned into an *r*. Dragnos in *Mad Eden* are like dragons, or at least this is how I read it. I am already inclined to see dragons everywhere. As a child I was captivated by all their possible forms—the beaked byrds and the earthwyrms and the cotton-mouthed wyrms that I, to my mother's horror, once tried to touch.

It was a nurse in the hospital who led me to *Mad Eden.* She had an autistic child and some traits herself, and she recognized them in me. She couldn't officially provide a diagnosis, but she recommended a psychologist who, after four hours of analysis, did, the psychologist sending my diagnosis via email three weeks later. The nurse had told me about *Autism as a Disorder of Prediction*, found its observations useful, and it was while searching for that article that I stumbled upon *Mad Eden.* The first installment was posted just one day before I found it, as if it were written for me.

But this is the wrong direction. I'm trying to tell this story the way a story is supposed to be told. This happened, which caused this to happen, which caused this to happen. To march resolutely forward along the clothesline of memory toward joy, but I've already lost the wire.

After—

After dinner—

After dinner, we—

Before my diagnosis, I complained to my colleague Eva about this failure of linear causal memory, and she suggested I consider the special theory of relativity. The theory of relativity insists that an event is affected not by the past writ large but by its backward-facing light cone, the area of spacetime from which light has traveled to reach it. The study of causality is really the study of light, Eva said. Eva studied the philosophy of science in college, started a PhD, and abandoned it when her thesis advisor, the only other Black person in the department, was ousted in a sexual assault scandal, an ousting that wasn't unjustified—he had been sleeping with students—but was unjust—the white professors who did the ousting had been sleeping with students, too. She'd considered returning to school for social work, but then she got the job at St. Cat, the Southern Trans Care Access Taskforce, where no one cared about the letters after her name. Her approach to life remained indebted to her coursework, hence the light cones. To arrange events in linear time—which is, according to Eva, to invent time, creating its linear flow by approximating it—you denote an event as your starting place, then consider its two light cones. One light cone expands outward from the event toward all of its effects, into what, in common parlance, we'd call the future. The other cone expands backward, encompassing all possible causes. The scope of the light cones is bounded by the speed of light. Thread these light cones and all associated light cones like party hats on a string, and you've charted one possible path of a particle through time.

So, okay. Here we are within the backward-facing light cone of the joy, which I imagine, inaccurately, as a roving searchlight, scanning across the detritus of all that had to happen for the joy to be. Liam hid a note in a ceramic pig. Quentin squalled in a NICU. The first dolphin ever trained to do so leapt through a hoop. This isn't helping.

Filter, maybe, by relevance. Take *Mad Eden*. It's safe to say that in the backward-facing light cone of *Mad Eden*, published online in 2023, are the *Etymologies* of Isidore of Seville, published around 625 and including this description of dracontites:

> [It] is forcibly taken from the brain of a dragon, and unless it is cut from the living creature it does not have the quality of a gem. For this reason, magicians cut it out of dragons while they are sleeping. For bold men explore the cave of the dragons, and scatter medicated grains there to put them to sleep, and in this way cut off their heads while they are sunk in sleep and take out the gems.

This is the origin, as I see it, of *Mad Eden*'s feud between magicians and dragons. Well, dragnos. And in the backward-facing light cone of the *Etymologies* is the New Testament:

> And behold a great red dragon, having seven heads and ten horns, and seven crowns upon his heads. And his tail drew the third part of the stars of heaven, and did cast them to the earth: and the dragon stood be-

> fore the woman which was ready to be delivered, for to devour her child as soon as it was born. And she brought forth a man child, who was to rule all nations with a rod of iron: and her child was caught up unto God, and to his throne. . . . And to the woman were given two wings of a great eagle, that she might fly into the wilderness, into her place, where she is nourished for a time, and times, and half a time.

And in the forward-facing light cone of these texts was DraconiteDragon on YouTube, posting walkthroughs of *Roblox* and *Minecraft* always with the same catchy intro song, and in the forward-facing light cone of that YouTube account was Quentin using the walkthroughs as a salve when he couldn't sleep, and then Liam, humming the intro song absentmindedly while threading a new drawstring through the waistband of Quentin's sweatpants, but I can't use this method to place Liam saying, somewhat desperate, to Quentin, "Anything else you need to get done while you're here? Anything else we should fix?" Was this before they fixed the drawstring? Were the sweatpants offered up as a response to this query? Or was it after—the pants fixed, the days stretching, Quentin on his phone, me on my computer, Liam bouncing between us? In what order do I string these party hats? How can I place the image of Liam rubbing a stain out of Quentin's khakis? Or the morning when, as we ate breakfast, Liam told Quentin about our courtship—how we had lived on the same street in Gainesville but for a year didn't meet in person, choosing instead to send handwritten messages, which we stuffed into an old ceramic piggy bank and hid all over town for the other to find until eventually the piggy bank was lost in Paynes Prairie, an asynchronous courting I still remember as glowy with excitement and intrigue, which ended when Liam invited me to coffee, and I accepted with trepidation—I don't like coffee or most teas, and I don't particularly like conversation—and we talked for an hour, and I spent the three hours after tracing every twist of our conversation, planning what I would say next time, if I was invited to coffee again? Or the image of Quentin tugging out slowly, from under the couch, a dusty rosary, its wooden beads dented as if chewed? And alongside these memories, I am supposed to somehow intersperse the hours I spent in front of my computer, helping a seventeen-year-old trans woman figure out how to continue the estrogen therapy her RN can no longer prescribe, or a nonbinary teen in Mississippi with vaginal atrophy find a local prescriber to adjust his dose of T, or a seven-year-old in West Virginia establish care with a therapist who can help her come out at school.

When researchers asked participants to take the tea bag out of the tea after three minutes or put butter on the table six minutes before hypothetical guests arrived, autistic adults performed less well than neurotypicals. When researchers asked participants to determine whether or not a flash and beep were simultaneous, autistic teens performed less well than neurotypicals. When parents of autistic children were given the *It's About Time* questionnaire, results suggested autistic children have trouble preparing for future events.

All of this is supposed to indicate abnormality, and you might, at this point, be ready to agree. After all, where are we in the story we are telling about Quentin's visit, which lasted some finite number of days divided up into some finite number of hours divided up into some finite number of seconds, which are defined as 9,192,631,770 periods of the transition between two hyperfine states of decaying cesium-133 atoms? This regimented and arbitrary clock time means little to me though it does make a certain poetic sense, looking out at the world, that our most accurate clocks carefully portion out decay.

One parent, filling out the *It's About Time* questionnaire, said of her son, He can get anxious if he feels that he is 'losing time.' We are losing time, loosed of it. And yet, in spite of this, I am rarely late for anything, and on the day that matters to us now, I am right on time to meet my 1:00 p.m. clients.

My first client is a mother and her thirteen-year-old son. They're living in Kentucky. He wants to be on puberty blockers, and both parents are supportive, and they have some money saved up. I meet with them on a virtual platform, as I do with all of my clients. Their box unfolds beside my box, revealing the mother's shoulder and back—she is leaning forward, slightly flustered, maybe some trouble with the technology. I eat a single blue candy and give my desk two light slaps for readiness. A ritual of sorts. Not religious, but adjacent to religion. We, at St. Cat, are not above prayer. For guidance. For protection. For the sort of dumb luck on which injunctions and court cases sometimes turn—let the defense lawyer be leaving this evening for his honeymoon, let the judge have had a filling lunch. I pull up the honesty attestation on my screen: This is a confidential meeting. Recording is not allowed. The attestation is an attempt to decrease St. Cat's legal liability, though we all know it wouldn't hold up in court.

I say, "Welcome, how are you," into my microphone, less a question than a tech check, trying to gauge whether they can hear me. Their background is low-lit—a cluttered kitchen, a whole chicken thawing by the sink. The angle of the camera is wrong, a downward tilt, so I can see the boy's shoes—Nike tennis shoes, new. The calls are scripted. I have a list of questions on a sticky note beside my keyboard, though by this point I have the flow memorized, a useful patterning. I know to ask about transportation before asking about insurance to make it less likely that I'll offer false hope.

"Doing fine," the mother says. "You want to introduce yourself?" This to the boy, who spins once in his chair, ends up facing away from the camera. "He's being shy now. Been going on about this for hours." I ask for his date of birth. She rattles it off and answers my next questions easily—commercial health insurance that won't cover out-of-state care, transportation not a problem, family in New York.

"Like I said he's been on about this for ages, decided recently he's gendered fluid."

"Genderfluid," her son corrects. Using the toes of his new shoes, he spins to face his mother. He says the word slowly, enunciating for her benefit, but his correction is useful for me as well. I've been taught to look for things like this. In a security training at St. Cat, the trainer described differences in language between the two political sides: "When one side is saying people with uteruses, and the other side is saying biological women, you can learn a lot about what media someone's been consuming by paying attention to the language they use." With her son there beside her, his look of impatience, I'm unworried.

"Isn't that what I said?" she says. Then, looking at me, "Well, we can travel, within reason. They can't come after us, can they? For taking him out of the state?" This is a more difficult question than it seems. "We haven't seen suits against parents except in cases where one parent is bringing suit against the other," I say. "Well, we're willing to travel," she says. "And we can pay." She says this abruptly, almost boasting. An appeal to some common value—sacrifice, maybe, or thrift. "We just want to buy him some time."

I explain about the direct flight that runs Tuesday evenings between Nashville and JFK, tickets just sixty-four dollars if you book well enough in advance. I explain about the nonprofit that links families traveling for care to volunteer drivers. I give them the phone number of our New York safe house. I suggest a specific doctor at a specific clinic. There's a three-month waiting list, but they're hiring on a new clinician, and I'll put in a word, see if I can get him in sooner. The boy no longer fidgets. I watch the side of his face as I say all of this, the slow kick of his shoes, which stops when I stop speaking. I explain that the medical system's legal team shut down a program that allowed patients traveling from out of state to pay less than the local, insured patient population. In this context, a shot of Lupron costs more than two thousand dollars.

"Two thousand?" the mother says, and the repetition warms me. This style of communication I understand easily, how her echoing of my words, her addition of an upward lilt on the final syllable, tells me the total is not within reason, the previously comforting bulk of her savings paling before the cost. I give her a discount code. With the discount code, the cost falls to seventeen hundred dollars. Buying time for her son must be set against buying food and gasoline. "That's every three months?" she says. "That's monthly," I say. The boy hasn't noticed her distress. He spins in his chair. He is facing me again. There is a ready expression on his face. His mother clasps her hands tightly. She provides for her son. The chicken is expensive, maybe free-range. His sneakers are new, the ones he wanted. She is quiet. "That's our best option?" Her tone is polite, an edge beneath.

I tell her to double-check the insurance coverage. Most companies with out-of-state exclusions still cover prescription medications, and in some cases this includes blockers.

"And if ours doesn't?"

I tell her that Depo-Provera is an option if it's the menses that are especially distressing. It's billed as birth control, and it's inexpensive. She softens a little at this. I should tell her that Depo-Provera also causes increased chest size in some people, a side effect likely to distress a thirteen-year-old boy, but I am unable to bring the words forth, unable to rupture the fragile return of her hope. It shouldn't come to that, and if it does the doctor will tell them, so I finish by laying out the logistics.

My next client is a forty-year-old trans woman on Oklahoma Medicaid. She needs a genioplasty, and even if Medicaid would cover it, no one in Oklahoma will perform it. I ask about primary care, hormones, but she's got that covered. I suggest a local community clinic that I know takes Medicaid. "It's a primary care clinic, but they'll know more about options for surgery locally," I say, and she says, "I told you I'm not looking for primary care." She's frustrated. She thinks I'm not understanding. I am understanding, I just don't have much to offer. Finally, I say, "How attached are you to the place you're living?" "It's home," she says, "but that doesn't mean I wouldn't hop a train if somebody handed me a ticket." I give her a list of states in which Medicaid covers facial surgeries. "How am I supposed to get there?" I have little enough to offer—a cab voucher, the link to a form on a nonprofit website that might get her five hundred dollars if she completes the application to the letter. "But I mean how am I supposed to get there. I have a life here." Increasingly desperate, I give her the name of the person who runs a trans support group in Northampton and often has leads on inexpensive housing—room shares and cheap studios. "I'm not saying this is the best option," I say. I show her an example of a crowdfunding page that raised two thousand dollars for a family's journey from Florida to Connecticut. "This is your professional advice?" "My professional advice is that you talk to a primary care provider and go from there." "That's not going to help. I'm not looking for primary care." I gesture to the crowdfunding page on my screen.

The call ends, and I am alone. Liam and Quentin are elsewhere. "See you later," Liam said, and I echoed, "See you later." "Love you," Liam said, and I echoed, "Love you." I used to think little of these echoes, how often my responses add meaning not through the words I choose but through the specific rhythm with which I repeat them. Didn't all lovers create their own nonsense languages? Weren't all rituals of greeting and parting repetitive, a variant of the peace, my favorite part of church services as a child? But after the hospital, I tended to these echoes, considered them proof of some autistic legitimacy. "Don't have too much fun without us," Liam said, and I echoed, "Don't have too much fun." Where were they headed? To update Quentin's wardrobe? To eat two-dollar empanadas? I only know I am alone. My memories of aloneness have a specific quality. I shift in my chair when the call ends, a contortion that travels inch by inch up my spine like the rippling muscular contraction of a shedding snake, an attempt to rid myself of the loose energy of that call, how it edged close to despair, and of the stress of the work, its inchoate danger. Liam often worries about aiding-and-abetting clauses in certain state laws and potential subpoenas from government prosecutors, but this is unlikely. No patient navigators have been prosecuted thus far. Illegality only matters if it's worth someone's time to point it out. This doesn't mean there's no risk. When I joined St. Cat a year ago, my supervisor Amalia suggested using a paid service to scrub my information from online databases and getting a PO box for all mail. I laughed at her concern. Liam and I rarely stayed anywhere longer than three months. Even our friends couldn't keep up with our shifting addresses.

Still, there is a shiver stuck between my vertebrae, which I dislodge by arching my back, bringing my shoulder blades in and down, my hands reflexively lifting, taut and bright, fingers bent back, tendons standing out. My hands find my head, and the sensation of fingers against temples, a gentle scraping, is as good as the first stretch after a night of sleep—a rough waking sensation, coming back to myself. Warming up, I touch the pad of my thumb to my first finger three times, to my second finger three times, to my third finger three times, to the pinkie three times and back again, a pleasant feeling of speed and mastery, like playing scales on a piano. This is a good feeling, but not the feeling I'm searching for. I'm searching for the sunny, toenails-to-the-sky feeling one gets at the pinnacle of a swing's arc. A feeling capable of dragging me through layers of sentiment, out to the very edges of human sensation.

I don't quite get there. I am fumbling and tentative, as I was when I first began masturbating, always stilling my fingers just before orgasm, afraid of that rush of unbridled sensation. Not that stimming is like orgasm. It is—not exactly like but an adjacent feeling, intense build, satisfying release—but we can't tell people that. They already think us obscene. Like orgasm, the feeling of stimming is hard to control. Attempt to corral it, and you will lose it, the act becoming useless pantomime or, worse, parody. I've watched videos in which auties say, "It'll be easier than you expect. You're not actually learning a new way to be. You're remembering an old way of being that you've suppressed for years." And this is true, the movements and patterns come quickly. My fingers, which I often deride as clumsy—and they are clumsy with things like spoons and car keys—are deft with repetition, but still, watching those videos, I sometimes feel like a fraud. And fearful, too: What if the mail comes, and the deliverer looks in the window? What if I am seen? I asked Liam to film me once while I shook my hands to the beat of a song we both liked, and they kept the camera rolling as the sensation built, took me. A mistake. Watching the video later, I didn't recognize the person lying on their back on the floor of the kitchen, using their legs to spin around and around and laughing—a harsh, loud laugh not like my usual laugh. Not inhuman, the opposite.

I looked human. Raw, unfiltered human. In other videos I have a tense, curated air, something careful, metallic. I was rarely caught off guard. In photos of groups of people—at work gatherings or family parties—I am often the only person looking, stone-faced, directly into the camera. But the person in Liam's video was unaware of the camera's eye, lithe and uncouth, their shirt wrinkled up in the back by the spinning so that their belly showed. I deleted the video. Now, before allowing my body to move in the ways it desires, I ensure I am alone. Even Liam's gaze is too much. When they return with Quentin I stop immediately, full of that bad feeling I know is commonly called shame.

Liam makes dairy-free risotto for dinner. Risotto was one of three dinners I would eat, and with leeks and mushrooms it was by far the fanciest. Both Liam and Quentin were lactose intolerant. "Runs in the family," Liam liked to say. Honeycub eats vegetables and flaxseeds, part of a carefully determined diet. Quentin feeds her before feeding himself, coaxing her also to take a shard of diuretic to ease the swelling in her feet.

At the table, into the thick silence that often settles over our meals, Quentin says, "I've been dating."

"Who?" Liam says, immediately ensnared. Quentin has chosen his topic well, though he balks at the question. "Different girls," he says eventually. You wouldn't think it from the shit you saw on the news, he continues, but Florida girls like trans guys, or a certain sort of Florida girl does, and there are plenty of those sorts of girls in Tampa, and he's been fucking them, and it feels good to fuck them. He pauses again, not looking at us, flirting with our disapproval. He must know this, must know we won't approve of his phrasing—*Florida girl, fuck them*. Does he want our disapproval? Perhaps not. He wavers now, backtracking, explaining that his appetite has surprised him. He'd thought, somehow, that he'd never be that kind of guy.

"You're being safe?" Liam says, more mildly than I expect. "You're treating them well?"

Quentin shrugs. He picks the girls up at clubs, mostly, and they're out of his place by morning. Dating is maybe the wrong word, he says, now looking a little afraid or maybe apologetic. Dating is probably the wrong word.

"How are you getting into clubs?" Liam asks. Quentin shrugs uncomfortably, rubs Honeycub's belly with his knuckle.

"You're being careful?" Liam says, a variant of their earlier question, and I echo, to my shoulder, "You're being careful?" I say it softly, so the repetition won't strike Quentin as a reprimand.

"They're the ones that have to be careful," he says, but at Liam's look of immediate, severe outrage, he continues, "I'm careful, of course I'm careful." He puts Honeycub on his shoulder.

"You sanitize your toys?"

"I don't have *toys*."

"Quentin."

"Imagine how it'll be when I'm on T." He wants the increased sex drive, the enlarged clitoris. He wants, someday, the minor surgery that would free his clitoris to function more like a cock, a thumb of a penis. Fuck size. He says all of this shyly, as if testing it out. I think he hasn't said it before. Then, more shyly still, "I'll be able to get it, right? I haven't looked into it, but you said."

Quentin had gotten emancipated in part to get away from his father and in part so he could begin the T-regimen hormone therapy his parents refused to consider, a dream that had ended before it began, the emancipation process dragging on, and the new Florida Department of Health guidelines released before he was eligible to make his own medical decisions. He'd chosen college in Missouri, a decision I'd helped him make. University of Missouri was the only school in a state without a care ban that offered him a scholarship. He was reluctant—his mother lived in Jonesboro, Arkansas, five hours away, closer than Quentin would have liked. Quentin would have preferred Oregon or California, but he didn't get in there. Missouri was the best option. When Missouri signed a care ban into law, he sent me a meme of a dog in a burning house, drinking a cup of coffee. "Don't worry," I told him. There's a continuation clause. If he starts testosterone before August 28, he can stay on it.

Now they are both looking at me. I have been called on. My body is staticky with the steady double gaze. I scrub my eyes. I say, "Yeah." I should say more, they are looking at me, but my vision is so blue I can't concentrate through it. "We should make an appointment now," I say finally, and Liam, forgetting themself in their relief, says, "Good Ro, best Ro," and I, helpless, call back, "Best Ro," and Liam, seeing it through, resolute in spite of Quentin's look, says, "Best Ro, good Ro," and I say, "Good Ro," and Quentin says, "What kind of fruity thing is this?" and Liam doesn't answer, opens their laptop, plates pushed to the side. They find the university's clinic page, click around to the student health center, but the gender care offered there extends only to affirming intake practices. They find the med school's website and browse for a while, Quentin looking half at the computer, half at his phone, perking up when Liam finds a page about voice therapy. Liam identifies a primary care provider who prescribes hormones but can't make an appointment on a Saturday night. Quentin will have to call Monday.

"It'll work?" Quentin says, looking over Liam's shoulder. "You're sure?" Honeycub is gently chewing on the lobe of his ear. "This is Ro's job," Liam says. "It will work," I say at the same time, and then, to escape the pressure of their worry and expectation, I open *Mad Eden* on my phone. I pick up at the place where the dragno brings Nova to the islands of proficiency. The original scientific article describes the islands of proficiency as areas in which autistic people perform better than allistic people, including mathematics, static form coherence, visual search, block design tasks, calendar calculations, musical performance, and drawing abilities. In *Mad Eden*, the islands of proficiency are the Edenic sky gardens of the dragnos, the source of their magic and their refuge. The islands float from place to place, blown by the wind. The dragno puts Nova down on one and says:

I am Cardinaux, raymaker, leader of the resistance. Magicians run before me. I feed on time and digest space. I have unfolded more times than any other dragno, and each has left me stronger. You might know of me.

Nova doesn't. Specific dragnos aren't included in the histories of the magicians. They are uncommon to see, would rather stay away from the magicians' city. Magicians who survive getting close to dragnos are

found with alarming stereotypies that cause self-injury. They're chained up for their own good. They often die from their injuries.

Better, Nova thinks, to be digested by a dragno. They attempt to stand. If they are to be dragno feed, they at least want to die standing up.

"It's such a ridiculous trope," Liam says, reading over my shoulder. "Why does it matter if you're on your feet when you get eaten?" Liam, when depressed or ill, struggled through life from their bed or reclined in a chair and hated the ableism, the militaristic tropes common in stories like this. I nod in agreement with their critique, then I shift away from them, hiding my screen, shielding the words from their critical gaze.

"They're totally obsessed," Liam says to Quentin, trying to draw me back into the conversation. "They're like this with anything about autism right now."

I ignore Liam, who isn't wrong. Before my diagnosis, I'd have had no interest in *Mad Eden*. Now, I'm fascinated. In the first installment, Nova learns that everything they knew about the world is wrong—dragnos are not the hunters but the hunted, pursued by magicians for the magic of their islands, and Nova is not a magician but a scale, their magical abilities evidence of their bond with Cardinaux. When I was first diagnosed, I felt my world similarly upended. Autism explained my love of libraries, my refusal to drink carbonated beverages, even the position in which I slept. The nurse who first mentioned autism told me, "You need to make different choices. I've seen patients who lived like you through their thirties, masking hard, interacting with people day in, day out, and they wind up back here in their forties and fifties with their brains fried." I was unconvinced, unwilling to change my life. When Cardinaux gives Nova a similar choice—cement their bond with him and join the dragnos or return to the magicians—I want Nova to choose the dragnos.

Liam has for some time been saying, "Ro, earth to Ro." I look up. Quentin is talking about a new vegan cheesecake at a bakery chain. "They deliver here," Quentin says, a rising excitement in his voice. "They deliver to the fucking middle of nowhere. Did you know you could get delivery?" "No," Liam admits, and Quentin shows us the screen, too quickly for me to make anything out but the price, a walloping twelve dollars per slice. He grins at us, excited by his ability to teach us something. "Do you want to try it?" He moves his fingers quickly over the screen of his phone. "We could order."

"We can't." I say this too fast, too loud. It sounds harsh. I know it immediately from the look Liam gives me, one of censure, and the look Quentin gives me, abashed. I don't apologize, I just say, "We can't spend thirty-six dollars on cake," and though I am proud of this choice, an autie's allegiance to clarity and honesty, it causes Quentin to hunch down over his phone, and I think I should have accepted even though it would be more than half our grocery budget for the week. We could have split a piece, we could have made it work. Quentin says, attempting to reestablish affinity, togetherness, "You want to know what's fucking crazy expensive is packers. My friends and I made our own." He looks up from the phone, still hunched, uncertain. "I guess maybe you don't want to see."

"We want to see," Liam says. There's nothing else to do. Liam confessed to me early in Quentin's visit that they wished we had a television. Quentin disappears into the bedroom and emerges carrying a gel-filled condom that he's tied off at the base like a balloon with a length of pink ribbon, which is what he uses to secure the condom to his waist. "My buddy only had pink," he says. It isn't an apology. He is emboldened by this act of tentative exhibition, even by the pink ribbon. It suggests something, some comfort with yourself, tying your packer onto your body with pink ribbon. He is looking mostly at Liam. Liam is the person he hopes to impress. I am peripheral. He doesn't know, cannot know, that the desire for a penis is the one thing Liam has talked about not understanding, the one thing they have never wanted or believe they ever could want. We've agreed that I will not get a packer, though I might want one. I enjoy walking around with our dildo strapped to my thigh, and Liam finds this easier to understand—the positioning still too alien to mimic a human penis, divorced from any recognizable maleness.

"If you touch it through clothes it feels pretty real," Quentin says. "This one woman, I fooled her. I think I did." He grabs a kitchen towel and places the towel over the packer in his hand, his gesture performative, magician-like. I half expect him to disappear it. He proffers the cloth-covered packer. He wants us to touch it, the way a man might want you to run your fingers over a board he sanded to level, admiring his handiwork, but it is also, per his previous words, his penis, Quentin's, our seventeen-year-old son's penis, and this makes us reluctant, uncertain about propriety. Liam says, "Wow, I'm impressed." I say, "Wow, I'm impressed." My iteration is a little louder and more forceful than Liam's, and it works.

Quentin, satisfied, returns to the bedroom to put the packer on again, emerges in the low-slung pants he wears to show off the band of his boxers, and I see, now that I know to look for it, the line of pink running above his hip bones and what appear to be, beneath it, faint bruises, even a thin red line on the left that looks as though, if I touched it, my finger might come away with a little blood. Liam sees this, too. They say, "How much can it cost? A packer," and then we are all on the couch, Quentin in the middle, Liam's laptop whirring on his lap. Quentin clicks from site to site, navigating us rapidly through a world he's clearly explored at length, and we are parents still, or at least we are firmly situated within the delusion I associate most strongly with parenthood: that with a little time, a little money, we can offer Quentin the sort of adolescence we didn't have—abundance and acceptance—and that this will ensure Quentin's life is better than our lives, more free of suffering.

The packers are more expensive than the cheesecakes. They require accessories. You need a way of suspending the packer, and Quentin is concerned that the harnesses and joeys, which are cheaper than the boxers, will chafe, so in the end we settle for a small limp penis and a pair of gray boxers, paying an extra five dollars for express shipping to ensure they'll arrive at our cabin before Quentin leaves, since he's said, and we agree, that he can't very well have it shipped to his college apartment.

"Sometimes I forget he's seventeen," Liam says that night. They have another mentee, whom they helped through grad school and with whom they sometimes exchange work, but she's twenty-three, and that relationship is more clearly defined, easy. Quentin is a child. We have tucked him into the couch like a child, pulled the sheet tight over his torso and dug with our hands into the gaps between the cushions. He protested at first. It was ridiculous, no one had tucked him into bed in living memory, but he didn't sleep well, Quentin. He hadn't slept well in years, and by the end he'd gone still, smiling, enjoying the process, the squeeze of the blanket, which I know from experience is a reliable comfort, and also what the blanket signified, that specific sort of care that seems capable of eternal protection, though such protection is always a delusion, a trick, or it seems that way to me as we step into our bedroom and close the door behind us, since immediately we begin to argue.

There should, I know, be a reason for this argument, a nod to causes. Try this: It was late. We were both tired. We were stressed by Quentin, the pressures of hosting. I had a butt-itch feeling in my body, a pulsing tension at the base of my spine that I tried unsuccessfully to dislodge by clenching my thighs, my butt, my fists. There were ants in the kitchen. I was bleeding and disliked the internal press of my menstrual cup. There was a dead mouse in the spring trap in the pantry whose body was starting to smell, and I insisted Liam had promised to remove this mouse, and Liam insisted I had promised, and we were both worried the mouse's body would offend Honeycub. There was the problem of the bus stop on Wednesday, more precisely our needing to be there, to see Quentin onto the bus that would take him to Missouri. There was the problem of Missouri itself—its distance from us, its probable transphobia, its concealed-carry laws, how Quentin would get from his apartment to campus without a car. I had suggested getting him a car—nothing fancy, I found a used sedan online for three thousand dollars—but Liam had said, and it was true, that this would be an irresponsible financial decision. And the crickets were so loud, and the air-conditioning was so expensive, and the bedroom was so hot, that we hadn't been sleeping well. All of these things could, conceivably, be reasons.

Still, the argument is a surprise. It arrives in front of us fully formed, like the quantum particles that arise in a vacuum, an initial effect without perceptible cause, one responsible, according to particle physicists, for the big bang, which is to say, everything. "You can't promise him that," Liam says. This is the first line of the argument I remember. It wasn't an argument yet. Liam's voice was low—not angry. Concerned, maybe. "Him" refers to Quentin. That's easy. But "promise"—what have I promised him? The car? Happiness? Have I become the sort of person who insists my thirties are better than my twenties and expects others to take heart, who is impatient with the desperation of youth? "You can't promise him that," Liam says in my memory, and I know they are correct. I'm wrong for promising whatever I've promised. Some delusion of parenthood, maybe, but no, I remember now. I'm not attempting to be a good parent, but a good employee, to do my job well—it was T. That's what I had promised. Quentin's ability to get testosterone in Missouri with his student health insurance.

"He has until August," I say. I sit on the single chair in our room, a wooden ladder-back. You can't easily sit on our bed—a mesh tent surrounds the mattress, protecting our sleeping bodies from mosquitoes and roaches. The only other furniture is a dresser, which holds our clothes. Atop the dresser are my wallet, a mangled candle, a plastic safety whistle, and three ceramic dragons I've had since I was a child. Liam says, "Unless you're handing him a prescription, you can't promise that."

Once, in Colorado, Liam went four days without the medication that allows them to sleep. They didn't realize until they signed on to the virtual appointment for a refill that it wasn't possible for the psychiatrist to meet with them when they were out of the state, and it wasn't possible to refill the prescription without a meeting. Liam searched, frantic, for a psychiatrist licensed in Colorado, but the psychiatrists in Colorado didn't take their insurance and when they finally paid out of pocket for an appointment at a large hospital—the only place without a months-long waiting list, an appointment that took dozens of phone calls to find—the hospital sent the prescription to the wrong pharmacy, and it took another two days to get a pharmacist there to cancel the prescription, which had already been filled, and transfer it to the nearby pharmacy in Colorado, and when they showed up at that pharmacy, three nights unslept, to pick up the pills, the total came to $195.66 due to insurance copays and some other fee, and they burst into tears at the counter. The person working the register, after they'd blubbered an explanation, said, "I get it. I started working here after I went a month without my ADHD meds. My doctor messed up one number in the prescription code and wouldn't admit he'd made a mistake."

This all happened in the early days of our dating. I was still in Florida. Liam had mentioned via text the trouble with prescriptions, but I had never taken medication and had struggled to relate and had said I was sure it would work out, a response Liam told me later they found unhelpful.

"You're the dad, and I'm the mom," Liam says now. "You make this promise, I'm the one that has to see it through. I'm the one that's getting calls about intake paperwork and buses. I'm too involved, I never wanted this."

"Quiet," I say, worried Quentin will hear. It is a mistake, saying this. Liam hates being told to be quiet. "I don't want this," Liam says, their voice deliberately, defiantly loud. "It's too much."

We come to distress the same way—quickly, our bodies ready for the surge of adrenaline, the trembling certainty. I almost wrote anger above, but I don't know if it's anger Liam is feeling. We rage, but it is possible to rage in response to fear or disappointment. I understand Liam's emotions as I understand my own, a binary understanding—calm, not calm. We were both, as teenagers, taken by our parents to doctors, who were asked how to manage our fits. My mother insisted my attacks weren't emotional but physical, though they expressed themselves as emotions did—tears, shouts, on one occasion my fist through the drywall in my bedroom. In boys, maybe, our embodied distress would have been only mildly censured, but we were raised as girls. Our distress wasn't meant to be expressed through fists. In both cases the doctors dismissed our parents—panic attacks, they said. Now, I imagine that with the right background—something abstract in black and silver—with two spotlights in purple and blue, with the right music—Helado Negro, maybe, "What's best for you and me? What's best for you and me?"—our arguments could be a sort of dance. They are primarily physical events. We do not hurt each other, though this doesn't mean we are not violent. Liam turns their distress on objects. I turn my distress on myself. In this sense, we are not antagonists but collaborators, our conflicts choreographed. Liam stomps, Liam sits. I stand, I jump. I slap my thighs with open hands. I say, "I don't understand why you invite people over when it stresses you out."

"It wouldn't stress me out if it didn't stress you out."

"It wouldn't stress you out?"

"I have to get better at ignoring your stress."

"Ignoring it?"

"I actually like people." This remark is punctuated by a slap of the floor. "I actually like occasionally interacting with people other than you." I lean against the wall and half slide, half roll along it, the textured drywall comforting against my temple. "It's always going to stress me," I say. "That's not changing."

"I used to think that was true," Liam says. "I used to think the best predictor of future reality was present reality, but I don't know if that's true with you." When I fight with Liam, I remember they are a writer, that they occasionally weaponize words professionally in essays and book reviews. They have said they write best when emotional. The more distressed they are, the more eloquent their language. The words transmit their emotion as if the emotion itself is the words, and they told me once they could wind themself up or down just by speaking. "He'll be all right, won't he?" Liam says, winding down.

"I don't know. It'll be hard—"

"Forget it. Forget it, forget it." Liam slaps the floor three times. "I forgot to never ask you for reassurance." I go still. There must be some connection, some causal relation between Liam's actions and mine, but with Liam's hands slapping the floor and my body wedged into the room's corner, each expression of agitation feels isolated and senseless, as if scripted for us by a playwright not beholden to meaning.

Liam says, "I wish it felt like we were in this together."

I say, "I was reading."

Liam says, "It's like having two children."

I say, "You could have let me keep reading."

I say, "I didn't choose this."

I say, "I don't make the rules."

Liam says, "Why am I waking up every day at seven? Why am I driving to get groceries in Lake City when there's a store right here? Why am I eating beans every fucking night? You literally make the rules."

But those rules are useful, I think. They keep us safe.

Liam says, "Could you just pretend to understand what I'm feeling for once?"

Everything is thickening around me. The thrill of adrenaline is gone, replaced by a seeping slowness. It is how it would feel to become a tree, the beat of my blood slowed to sap, gentle ooze. "Okay," I say. "Forget it," Liam says at the same time.

I lift the safety whistle from the dresser and stab my arm with the edge of the mouthpiece, trying to puncture the slowing feeling. I did not want to be a tree. If there were a knife I would use a knife, but Liam kept the knives in a safe. If there were scissors I would use scissors, but Liam kept the scissors in a safe. "Stop," Liam says. "Stop it now."

The autistic disability justice advocate Lydia Brown

insists that doctrines of personal freedom should extend to autistic stimming even when, from a neurotypical perspective, such behavior looks like self-harm. If an autistic person's go-to stim is to stab their hand with scissors, Brown says that's their right—"Well, it's not an emergency . . . they're not stabbing themself in the neck and they're not stabbing another person with scissors." I've said this to Liam. When we're broken up, Liam said in response. When I'm dead. When I'm gone. Until then, no, absolutely not. I can't watch that. I absolutely cannot watch that. So I stab my arm with the whistle instead—a blunt sensation, dull and unsatisfying. I say, "Nothing is good." I say, "Bad bad." I say, "Bad bad bad." Words that appear as ridiculous, written out, as would the words we whisper during sex.

Remember the joy hadn't arrived yet. The joy was still ahead.

"If something happens to him," Liam says, "it will be on us. We are responsible." "No," I say. The treeing is happening again. It is difficult to move. I am slowing, slowed. "Yes," Liam says. "You're responsible, too. I can't be the only person responsible."

There is a shifting of floorboards in the next room. I wonder if Quentin is listening.

Liam says, "I just have to remember that I can't rely on you, that you're not that kind of partner. That's fine. I didn't choose to be your partner to have someone I could rely on. Can I count on you to turn the air down when it's a hundred degrees inside? No. Can I count on you to pay for more than half the Wi-Fi bill when you're making four times as much as I am? No." They've gotten carried away by the rhythm of these sentences. I say less and less and they say more and more. "Can I count on you to entertain our guest for one morning by yourself so I can write? No. Can I count on you to say just once that everything will be okay just to hear, just once, in this fucking cunt fucker of a world, from my partner, the person who has promised to stand beside me in all things, that things will be okay?" I reach for words with which to respond to this question, but—

I reach again—

I reach again—

English is the language I was born into but it has never felt like a friend to me. Even with the response to their question in front of me, implied by the parallel structure, a rhetorical trick I admire, my words won't come.

Liam notices. They always noticed. They noticed everything—it was their gift and their burden, to notice everything. They make a fist with their right hand and rub it in circles over their heart. *Sorry.* I always feel relief at this moment, the moment when spoken language, however hard I attempt to command it, refuses to answer my summons, and I am—through failure—freed from its yoke. The relief is like the moment when, after swimming upriver to the point of exhaustion, you stop swimming and let your body be carried by the current. I don't know why sign language is easier. Maybe my hands are nimbler than my tongue. Maybe it's the magic of second languages, the magic Liam loves—how a less familiar language forces something like clarity, makes it harder to hide within syntax. Maybe it levels the field between Liam and me. Liam learned sign alongside me when they understood that English alone wouldn't suffice for any real discussion. A gift. Liam wasn't especially adept at sign. It came more easily to me. Now, Liam points to themself, makes the sign for *don't want*, which is the sign for *want* with a twist of the wrist at the end, so that the bringing toward becomes a pushing away, an appended movement of repellence. Then they sign *child*, moving their hand as if patting a child on the head. *Don't want. Child. Don't want. Child.* They sign it again and again, their hands moving in a loop, turning the last sign into two slaps against the floor, so the phrase begins to have an audible, percussive rhythm, and Quentin surely knows something is happening, but he is circumspect and will leave us alone, I think.

I know how to say with my hands the things I might say in response to this—*It doesn't matter*, or, *But we have a child*, or, *If you can't show up for him, okay*. I don't sign any of those things, don't expect they would be helpful. Liam taught me a phrase to use in moments like this—*It makes a lot of sense that you're feeling that way*—but I don't know how to sign that. I have the signs, but not the grammar. Instead, I sign, *All okay*. Then I bring my hand forward from beside my cheek into the space ahead of me to indicate the future. In ASL, time is relative to the body of the signer. The future is in front of you. The past is behind you. Your body is the present. Time is locational, personal, as in physics. It exists on a variety of individual axes. I sign, *Tomorrow*. Then, *Quentin go where?* I raise my eyebrows to indicate that the question is rhetorical, then sign, *Hotel. Why?* Then, *We need alone.* "What does that mean?" Liam says. I sign it again. Add, at the end, *I pay will*, swinging my hand forward into our personal future. Liam scrubs their head with both hands. "You're asking me to kick Quentin out?" I sign, *Our house quiet, calm, nice, will be.* "We're not kicking Quentin out," Liam says. "Not everything is about you."

I go quiet and still. I am quiet and still, all the way down. "Ro," Liam says. My arm throbs, a faraway throbbing, not sharp enough to be useful. I punch that arm, punch and punch until Liam's hand wraps tight around my fist, and then all of Liam is wrapped tightly around me, snakelike, and they say into my ear, "I don't know why I said that. I don't think you think everything is about you," and at some point we move to the bed, and the static is so big, a static that isn't about Liam's comment—that alluring, too easy cause and effect—but about the presence in the next room, about having eaten risotto instead of black beans, having gone to bed an hour late, nothing being quite right, a slow buildup of static like on a balloon rubbed against a pant leg that at some point, if it isn't siphoned off, will send a shock, and the shock zaps through my abdomen, and Liam says, "Okay," and Liam says, "Come on," and Liam presses hard with their fingers on the muscles of my back, searching for a competing sensation that can cut through the shocks though the shocks are not stoppable once they have begun. Liam continues until the static is eased. Then I sleep, Liam atop me, the way we routinely sleep, their body draped over mine, its weight a comfort, the weight of an animal atop another animal.

You could say that it was in the aftermath of this argument that we first felt the joy, those earliest tendrils, but I don't think so. It wasn't joy then, not yet joy, not quite, though it's true that the next morning we were sweet with each other, sleep having shed us of our distress. Liam said, "Henlo," a private greeting, which came from an email Liam got from their editor's assistant months before that began, "Henlo, sprry for the delay." We use it regularly, at once a greeting, a welcome, and an expression of happiness. We sometimes sing it all day, back and forth. "Henlo," I call, and Liam responds, "Spree!" "Henlo," Liam said that morning, and I smiled back at them. In the kitchen, the sun through the window had cast a hopscotch pattern on the floor. I hopscotched, and Liam hopscotched, and Liam said good morning to Quentin, who was on the couch scrolling on his phone, and Quentin said good morning to each of us, and I said nothing and no one expected me to say anything. Outside, a sparrow sang. The sparrow's song uses the same fourths and fifths that often characterize human music, which means their songs sound pleasant to human ears. I went to step out into the garden, and Quentin said, "There's a gator out there."

Paradise has many definitions. Don't look askance if I insist this was ours. In the beginning, there was a garden, and in the garden, there was a dragon.

Autism as a disorder of predictien

1. INSISTENCE ON SAMENESS.

This is the island Most-of-Sky, Cardinaux says, and Nova hears his speech in their mind. *Welcome home.*

Nova sees figs and apples, streams and rivers. The sky is gold. Their legs tremble. They give up and sit down. "What is the hidden scale?" Nova says, thinking of the dragno in the magician's libby.

You are, Cardinaux says. *The magicians hid you from me.*

"But I'm a magician."

You are my scale. I am a being of mind and spirit. As my scale, you link me to the physiological world, the world of muscle, brain, and heart. We share a bond across species. If you stay in this partnership, over time your body and brain will become more like mine, and my body and brain will become more like you.

"Is this happening because I'm so bad at insisting on sameness?"

Cardinaux hums and Nova feels it in their body. *To survive with dragnos, it helps to constrain your observations to what happens in the moment. It's better if your interpretations are not influenced by past history and do not presage future events. When this is difficult, we say,* I'm walking on uneven ground.

"Have I become mad?"

Cardinaux tenses with anxiety, and Nova feels this, too. *It happens sometimes, that a mind cannot survive the bond. I'm attempting to avoid that fate by not engaging your predictive ability. Do you feel as though you've been overwhelmed by a relentlessly magical world?*

"I feel anxious, as I often do."

Exceptional! Then you were already mad. And this is Mad Eden.

The alligator in our paradise is four feet long. A juvenile, three or four years old. That or their growth has been slowed by some aspect of their environment, which is possible given that they are in our narrow, murky retention pond, which is a poor habitat for any creature. They are orange, stained perhaps by rust from the drainage pipes.

They are not a surprise to me. They have come to the pond twice before, both times on the day my period began. I put in my menstrual cup last night and have been waiting, since, for their arrival. Right on schedule, drawn perhaps by the same lunar rhythm, they've come. Let scientists insist that autism is a predictive disorder, but, too, let me say this: I am good at predicting the alligator.

At the pond's edge, the alligator appears to sleep, but they come to attention at the slightest disturbance of the water by anything alive. Touch sensors on their jaw enable this sensitivity. Up close, they'd appear like sunspots or freckles.

Quentin says, "If it was my yard, I'd shoot."

Liam, pouring oats into a pot, says, "You don't have to shoot things to prove you're a man, Q." I say nothing. Most days, speaking is possible for me, but beginning to speak each morning is like choosing to dive into very cold water. It's okay once I'm in, a little uncomfortable, but I dread the plunge. It's a Sunday—no work meetings, no clients. I feel the lure of a silent day, but when I walk to the window seat, Quentin follows. Honeycub rests in his hand. Quentin sits on the butterfly chair next to the window seat. I watch the alligator. Quentin watches me, sideways on the chair, a position which is deliberate, I realize, as he says, quietly, "You and Liam are happy together, right?" I do not respond. I am perplexed by the question and vaguely nervous about talking to Quentin without Liam, being solely responsible for the conversation, a nervousness I always expect to fade, thinking I will grow bolder with time, though I don't. Quentin continues, "How do I get something like that? Something healthy?"

His expression is fixed and serious, though I can't identify the source of this seriousness. This is typical of conversation with humans—emotion without context, intensity without clear cause. For some weeks after, I will wonder if this question proves it was Quentin who first noticed the joy, though when I suggest this to Liam, repeating his question and my interpretation, they will suggest that his question implies not admiration but worry, that Quentin had heard us the night before, that he is asking the opposite of what he asks.

I think about the trainings I give sometimes with Eva. Eva is the lead trainer at St. Cat, and I assist her as my schedule allows. At one of those trainings, a school nurse asked how she could convince two lesbian girls to come out to her. She was worried they were too caught up in each other, and she wanted to help, but they wouldn't talk to her.

After the training, after we answered her question by suggesting she wear one of our free pronoun pins on her lapel, the sort of answer we always gave—straightforward and easy to execute and beside the point—Eva said, "Do you think she was right?" I said, "Sure." We'd talked, Eva and I, about early signs of queerness, how the bullies and teachers sometimes knew before we did. But Eva wasn't asking about queerness. "I've realized with Darcy," Eva said, "that this is my first truly healthy relationship." "That's interesting," I said, nodding to invite Eva to continue. I am unsure whether I want her to continue. A few years ago, Eva and I were in a relationship, or I thought we were. I was pretty sure, though I am often wrong about these things, as when I went to break up with my college girlfriend at an ice-cream shop, and she said, in response to my carefully rehearsed speech, "Were we dating? I didn't realize we were dating." My relationship with Eva, if it can be so named, was geographically and emotionally distant, choices we had made deliberately based on the sort of relationship we'd both wanted at the time, so I'm not sure what Eva is saying now about that connection, what is being thrown into relief. "Isn't that fucked," she says. "Halfway to fifty, and I'd never experienced a healthy relationship."

Quentin is watching me with the cautious look Liam gives when I whimper or laugh aloud at a memory only I can see. I don't have an answer for Quentin, as I didn't have a response for Eva. The word healthy brings to mind thin, seedy crackers and thinner women in yoga pants. I don't know how to apply it to my relationship with Liam, who swallows three pills nightly to continue living, pills with potential side effects like cerebral ischemia and choreoathetosis, words I've looked at but haven't looked up, believing that refusing to know has some protective power. My arm is dotted with blue bruises in the shape of the safety whistle's mouthpiece, a school of blue fish, floating up dead on the surface of my skin. I don't want a healthy relationship any more than I want a healthy diet, which would require me to deviate from the foods I eat daily—yogurt, black beans and rice, the six-packs of green-tea mochi on which I spent any discretionary income—but I can't say this to Quentin. Liam would be disappointed if I did, and there was a ferocious need in Quentin that stopped me.

Quentin is still waiting. It will hurt, to speak. I will speak, for Quentin, if I can think what to say. I want Liam to interrupt, but Liam is adding shredded coconut to their oatmeal and to Quentin's oatmeal and to my yogurt, and Liam in the kitchen thought of nothing but the kitchen, and then I am saved by movement in the garden.

The alligator has noticed something. I notice the alligator notice, and though I see nothing—no possum or raccoon or small deer—I know what the alligator will do. The desire and motivation difficult to parse in Quentin is easy to understand in the alligator. They lift their body onto four hinged legs, which spin round in their sockets like the joints of an automaton. I lean forward as they enter the water, making no splash, and Quentin shifts beside me. We are aligned. The alligator is perceptible only as a V in the water, and it is clear the moment the alligator decides to kill whatever creature they've observed—their speed increases, their path straightens. When they are near enough, their speed triples, and they spring onto the far bank, and I understand from the rippling movement in the vegetation there that they have caught a snake. A long one, longer than the alligator. "Python," Quentin says, though pythons aren't usually seen this far north. The alligator has caught it in the middle. The alligator rolls once. They twist their body in that motion common to predators, that quick shake of the head. It doesn't work. The snake ripples like a ribbon on a baton and is not killed. The alligator rolls again, a mistake. Now the snake is wrapped around the alligator's middle. The alligator bucks, and I think for a moment the snake has bitten them, but the buck was tactical. The snake is no longer wrapped around the alligator. Now I expect them to finish the snake, retreat into the water. Already, some of the snake is swallowed, but the rest of the snake disappears into the reeds, and when the alligator attempts to return to the water, some force exerted by the snake keeps them in place. The alligator attempts to walk backward, a rhythmic stepping, legs rotating in reverse, but the alligator doesn't move backward. Only their tail is in the water.

Quentin looks with me out the window. This has always been my image of love. Not two people gazing at each other, but two people, side by side, gazing at a third thing. And here it is, I know it, the earliest tendril of pleasure. The first. The words I have to set it apart are all temporal, but I wish to attend not to time but to scarcity. Not that we were without pleasure before—we had moments, even days—but here begins the season of pleasure, and as the early days of winter are thrilling in their chill, the season's beginning offered the greatest contrast to what had come before.

Liam's phone rings. Our neighbor has seen the alligator from across the pond and wants us to do something. Call an exterminator. Call animal control. I have read a great deal about dragons, so I know they can be killed—with loaves of boiled pitch, fat, and tar, with linden shield and ancient sword. But there is nothing to do, we decide, about the alligator who is trapped on the far bank of the pond. They are forsaken. It isn't a good place for an alligator. The best alligator habitat is farther south, near Venice or Port Richey, beneath the heron and stork rookeries, a facultative mutualism in which alligators offer the nesting birds protection from snakes, raccoons, and possums, and the birds feed the alligators, one of five mutualisms featured on a YouTube video called *5 Animal Friendships That Will Melt Your Heart*. (1. How industrious the oxpecker. 2. For the fig wasp always eats first of the fig. 3. How sweet is the dream the squash bee dreams in the cradle of the squash flower. 4. That the shark never hungers for the remora. 5. That the gator never hungers for the stork.)

That the dragno, a creature of mind and spirit, is linked by their scale to the physical world. Liam, too, was a creature largely of mind and spirit. Without me, they lived on ramen and went long periods without sleep. They could suppress the need to pee for hours, went days without drinking water. With me, they eat three meals a day, sleep nine hours at night, hydrate regularly, shower regularly. We've talked about how these rhythms steady them, how my routines tether them to the physical world. Can it be as simple as this—that Liam is a dragno, and I am their scale? **A bond across species**, like the herons and alligators? I decide to leap. *Mad Eden* has done it, has made the speaking possible. I say to Quentin, "Our relationship is mutualistic."

So the first tendrils of joy come upon us. How to describe them. They aren't warm as the sun on the backs of our necks. They don't melt in our mouths. They aren't the minor conveniences that we write off as luck and treat with the skepticism a sudden change in fortune deserves: the temporary cessation of our check-engine light, which has been glowing steadily on the dash due to our off-brand gas cap; the trip to the beach, where Liam sits topless in the dunes for the first time, a triumph given they haven't particularly liked the new contour of their chest. When the wrap came off for the first time postsurgery, they sobbed—"I don't look normal, I don't look normal"—but now they sit bold and upright, their scars faded to almost nothing, and we all wait for a barbed comment or a sheriff sent our way by someone worried about public decency, but—nothing. Not even the night that, heedless of the heat, which is severe, we push the furniture up against the walls of the cabin and dance, and I let my careful movements go a little, rapidly extending and relaxing my hands. This new movement is motivated by an emotion beyond my lexicon of calm and not calm. I have no word for it—my darting, loose hands, the swing of my shoulders, the sensation that builds with each beat, mounting toward ecstasy. I continue until the feeling edges into discomfort, then nausea, an internal vertigo. Then I stop and remember I'm not alone. This moment of remembering is sharp, nearly panic. Only once before—when Liam filmed me, disastrously—have I felt this nameless emotion in the presence of another person, and though I flinch with remembered embarrassment, the embarrassment is only that—remembered. Neither Liam nor Quentin is looking at me. If I move strangely, neither notices, and I recognize this moment as a new fellowship. But the joy isn't that. It's not the victory of opening the door of the microwave one second exactly before the beeps. Not the carton of blueberries from our neighbor's garden, more than we can eat in our morning yogurt. Not the gift of cantaloupe with its tessellated rind or Quentin waltzing away with the cantaloupe under his shirt, saying in a posh accent, "With child, I'm with child," and squealing like a child when Liam tackles him to retrieve the melon and slice it. Not the cooking spree these gifts inspire, the muffins and reductions and scones, though the luxury of plentiful fruit, plentiful food, eases something that isn't hunger, some other stress that has been, until now, constant and unspoken. Not Liam's completion of the translation of a long and difficult passage in which the Spanish is little-punctuated, flowing in clauses beginning with como. Not my client in Mississippi who got the letter she needed, not my client in Oklahoma who has a crowdfunding page up and has raised $350 so far, not Quentin managing to schedule an appointment at the university hospital's gender center and afterward shimmying his shoulders in victory. I'm describing events, but the first tendrils aren't events, they're texture, coarse threads stitched through the machine-woven cotton of our lives, a thing we snag on, opening the freezer to grab a frozen blueberry and pausing there to watch as a drop of water slides behind the ice molded against the rear wall, so like a red blood cell in a vein, or the reliable beauty of holiday string lights draped from the eaves of the porch, which flicker above our heads on Quentin's last night, as we gather around a small bonfire in the backyard. I tell the two of them that our minor fire is an echo of the larger animal bone fires lit centuries ago to ward off dragons. The alligator has not moved from the far bank, not for two days. I can see its silhouette for a moment as Liam throws another log onto the fire. We are all mesmerized by the spray of sparks. For once the tingling in my body is a shared sensation. For once the strange way I come to the world, my heartstrings pulled more easily by perfectly aligned windows than by words of adoration, my tears more easily motivated by spoiled yogurt than by death, for once the weird tenor of my responses is shared. The valediction looms. We all cry, and I think the tears are not for grief but for the thrill of fire, how the wind whips the flame and the flame bucks, an elemental call and response, and none of this describes the tendrils either, not exactly, they were something we tried to understand but that evaded our grasp as they evaded language. We don't discuss them. We treat them like gossamer—as if, given breath, they might come loose and be lost to the wind.

Quentin says little on the drive to the bus station, watching videos on his phone, which is a new model, a last gift from his mother. A year ago, when Quentin was newly emancipated, a man at the youth shelter asked him, "How is it you don't have a home but you've got the fanciest goddamn phone I've ever seen?" Quentin tells me this story and laughs and laughs. At the bus station, he doesn't laugh. He slouches over his bags, dragging his duffel forward as the line crawls, his digital ticket ready. His hugs are quick, perfunctory. Confident, I think, but when I suggest this to Liam on the drive home, they shake their head. "Terrified," Liam says. Unwilling to show it, and unable, therefore, to express any other emotion. Liam is moved by Quentin's terror, sick with it. They spend the drive back listing the reasons it would have been impossible for us to drive Quentin all the way to Missouri. (1. Our car has two hundred thousand miles on the odometer, and the check-engine light has come on again, perhaps warning us about the state of the engine. 2. Our front tires have little tread, and out of thrift we haven't yet replaced them. 3. Liam is behind schedule—that colloquialism in which to be staring at time's backside is to be in danger. Their translation is due to their editor in October. They should be nearly finished with a solid draft. They aren't.) "Four," Liam says. "Quentin didn't ask us," I offer, and Liam says, "Quentin didn't ask us?" and I say, "Didn't ask us," and Liam says, "Didn't?" and I understand from this exchange that I am incorrect. Liam never lists the fourth reason.

Neither of us says anything about the waxing relief, which is another, fatter tendril of contentment, this one so thick and meaty you could stick it with a needle and draw blood. We are aware of it, but it is a guilty contentment. The only thing better than guests is no guests, we do not say, and since we haven't mentioned our relief aloud we cannot mention, aloud, the dread we feel when Liam's phone begins to vibrate in their pocket. Quentin is calling. His second bus isn't coming. There was flooding in Tallahassee, the roads were closed. We're twenty minutes from home. He's ninety-five miles away, and I can't argue, this time, that he hasn't asked us to help. His voice on the phone is panicked and clear—"Can you come?" He doesn't know the town, and it's getting dark, and this woman keeps offering to share a ride, which is creeping him out, so he's locked himself in a stall in the men's bathroom at the bus station, and if he leaves he's scared the woman will offer a ride again, and if he stays he's scared he's going to get arrested, his pee sounds wrong, it doesn't sound the way a man's pee would sound, and if he can hear this difference so can everyone else, and his voice is too femme, he doesn't know what to do, he can't do it, he can't handle it—college, another bus ride, living on his own in a new state, in this country. Can we come? He wants to go home. He wants to live with us.

Liam talks him through the plan, which they invent on the spot—a hotel for the night, a flight out in the morning. No more buses. "We'll cover both," they say. They insist. While they drive, I book Quentin a flight leaving the next morning and a ride to a nearby hotel. "The woman is probably gone," Liam says. She's probably just lonely, but give it a few more minutes just to be sure, and go. Go go go. The rideshare is there, waiting for him. We stay on the phone until Quentin's in the car. I track him from bus station to hotel. Liam instructs him to get up to his room, take a shower, it'll help. We hang up.

Liam says, "Our soul of flowing water, his soul of thirst," a bastardization of a line from the poem "Fugue" by Lucie Delarue-Mardrus, who wrote it and other poems to her woman lover in 1902. Liam read her poems to me in French in our first weeks living together, when I struggled to sleep beside them. The poems were soporific, the French meaningless to me unless Liam paused to translate a phrase or a line, as they did this one—Ton âme d'eau fuyante et mon âme de soif. The next line—S'uniront-elles ?—we usually leave off, as it is more romantic. It hadn't been romantic, those first months together. I was wary, Liam coiled. But we still repeat that other line, years later, to mean two opposite things—complement and sacrifice.

In this moment, it's sacrifice. The money for the flight and hotel will deplete our meager savings. Still, we are relieved. It was a relief to be useful, to find ourselves capable of answering Quentin's call. He'd needed help in the spring, was stuck in a low-paying job with a terrible boss. He'd thought about leaving. After a particularly bad shift, he texted us asking if he should quit, but Liam was depressed and hadn't, for two weeks, replied, and he hadn't quit. He was fired a few weeks after for arriving late to a morning shift, and Liam blamed themself. Liam was often depressed in the spring. Now, in early summer, they have the energy that follows depression. It is not hard to make a decision about the hotel, to book the midmorning flight instead of the cheaper flight that leaves at six, not hard to show up for Quentin. When I mention this ease to Liam, they say, "I feel all-powerful," and laugh at my look of sudden alarm, which has to be laughed at, as it mirrors the alarm the world has for anything suggesting mania. "Not in a god way," they say, "more like I've been training with a weighted bat."

I've never been good at noting Liam's spells of depression or tracking the ebbs and flows of another person's mood. The first person I ever dated once called me after a weekend we'd spent in the Blue Ridge, hiking and staying awake at night to have long, twisting conversations about who we were and would be, to say he'd been in the hospital the week after our trip together, had to adjust the dosage of his medication. He'd been hypomanic that whole weekend—wired, out of control. Had I noticed? He'd asked brusquely, and I had the sense that the question was a test, that I should have noticed. Not only noticed, intervened, and I could only say that I hadn't. He was energetic, sure, ready each day for another eight-mile hike. He was awake when I fell asleep and awake when I woke, but I've often needed more sleep than other people. I'm bad at recognizing the blurry line between personality and pathology. I say this as Liam drives us toward home, an apology of sorts, and Liam softens. "Of course you're bad at it," they say. "It isn't a line. There's nothing there."

In a paper called *The Experience of Time and Its Disorders*, Thomas Fuchs postulates that manic and depressive symptoms could be caused by abnormal acceleration or retardation of one's experience of time, a desynchronization of personal time from consensus time. "That doesn't match my experience," Liam says in the car when I mention this. "For what it's worth. A narrowing of the specious present, sure, but having longer hours in a day doesn't motivate me to do anything with those hours." I tell them that autistic children and adolescents are less adept, in clinical trials, at thinking backward and forward in time, less likely, if given three related events, to correctly sequence them.

"Can I change the channel?" Liam says.

So I tell them about the second installment of *Mad Eden*, which I've read five times. On the islands of proficiency, Nova meets the dragnos—reclusive creatures who would happily spend their whole lives on their islands if not for the need to battle the magicians seeking to steal their magical homeland.

The sentences of *Mad Eden* are often awkward, an awkwardness that makes sense if you trace the words back to the original article. For instance, the word eat doesn't appear in the original article, so Nova can only **digest** the magicians' simple roots and the dragnos' figs.

In the second installment, Nova, in spite of studying for three weeks what other scales have studied for seven years, easily becomes the best in their class. When they are given a test consisting of one question—**Why?**—in which to answer **Because** is to fail and to answer **Why not?** is to pass, they pass easily. At first this gains them popularity, but over time admiration turns to resentment, then suspicion. After Nova calls the dragnos **y'all**, a word only magicians use, and gives a long monologue about **the minimalistic movies of Heider and Simmel**, Cardinaux warns, ***Don't say you were a magician so clearly***, but the damage is done. Among the scales, Nova is increasingly suspected of being a spy, sent to help the magicians locate the islands of proficiency.

"Which will turn out to be true, but it won't matter. Nova will save the day, fight off the magicians, and become universally beloved," Liam says, and I yelp, slap my hands over my ears too late. "It's a classic self-insert story, you're supposed to see yourself in the main character," they say. Their words rankle. I have, after all, inserted myself. **Nova has poor postural control and is unable to catch a ball. Even with the dragnos, staying on a script is their sole means of keeping anxiety at a minimum.** Seeing myself in them doesn't feel like being manipulated. It feels like being known, like intimacy, an intimacy I no longer want to share with Liam. I tell them instead about St. Margaret of Antioch, who, according to legend, slayed a monstrous dragon by bursting from its stomach and is now the patron saint of women in labor.

"Neat," Liam says, and I go quiet, tracking the mile markers with my eyes. Mile markers are like fan blades. You can hold your gaze steady and let them blur by or follow them, each one speeding by crystal clear. I shift between these two modes, enjoying myself.

Quentin calls. He has showered and is feeling better. He's watching walkthroughs of *Diablo III* on his phone, hungry but unmotivated to get food. I sign, *Get food, we pay?*

Makes sense, Liam signs, tapping forefinger to temple, a sign that mimics the sign for *cents*. The English words are homonyms, which you wouldn't expect to matter in sign, but it does matter. The signs are etymologically linked by a long interplay between American Sign Language and English.

I tell Quentin to order food, whatever he wants. We'll send money. He demurs at first, but eventually orders fast-food tacos. When I've hung up, food on the way, Liam says, "We couldn't have done it. We couldn't have driven all the way back." "The car probably wouldn't have made it," I say. "I have to work," Liam says. "I've hardly worked all week." Liam talks about an etymology that has them stuck. Not badly stuck, but they're uncertain how best to proceed. They explain it to me as we drive, inviting me into their work, a generosity. Near its finale, the sentences of the book they are translating hinge on the etymology of *miedo*, from the Latin word *metus*, meaning fear. The book offers the etymology and then moves into several paragraphs of wordplay, riffing on the etymology to bring thematic threads together. "And I can't find any English words with the same root." The English words for fear mostly came from Old English. *Fear* itself from *fǣr*—peril. *Worry* from *worien*, that killing motion, as when the dragon in our retention pond worried the snake. *Dread* from *drǣdan*. *Terror* was from Latin, but the root was *terrēre*. *Scare* was from Old Norse, as was *awe*.

"Miedo always makes me think of médula," Liam says. "Fear and marrow."

Médula from the Proto-Indo-European *medhyo*, which also gave us *medio*, *Mesozoic*, *Mesopotamia*, *amid*, *midriff*, *milieu*, and *mezzanine*. A word plump and fecund as an ant queen.

Miedo and medio. The deep middle of a fear. Half a fear. Fear by halves.

"Fair," I say. It has a sonic resemblance to *fear*, as *medio* has to *miedo*. Half and half is fair.

"But the issue is the etymology, or really what to do after. I can't translate the wordplay without the etymology."

Quentin texts. He has his boarding pass ready to go for the morning flight.

"To the menacing Midwest," I say, still thinking of miedo and medio. "With only two mortifying middle-aged meddlers to mediate the monstrous milieu with meticulous—"

Liam gasps. "That's it."

"What?"

"Meticulous. Look it up."

From *metus*—meaning timid, full of fear.

"It still doesn't quite work," Liam says, but they're smiling at the windshield.

"You're a one-track pony," I say, and laughter shatters me.

Liam looks over at me, one eyebrow raised. "I don't think," they begin, but I wave away their protestations. *I know, I know*, I sign, laughing too hard to speak. I said it wrong.

Liam laughs a little at my laughter, then Quentin calls again. He's eating. It was so awful, he says. The woman told him to sit beside her on the bus, in the window seat, but she hadn't stood up to let him in, and as he slid past her, she touched his crotch. An accident, maybe, he wasn't sure. But he was sure, after that, that she knew. She wasn't fooled by the packer. She talked the whole ride about her husband and her two boys she'd just left and the retail job she'd just quit, and she asked Quentin where he was headed, and he told her, hadn't thought to lie, and she said maybe she'd head that way as well, and he was trapped like that in the window seat for an hour, beside this woman who knew and who might do anything with the knowledge. Liam knows what to say—he did a good job taking care of himself, he was right to call us, he's safe, there's a free shuttle from the hotel to the airport, don't forget to set an alarm, and with time Quentin's responses are slower to come, sleepier, and Liam instructs him to rest, hangs up. Liam says, into the silence that follows the call, "In the marrow," and I say, "In the marrow," and the repetition isn't mere echo, but a way of wrapping us up, my favorite moment in conversations like this one—the moment in which echo becomes motif. I will think about this later, when I reconstruct these days, attempt to recognize within them the catastrophe to come. I will remember how we drove through the night with headlights that needed new bulbs, fast and unconcerned, and I will remember that there are whole etymological gaps in our language of fear.

A gentle peace sustains us through the rest of the drive. I wouldn't have called it joy. Relief, I might have said. Contentment. Liam says, "We have a good life together," and I say, "We have a good life together," and I say, "When we get home, bed?" and Liam says, "Bed?" with a teasing lilt to the word, and I know we are both thinking about sex. It is easy to locate myself in our shared meanings. Echolalic conversation. Indistinguishable, to me, from the language of love.

I know most people prize adaptability in all things, from employees to hiking poles to muffin recipes, but there is something to be said, too, for the precise steps of a ritual honed over years, every touch, every sound, every contact point between bodies already known, metered, ordered. Isn't this what we prize in religious ceremonies of worship, and isn't sex worship of a sort?

To begin, I put the pendant of a necklace in my mouth. We keep our clothes on. I dislike the sensation of skin against skin, and Liam doesn't always like the way their chest looks without clothes. Liam takes my left earlobe in their right hand and pulls twice, a milking movement, and my body lets down. My fingers play from their rib to their elbow and back again, skating across the sensitive pit of their arm. We do not progress if this tickles, only move forward when my touch makes them pull in breath and hold it. Then they kiss my face and neck while I say the word, "Kiss," again and again. I don't like kissing, can't manage the timing without deliberate mental effort, but I do like the word, the hard kick at the beginning and final sibilance, a downhill word, a word gravity wants you to say. Sometimes, we trade the bead, passing it back and forth. Sometimes, we let our mouths rest against each other, comforted by the hard barrier of teeth. Sometimes, we tug with our fingers at the other's lips or run one finger pad along the gum. At about this point, one of us usually needs to pee. When that person returns, we've lost some momentum. This is important. We settle into back scratches, foot massages, touches often categorized as platonic until we are again at the point where a single touch elicits from Liam a gasp.

I don't like to be touched, I like to be compressed. Liam, knowing this, will loose all their weight on me at once, their legs pinning my legs, their pelvic bone teasing my clit, pressing just above and off to the side, nearly in the place that I want it, their chin on my chest, and if I lose all my breath in one hard exhale, we continue. This part of sex has changed since the hospital. A clear before and after. I still like to be pinned, that helplessness, how Liam sometimes pulls my shirt up over my face, a pleasurable muffling. I still like it, but the liking is narrower now than it was, the line between arousal and panic so thin that Liam at first asked not to navigate it, and for weeks we stopped at back scratches and foot massages. When I chafed at this, Liam said, "Give it time."

Time, whose earliest accurate description is just this: heat, traveling from the hotter body into the colder body, as I am beginning to sweat beneath Liam. The distance between the past and the future is quantifiable—sped particles, sped breath. Time's arrow is heat or, more precisely, the disorder we sense as heat, what Clausius named entropy. I suck air through my shirt, and the molecules in my lungs become more disordered. I move to align my clit with the hard edge of Liam's pelvic bone, and Liam says, "Oh, does she want something?" A deliberate misgendering.

Zoom in further, and time loses its directionality. At a quantum level, effect can precede cause. My breath slips from my mouth, and I can't recover it, and as if Liam knows before I know, before my body recognizes panic for what it is, they are gone, kneeling at the end of the bed, as far as they can go given that the mesh tent surrounds us, and when I ask how they can tell, how they know before I know, they say, "I watch you," and I think of the study showing that up to eleven seconds before a person consciously makes a decision, neural activation patterns predict the decision they will make.

When I am calm again, I tackle Liam, landing them on their back, and for a time, half a time, I lie atop them and root around in their hair, like a chimpanzee grooming another chimpanzee to eat the grubs. Then Liam flips me onto my back. Time can be this, too. Oscillation. Some early clocks pinned time to weight and gravity, to sway. Our brains do not tell time like clocks—no crystals, no pendulums, no decaying cesium. Instead, a cascade of neurons keeps our internal time, and maybe it is possible to sync these neurons as you can sync menstrual cycles, can sync breath—we reach at the same time for the strap-on.

I wear it, the dildo that is striped pink and blue and looks like a dildo, mushroomed from my thigh, a pleasantly alien thing. Liam lowers themself onto the fruiting body, and grinds painfully against me. The pain is a necessary part, pairs with the stroking of their finger on my clit, which is gentle, and the trouble with time's arrow as a description of the universe's movement toward entropy is that it relies on disorder, which is itself difficult to define. The theoretical physicist Carlo Rovelli, describing this in his book *The Order of Time*, uses a pack of playing cards as an example. He asks the reader what order of cards is most orderly—arrange the cards by color, first red cards then black, and you have a numerically disordered group. Arrange the cards by number, and the suits and colors are disordered. Any linear ordering along one axis introduces disorder along another. This is perhaps clearer still if one attempts to order more complex things—people, for instance. Try to line up people along one single linear axis in the most ordered way. It's impossible. No one person is, objectively, more like or unlike any other. It's our very inability to see this, to understand how equally like and unlike every person and every atom is, that creates time. When people talk about an intuitive understanding of cause and effect, of linear time, what they laud is the blurring of perspective that comes from an inability to ever see any given object, animal, or event in its full complexity, and this is why I cannot wear the strap-on forever, that word that suggests stasis. I can wear it for hours, and I do, the shaft protruding through a hole in our oldest pair of blue jeans, but I cannot wear it forever. The strap-on will be perceived by the shopper at the local grocery store not in all its complexity but as an object easily categorized as queer, weird, obscene—and time, as it is understood in physics, is what this inability to see the world has created. Time, Carlo Rovelli writes, is ignorance.

Liam rolls off me. I whir. A happy whir. "My little robot," Liam calls me in these moments when happiness takes me away from language into a noisy, alternate space. The whir is both a sound of pleasure and pleasure itself, something between a whistle and a sustained rolled *r*, a massage of the vocal cords. It is the most precise expression of what I feel in those moments just after orgasm. I feel whir, and I whir. The whir shifts in pitch, tracing precisely the tides of that sensation, higher when it peaks, lower as it fades. I lose myself in the expressiveness of it, how I can send the whir spiraling higher in my chest and feel my joy follow it, as if the sound creates a place feeling can inhabit, though the feeling also creates the sound, the two loop back on each other, a not-impossible thing, that time is a circle with no beginning, that by moving only forward in time one could return to the place where one started. It has been done, at least on paper. Time is ignorance.

My head is on Liam's shoulder. Beneath my ear, their heart beats fast. They say, calling me lightly, "Don't need a man to have a good night." I am supposed to say, "Evelene," completing the line of the song, but I don't. My eyes look past the point of their chin. I focus my eyes, then unfocus, the world blurring. Focus and unfocus. When my eyes are unfocused I can see things I can't see when I focus them. The line of Liam's chin becomes doubled and translucent. I can see through their body to the candle on the dresser behind it. When I focus my eyes, the candle disappears. I make it appear and disappear, a kind of magic, and I am caught up in this magic trick, the whirring a happy hum in my throat, appearing and disappearing the candle when I realize, in a moment of focused vision, that Liam's chin is shining. It glistens in the low light. Moisture. Their chin is wet. It could be saliva, but we don't kiss like that. I look up at the rest of their face. Their eyes shine. They are crying. Their eyelids are soft, scleras red, nose running. They have been crying for a time, and times, and half a time. I take my whir low then high, the pattern of tones that signifies a question, and they shake their head to mean I shouldn't worry. I pivot into the questioning whir a second time.

"I just wish we could be together," they say. "After sex. I want to talk to you. I want to hold you, but you're gone."

They are crying loosely now. "You're gone," they say again, and I shake my head. I focus through the whir, sign through it, point to my chest with an index finger and then use my flat palms to sign *here*. *I*, I sign. *Here*, I sign. There is no to be verb in sign language. The body is the being, my teacher typed when asked to explain this. It would be redundant to sign with the body what the body makes clear. But I feel the lack of the verb in that moment. The signs don't convey what I want them to convey, that I am emphatically present. I am here. I sign *I*, then *here*, then *I*, eyes wide and cheeks puffed, offering the repetition that sometimes approximates this emphasis, but this, too, falls short. I'm sure there's a way, using sign, to emphasize presence. I might have used *with*, bringing my hands together, signaling our closeness. I might have run a curved hand down the length of my body. I might have used *we*. But these options only occur to me now, which makes it impossible that they could have occurred to me then.

What I understand, in that moment, is that I have accrued a small debt of language. I owe them the affirmation I can't sign, that confirmation of presence and love. And, too, I understand that they will not demand or even request it, no more explicitly than the request of their tears. "I want to hold you," they say, but they don't try to hold me. They don't stop me whirring. And despite the tears and the debt, the whirring is a joy. I will whir until the whirring has finished with me.

The next morning, I walk down to the pond's edge, where the alligator still has not moved. This lack of movement doesn't necessarily mean the alligator is dead. Alligators can maintain dormancy in their mud holes for weeks in winter, brumating, waiting for the warmth of spring, which they feel, first, in the blood of their scutes. I am cautious. I wear waders that come up to my thighs, which I have been wanting an excuse to wear. I walk slowly into the retention pond, skirting the deeper water, keeping to the shallows near the bank, thinking of a video I watched in which an alligator dragged a thrashing pig into the water and from the shore six other alligators entered the pond and swam toward them. The alligator does not move as I wade through the pond. The ripples I make slap against the underside of their jaw. They are half on the bank. The body of the snake protrudes from their mouth. The snake's front half is coiled around the alligator's hind legs and stomach, a crushing coiling, which killed the alligator. This prevented the snake from being swallowed, but didn't save the snake's life. Flies rise from the alligator's exposed tongue.

Given that the alligator is dead, my task is to drag them farther from our house, to a spot in the forest where their decay can proceed without the stench of it permeating our four walls, and I will drag them, later, after uncoiling the snake from their body, a difficult task, working against the rigor of death. I will take both back feet, the thick tail pressing against my hip, and I will walk backward, surprised at their heft, their dragged body gathering dirt and leaves, so that by the time I set them down they are lying on a pile of twigs and dead foliage, almost a pyre. I will do all of this, but first, I squat in my waders and consider the alligator. When I was very young, I read that dragons are alligators' afterlives. I believed it for years, believed that the skies above my home were, therefore, more densely populated with dragons than other skies. As a child, I searched for any excuse to hold alligators, to be near them. I believed them dragons-to-be, and this belief still has some power over me. I consider the hind leg with its clawed foot—so dragon-like. Dragon-like, too, the webbing between the toes. How delicate and thick the skin there, scaled with tiny plates. Faint webbing also connects the alligator's leg to their body, creating a flap, not a wing like the wing of a bird, but a flap of skin that might make gliding possible, and I look at the snake and think of what Edward Topsell wrote in 1607: Except a serpent eat a serpent, he shall never be a dragon.

I touch the claw first, that gray, thickened nail, a piano hammer of keratin. I work my way up the digits to the webbing and manipulate it with my fingers. I touch the sensors on the jaw. The neurons that process such touch are dead, but still I imagine how it would feel to have fingers on those too-sensitive bumps. Would it hurt the way whispers do, grating against the hairs of my ears? I put my hand into the alligator's mouth, touch the rough teeth, the tongue, the ribbed roof.

I still hadn't talked to Liam since our sex the night before, and I worried this was selfish. Often, when I couldn't speak to Liam I could speak to strangers. I could be naked and sprawled on the kitchen floor, bawling and knocking my head against the cabinets, but if the doorbell rang, I was up in an instant—clothes on, eyes dried, cold-water compress to both cheeks, a hard shake of the head, and I answered the door with an easy "How do you do?" A survival instinct or a Southern instinct, bred into me by my mother, a ruthless keeper of appearances. Though Liam never commented on this pattern, I worried about it. If I could be snapped back to perfectly functional speech by a Girl Scout or a Jehovah's Witness, was it really impossible for me to snap back for Liam? Can't or won't?

Little is known about alligator communication. A report based on observations of gators at Gatorama describes the bellowing of alligators as contagious. The bellows spread from one alligator to the rest in the early morning, the reptiles joining their descendants, the birds, in the dawn choir. Alligators do not have a larynx, yet they hiss, growl, and roar. They can even create infrasound, though it should be impossible for an animal the size of an alligator to create infrasound, which is otherwise reserved for whales.

I return to the house, find Liam at their desk, staring fixedly at the little letters on their screen. Like the alligator, I use my body to create an impossible sound, a sound that approximates the word "Done," and Liam says, "Thanks. Good Ro, Best Ro." We are not talking about the alligator. They are grateful that I am speaking again, that I've returned to them. They relax. Cause, effect.

Looking back now, I consider that if you run my actions backward, I bring the alligator to the pond and feed a snake into their mouth, working a sort of magic that, days later, brings the alligator to life, but I don't think of this then. I live only forward. I don't think of *Mad Eden*. I don't think that the alligator might be related to the joy, though I should. Consider how many songs and poems of jubilation have heralded the good fortune of a man sitting alongside a slain dragon, like this excerpt from *Les Chétifs*:

The beast fell unconscious from the blood it lost.
When Baldwin saw this, he raised his head.

Were someone to give him a valley's worth of gold,
He would not be so joyous as he was about how things
turned out.

I don't think any of this at the time. I assume—and wouldn't anyone?—that the alligator is just a reptile. A simple dinosaur.

Autism as a disorder of predictien

2. THE PIA HYPOTHESIS AS A PARTIAL ACCOUNT OF THE AUTISM PHENOTYPE

A dragno is not a common animal. To stay on my back while in motion, you need to detect where I am in space. Given that our bond allows mindreading, this should be simple, but there is a second crucial step: anticipating where I will be so as to intercept my body from moment to moment, Cardinaux says. *This isn't prediction as magicians understand it. It's more like a musical performance. You have to know what note I will sing next and sing it at the same moment.*

"How?"

It helps to practice a set of repetitive behaviors. We call it stimming. Leg-swinging is a good place to start.

Nova tries, and the feeling is magical, like the joy of finding a unifying theory for a chaotic pattern, as though the underpinnings of the capricious world could be perfectly understood.

Now, try it in motion, Cardinaux says. Cardinaux sings the note of a dive and down down down they go at a fearsome pitch. Balanced on Cardinaux's dorsal frith, Nova loses their hold and falls. Cardinaux catches them immediately, saying, *The bond between dragno and scale is not restricted by time or space. When a scale falls, wherever they are, their dragno will catch them.*

We are having a good day. This is what will be difficult to explain, later, to my therapist. That before the text, we are having a good day. We are driving—south, past Lake City. I am wearing my favorite shirt—a plaid cotton shirt that's comfy but also has a collar, which means you can wear it to dinner. Liam is behind the wheel. I don't drive except in emergencies. I am focused on the window, watching drops of rain catch other drops of rain and, overcoming both friction and gravity, slide across the glass. We are supposed to meet my coworkers for dinner outside. I've called ahead to ensure the outdoor seating is covered.

The dinner is meant to celebrate two things—Eva's recent engagement to Darcy, and Swaati being in town for a conference. It's rare that we can all meet in person. I've brought everyone tea in little bags. Gifts are useful—they suggest care without requiring spontaneity. I am nervous. My nerves were made worse by a stop at an enormous discount grocery store. Stopping made sense. The store was too far from home to make the trip worth it just for groceries, and black beans are forty cents a can there if you buy them in big flats. So we flashed our membership card, entered the store. Liam said, "You'll be fine. Stim if you need to."

At home, I'd been flapping my hands when I received good news and after long meetings. I was supposed to flap my hands in public, it was even an ethical obligation. I, as a white autie, should display the behaviors too dangerous for Black and brown auties in this country. It was safe enough for me to screech and flap my hands in a grocery store. But as I entered the store, I felt its immensity, metal and concrete, and some great force took me by the throat, and I managed just one limp shake of the hand. Instead of stimming by the black-bean aisle I cried quietly into my mask, and by the yogurt aisle I cried loudly enough that people noticed, a minor failure. But we made it out of the store, which, like restaurants and hospitals, was a place where one must measure success by survival. We made it out, our car full of cheaper groceries, our suffering repaid in spoil. We were a little late now—two minutes, three—and I was worried, and Liam was calculating the precise amount we had saved: twenty-two dollars. With twenty-two dollars, we could get four bags of vegan cheese, though we wouldn't. The money would go toward the next month's bills. It would change nothing. But we were having a good day. Our ease was still nascent, subtle as a single amaranth bloom. But it was there.

Then we began to lose time. Three minutes late became four minutes, then six. There was a wreck on I-75. We were still on the fastest route. We would arrive thirteen minutes late, and this was fine, Liam assured me, a reasonable time to arrive at a dinner with friends, but it meant I wouldn't be able to carefully select our table, my seat. I chose the restaurant for its vegan burritos, similar enough to the black beans I eat each night, and its outdoor seating with umbrellas for shade and cover from the rain, which is slackening now. I chose the time—seven, late enough that the day might be cooling. You will arrive at 7:14. We were okay. At my pleading, Liam pressed a little harder on the accelerator—72 mph, then 73, a kindness from Liam, who didn't speed, as we couldn't afford a ticket.

We're ten minutes from the restaurant when Eva texts the group—they're not serving the outdoor patio, there's a spot inside with windows, we'll grab a table in there? Swaati is first to say sure. Amalia is second. I am trying to figure out how to respond when Eva texts the group again—great got a table by the windows, we'll open them for some ventilation.

"What?" Liam says, attending as they always do to the minor muscular changes of my face.

"They got a table by the windows."

"Outdoors?"

"Sort of outdoors."

"Sort of outdoors?"

"Indoors," I say.

"Tell them to get a different table."

"I can't."

"You can't?"

It begins like this, a minor change.

"Then we can't go," Liam says.

"We've driven two hours."

"Sunk-cost fallacy."

"I can't bail." I have a rule: Never cancel on your friends. I have a rule: Don't eat inside restaurants.

"They're your friends, the whole point of having friends is being able to cancel on them."

"Swaati flew down from New York."

"For a conference. Which will happen again next year."

"I can't bail."

The world is full of traps like this one. Two inflexible rules that hitherto have run parallel break with the laws of geometry. Distorted by some great gravity, they bend and intersect, showing themselves to be in direct and immutable contradiction. And just like that, I have my hands wrapped around my skull. I am keening.

"Blame it on me," Liam says. "Say I have a migraine. Say we got a flat tire. Fuck, I'll give us a flat tire. We can meet up with them after to say hi."

I lean over, toward the window, knock my skull against it. I try to remind myself that my brain is encased in my skull, protected from the world, which is only delusion borne of electrical impulses, minor sparks.

Liam says, "I'm not eating inside. If you choose to eat inside, fine. You can go home with Eva and stay there until you have two negative tests."

"I have to go." Once an event was planned it took on, for me, certain qualities other people associated with the past tense. It was concrete. It could not be changed. This near to a meaningful plan, I have already catapulted myself into the future. What is brightest in my mind is not the dinner, but the evening after. It's ten at night, and we're back at the cabin. I'm eating green-tea mochi, two of them. Liam is reading a book meant to help with their translation. I'm scrolling through r/Auties, reading new posts discussing the author of *Mad Eden*. The installments are posted by user MadEden05, a throwaway handle with no other posts, which gives no clues about the author. Various well-known auties have been suggested. A few people are guessing AI.

I have my own speculations about the author—that they are late-diagnosed, like me; Southern, like me—but I don't post these. I have no desire to test the veracity of my suppositions. I have my headphones on, Adrianne Lenker is singing, "and my brain is like an orchestra, playing on, insane." It's a golden-hued future. We are hurtling toward it. The only threat to that future is a change of plans.

Liam says, "I need to feel like if a plan becomes unsafe for me, we can change it."

I say, "It's too late."

Liam wins by hitting the hazards and pulling off onto the shoulder. Suddenly, attending the dinner is a future decision. It hasn't been made. It will be made. We will make it. Except that the decision is impossible. There is no way to follow both rules. Death occurs to me then, a boring epiphany. Death is a way out of almost any conundrum. Hit by a car on I-75. Die, and no one will judge you for refusing to eat inside, for rudely sitting in a mask while everyone else eats, for eating with everyone else and thereby risking your partner's health, for eating with everyone else and then infecting an elderly woman I happen to sit beside on the bus the following week, who dies.

I hit my head. Hitting one's head, if done correctly, can be clarifying, causing an echo to vibrate lightly through the skull—sensation and sound twinned. Like very near lightning, when the thunder comes so quick on its heels the connection between the two becomes self-evident. In general, it takes up to one-tenth of a second for a sound signal to reach the auditory cortex. The brain waits. We are all a tenth of a second behind our own lives. When you vibrate the skull, the brain is forced out of the recent past into the now.

Liam is talking about now. They are saying the word. "Please," they are saying. "Can we not do this now?" Liam puts their hands on my temples, and I stop. I will not hit Liam. We need to be at dinner. The dinner has already begun. Liam says, "We need a plan," and pulls out their phone to call someone who can help, probably Trevor, their best friend and a physicist. Trevor is tall and soft-spoken and someone who reliably picks up the phone. He's anxious, but this doesn't cause him tears or panic attacks. Instead, he experiences indigestion. This is useful for us. We are dependent, occasionally, on the reliable substrate of an emotionally suppressed cis man.

Philosophers often attempt to create time-independent models of causation. Instead of saying that A causes B to happen in the future (A → B), these models suggest that A causes B in the future and C in the past (C ← A → B). On the level of language, this shift in thinking about causation creates a shift in tense. Instead of saying, If A happens, C will happen, we say, If A happens—in the past or the future—C would have happened. The trouble is that this makes it impossible to talk about what is happening right now, where Liam is saying loudly into the phone, "I don't, I blame the restaurant."

Trevor says something in a low voice. We are safe. We have exactly five minutes to lose our minds, and then we have to arrive, upright and presentable, witty and kind. Then Liam rends this safety, saying into the phone, "I'm not going." Liam opens their door, swings it wide. A car speeding past swerves into the far lane, laying on the horn. Liam leaves the door open, squats on the shoulder, their fists balled tight between their thighs. I get out, too, though there's nowhere to go. We are acting the way people expect us to act—unpredictable, dangers to ourselves and others, unable to keep our shit together.

According to the philosopher David Lewis, the highest-order causal thinking possible, which still separates human minds from the most advanced computers, is our ability to consider counterfactual possibilities. To consider the counterfactual, according to Lewis, one must consider the worlds closest to this world. To determine which worlds are closest, one must rank all the worlds that are not this world according to three factors: the extent to which they contain large miracles, the extent to which they contain small miracles, and the extent to which they contain series of events that match this world perfectly. Lewis's similarity measure goes like this: it is of first importance to minimize large miracles, of second importance to maximize regions of perfect match, of third importance to minimize small miracles. Every time a person asks what might have happened if, they are naturally performing this ranking system, minimizing miracles. In moments like this one—gone, heated, lost moments—I've always felt nearest to miracles. The rules of appropriate behavior dissolve and I am released into the infinite possibilities of insanity. Right now, for instance, I am sitting on top of the car. The metal beneath me is bright and hot through my pants. Liam is wandering along the side of the highway, violently picking flowers, tearing them up by their roots. I asked Liam once if they thought being neurodivergent meant magic was more possible for us. They shrugged. Liam was often frustrated by the relentless positivity of the neurodiversity movement. Asked by a friend whether, if there were a cure for bipolar, they would take it, they said:

"There is. I do." This was inexact. The psych meds they take offer management, not cure, but their response was effective in silencing their friend.

Miracles, of course, can be bad. I have just used our house key to rend the skin of my arm. There are several large, bleeding scratches. They are sticky, already beginning to clot. Miracles are, per Lewis's definition, bridges between worlds, but I don't know what world the miracle of my bleeding arm, or the miracle of the clotting of my bleeding arm, is supposed to make possible. Perhaps a world where we don't go to the dinner—I have no jacket and my colleagues can't see my arm like this.

The whole point of Lewis's model is that in the world closest to this one, the world that could be used to prove causation, everything is the same except that by some small miracle we are at the dinner, not stuck on this highway.

Liam is shouting into the phone, "Doesn't anyone care?" And they would care, my colleagues. They would care enough to insist that the restaurant seat us outside, but here's the thing—I haven't told them. I only tell people what they need to know and that, often, is little or nothing about my own life.

One problem with Lewis's model is that it can't account for backward causation, which requires a static view of time. In this view, the future already exists, meaning sentences about the future can be true or false.

I shout, a true statement, "We're going to dinner."

I shout, a true statement, "I can't miss this dinner."

Liam shouts back, a true statement, "They're your friends."

Here's the trouble: for Liam, the future is coming into being; for me, it is concrete. I see us there. We ate and talked and laughed. To say that we will not eat and talk and laugh is false. Nothing that happens between now and the future can change the future. To admit change, in that way, is ruinous.

I climb down from the roof of the car and there, in the grass on the side of the highway, is a single glove. One black workman's glove. It is much too large for me, comes halfway to my elbow, covers what I've done to my arm. Just like that, the solution comes. I see it all, what we will do, a memory of the future—how it was always going to go, not a choice, not an invention, but the discovery of a plan already complete. We will go to dinner. I will wear the glove. Liam will bring the flowers. We will order a vegan breakfast burrito (for Liam) and a vegan black bean burrito (for me), both to go. We will sit with our little containers in front of us, the sauces neatly stacked on top, our masks on. We will say, "It's been too long." We will look at photos of Swaati's dog dressed as a bat for Halloween. We will look at photos of the mountain in Tennessee where Eva and Darcy are planning to marry. Liam will say that it's beautiful. I will echo their sentiment, tracking them through conversation as I always do, following the paths they find for me.

First, I will go to Liam. I will tell them what's going to happen. "We're going?" they will say. "We're going to see your work friends now? We're going like this?" "Please," I will say. "I don't understand you," they will say.

"Trust me," I say. "It'll be fine."

And it is. I wear the glove. Liam brings six flowers, and they present these to Eva when we arrive, an engagement present. "Picked them on the way here," Liam says, and Eva says, "Why are you wearing one glove?" and I say I found it on the side of the highway, and Amalia says, "This is why I love you two. You're so whimsical," and Darcy jumps in to say they found their jacket on the side of a highway, that they want to dress themself solely in clothes they find on the street, highway chic. Liam waves their hands at me under the table, suggesting this is sarcasm, but as usual the identification is only half helpful. It doesn't tell me what is true.

Swaati says, "It's an American cultural phenomenon, isn't it? Thrifting?" Swaati lived for some years in Chile, some years in Germany. They just returned from an artist residency in Portugal. There is a pause. I say, "Yes. Definitely." I know nothing about thrifting as a cultural phenomenon, but I know what to say in this moment and I know when to say it, and those things are rare enough for me in conversation that I take advantage of them.

Eva mentions a documentary she watched on the ethical travesties of fast fashion. "That's interesting," I say, which you can say about almost anything. Swaati says, "I buy new, but only from lesbians," and Darcy laughs, and Swaati laughs, and I laugh, a second too late.

Liam says they want to live abroad, to cover up the delay in my laughter, which has embarrassed me. Liam is always watching, always attempting to put the group at ease, to placate here and tease there, an exhausting gift. This is one reason we're living in a cabin, our nearest neighbor across the retention pond. If it were up to Liam, we would live in a country where English is spoken rarely or not at all. Liam prefers communicating in other languages, languages in which they aren't adept enough to pick up every tonal nuance, where they can't manipulate syntax. Only then can they be themself. They mention this, and Amalia says, "I've set a goal for myself this year to date people who speak Spanish. English is my work persona, and I'm hoping if I date people who don't just speak English dating won't feel like so much fucking work."

I consider that I could interject here with a detail about the four-part songs of zebra finches, which are recombinant as language is. I wait for an opportunity to say this, filled with the soaring feeling the thought always gives me, and also with the stress of needing to interject at the right moment. If I were a cat, I would be crouched, sensitive belly to the ground, waiting for the moment to strike, that opportune pause, but before it comes Amalia says to Swaati, "Anyway, tell us about Portugal," and the conversation pivots with the agility of a mouse wise to the lurking predator, escaping me.

We attempt, when we meet up like this, not to talk about work. We talk about house repairs and gardening. When the server brings drinks we are sharing recent pet photos and Darcy asks me if we have any pets. Direct questions are usually a harbor amidst the broader conversational flow, but we do not have pets. "No," I say, and Liam, noticing that I am not in a position to elaborate, talks about the snake that has made a home of our bathroom, offering a photo of said snake coiled around the warm-water tap, and Amalia says, "I couldn't live like that," and I consider talking about the alligator dead on the shore of our retention pond, but I'm unsure whether this is too macabre, and before I can decide the conversation spins again with dizzying speed. Eva is talking about a new gender-neutral perfume, and I am attempting to reorient.

By the time chips and guacamole arrive, our attempt to avoid work topics has been sabotaged by our general enthusiasm for the work we do and by Eva flicking her phone on when the conversation slows and saying to Amalia, loud enough for the table to hear, "Carol isn't going to push the prescription through." Carol is a primary care doctor on tribal land in the Midwest who's been considering continuing to prescribe estrogen for a seventeen-year-old patient, testing the strength of tribal sovereignty. "She says she can't be sure the tribe would back her if the state comes after her." "That bill has teeth," Swaati says. The physician charged with a felony, the parent or guardian of the child charged civilly. We talk about sovereignty, the lack of case law, the difficulty of knowing how a court would rule if given the chance. This conversation is easier for me—I understand its purpose. Then Amalia says, "People are getting turned away by pharmacists in Florida," and we switch states. Eva says, about the Florida governor, "If he gets the presidential nomination, I'm out of here." We talk about racism, its possible protective power over our work. Most of the organizations that have been targeted are big institutions run by white people for white people. It's the white girls they worry about, the white uteruses they must keep at all costs from the knife, the pearly white breasts they picture when they write about surgeons cutting them off, their descriptions so graphic that Amalia has said, "You just know some of them are jerking off to this." St. Cat's clients are mostly Black and brown, and this, we sometimes say, means the work continues unnoticed.

When our food comes, Darcy and Liam are talking

quietly at the far end of the table and the rest of us are shoulder to shoulder, discussing what the aiding-and-abetting language in Mississippi's care ban means for us. We all join together for a moment when Darcy says, "This is delicious," and I say, a safe echo, "So delicious," though my burrito sits unopened in its to-go container. Eva laughs, and we fragment again. After the server comes by to fill waters, Swaati shoves their half-eaten enchiladas to the side and slaps down a sheet of paper—"Ten seconds to take a photo of this, only you didn't see it from me."

I photograph it without pausing to consider what it is, only reading the heading when Amalia inhales sharply and says, "Only for pharmacists," in a warning voice. "This can't happen through St. Cat." It is a recipe—Testosterone Gel, 500mL formulation. "Of course, it's for pharmacists," Swaati confirms, and winks at me.

Darcy glances over and Swaati folds the paper quickly. There's an awkward moment of silence, in which Liam's conversation with Darcy becomes audible—"Ro thinks unmasking is where you stop trying to act like a neurotypical person and start trying to act like an autistic person."

There is a beat in which I look at Liam—a panicked, stricken look—and then I am laughing. I laugh and laugh, longer than I should. Laughter is one way to pause conversational time. Now the rest of them are laughing, and I stick my straw up through the side of my mask and suck at my horchata, an expression of distress no one but Liam notices, Liam who will say later, as they drive us home, "I'm sorry. I shouldn't have said that, about masking."

It went pretty well, I am thinking. No one dumped a bunch of toothpicks on the ground. I can trust them. This is what Liam has shown me, what Liam is often trying to show me.

There are fairy tales told about my life. I know their shape. An elven child or a troll child is left in the bassinet of a human parent and is raised as a human. Or a gosling falls in with a family of ducks and is raised as a duckling. An eleven-year-old boy has no idea he's a wizard, a nineteen-year-old magician has no idea they're a scale. The child, the gosling, is awkward and ugly and wears broken glasses and is singled out for contempt until the day that their freakishness is revealed to be a gift of power. And then the scale or the swan, having been made aware of their importance to the world, mounts the dragno, spreads their graceful wings, leaves this world for another. To find out I'm a changeling at forty-five! soul554 writes on the boards. DAE feel like a diagnosis proves you're magic? hell0kitkat writes on the boards. Unmask! the boards and the books implore. Reveal your true nature. And I understand that these stories are better than the other, still pervasive stories, in which the changeling is beaten to death with a rock. But mostly my true nature is just me, alone in a room, plucking my hairs out one by one, and I'm unsure what this nature is meant to offer the world.

"I hadn't told them," I say, "about being autistic."

"I gathered," Liam says. "You were going to ask about accommodations at work."

"I was going to, I was."

"Eva's your best friend." This is true in the sense that Eva is the only person aside from Liam that I text on the weekends, the only person I go out of my way to see, the only person who regularly sends me blue heart emojis. Eva and I are sometimes paired together for trainings, and in our debriefs we talk about our parents and our fears and our loves. It is easier to keep up the friendship this way, funneled through our shared work.

"There's a bird and a stone," Liam says. This is a line from a poem by Victoria Chang, one that serves in our private language as a warning.

There is a bird and a stone
in your body. Your job is not
to kill the bird with the stone.

"It's hard, with your friends, to know what I can and can't say. It wasn't the easiest approach to an evening." They are steering with one hand, unwrapping the burrito they ordered with their teeth. They don't ask me to help, I don't offer. "You're scary sometimes. You know?"

I unwrap my burrito, hoping food will ease the tension in my stomach. "What do you mean?"

"How you can go from being one person to being another in one second."

"You did, too."

"Not really. I wasn't myself." They take a bite from the corner of their burrito. I take a bite from the corner of my burrito. "Are you upset with me?"

"Are you upset?" I say. "Are you upset, are you upset, are you upset, are you—"

"Okay," Liam breaks in. "I get it, I'm sorry. These are pretty good." The burrito is okay. I want to be home. I want to be home eating green-tea mochi, tonguing their smooth insides. "You just surprised me," Liam says.

I rarely surprise Liam. Beyond the predictability of my routines, they have studied me—my habits and reactions. They have me precisely timed. Once, as I struggled to beat a reCAPTCHA that was asking me existential questions about what constitutes a bridge, they counted down three-two-one to my groan of frustration. I can never predict Liam or myself. I thought, for instance, that Liam would be the one who'd have a hard time at the translation conference in the spring. They'd struggled with previous conferences—the late nights, the people, the constant stimulation. They returned from conferences talking fast, moving fast, a quicksilver version of themself. I loved being left alone. When Liam left for two days for a reading in another city, the solitude was welcome. But at the conference in the spring Liam was happy, elated. They loved their workshop, loved talking about syntax across languages. They loved the other translators, the polyglots. They even loved the food, which I found difficult to believe. I was the one calling twice daily to ask, "What are you doing now?" which I've since learned is a meaningless question as there is no true now across space, no moment in Liam's day at that conference that corresponded to the moment I experienced. To lie on your bed in Florida and ask your partner, "What are you doing now in Vermont?" is as ridiculous as asking, in the same circumstances, "What are you doing here in Vermont?" Vermont is not here or now. I didn't know this then, but I felt it, the supreme loneliness of local time.

The conference was on top of a mountain. Time was passing faster for Liam. They would age more, in their two weeks with the translators, than I would age alone in Florida. This divide was so palpable, and I was so unable to manage it, that finally they called the cops, even though we'd talked about cops, how much we hated them, ACAB, all of that, and the horror of active rescue, how it did away with agency, and agency was the only thing that made life bearable for either of us, the reason neither of us wanted to return to childhood. They had said, during this conversation, that the problem with alternative models of suicide prevention was that they failed to account for human panic. A comment that, looking back, felt freighted with prophecy.

Ludwig Boltzmann, after publishing his theories of time and heat, which would prove revolutionary, hanged himself at Duino, near Trieste, while his wife and daughter took a short swim in the Adriatic. His mentee Paul Ehrenfest, who developed a theory of time that helped, in one narrow way, to reconcile quantum mechanics and classical physics, shot his neurodivergent son and then himself. These deaths, and others, led a twentieth-century philosopher to suggest that time punishes with an early death those who dare approach its occult subject matter.

The night Liam called the police was unexceptional. I had cut my lower arms and upper thighs, and I was ashamed of this—it made me feel immature, I knew the world associated such behavior with teenagers, though I hadn't thought of it as a teenager, it hadn't occurred to me until my early twenties, my first friendship. Still, it was routine. A few years back, when I lived alone, no one would have known, and the cuts would have healed with time. A few years forward, and Liam would have stopped me easily. It was bad timing, that's all. I wasn't trying to die, I was trying to say something. When I told Liam this later, they said, "What were you trying to say?" But I couldn't think of any synonyms, any way to say it other than how I already had, which Liam had interpreted as wanting to die. Now, I think I was trying to say something about broken rules—buying the wrong brand of sweater, the wrong flavor of yogurt. This time, the rule I had broken was very important, one I'd had for years: Do not ever ask anyone for anything. I had broken the rule with Liam. This was the necessary risk of partnership. In the past, I had kept myself safe by insisting that partnership was not possible for me—but partnership had become possible, that was the thing, Liam and I had been living together for almost a year. We were eating the same meals. We were sleeping in the same bed. Liam had stopped commenting on my awkward movements, my heavy stride, the fact that when I walk across a room, the windows shake in their frames. I'd stopped startling at their appearance in the mornings, stopped twitching myself to sleep at night, Liam on the far edge of the bed to ensure we didn't touch. I'd become accustomed to them, the rule had given way, the impossible had become possible, and of course there was a cost to this small miracle. When they left for Vermont, I didn't feel the usual relief of solitude. I felt, for the first time ever in my life, painfully alone. Incomplete. Disoriented. For two weeks, I was sequestered in the cabin by the retention pond, where the precipice kept rushing up to meet my feet, so I flung myself to the ground to avoid falling, and I couldn't recognize my own life. So maybe it was about recognition, what I was saying, or about what was possible. I had tried using words with Liam, but they didn't understand—"You can do whatever you want today," they said on the phone when I tried to talk about the precipice. They listed possibilities, each one a stone on my chest, and when I panicked they said, "Easy. You have to calm down." By the time Liam asked if the cuts on my body needed medical attention, I was beyond talking. I texted them, I don't care, life is impossible, and then I stopped texting. I let their calls go to voicemail. They texted, Answer me. They texted, Tell me you're alive. They texted, If you don't answer, I have to call someone. They texted and called so many times my phone vibrated itself off the edge of the table and fell to the floor. They called Eva, then my mother, and when neither picked up Liam called the police, and what I'm trying to say is that aside from that one phone call it was just a Saturday night, it wasn't exceptional. A nurse later called the cuts a suicidal gesture. Not an attempt, a gesture. It was the right word.

"Henlo," Liam says, calling me back to the car. "Are you there?"

I say, "Yes," answering the question they asked. I am there, far from the car, dipped in fluorescent memory, my burrito forgotten. But they mean, are you present? Are you with me in this localized now, in which my burrito has tipped in my hand, loosing a clump of beans and sauce. They land on my favorite shirt, and I panic, lift the beans to my mouth with my fingers, which smear the sauce into the cloth, and Liam says, "It's okay. It'll come out," and I look down at my feet and see the sachets of tea, which I've forgotten to give out, a common mistake, my memory erased by the pure, bracing anxiety of interaction. I once flew to visit Swaati with a pair of earrings and didn't realize until I was back home, unpacking my bag, that the earrings were still there in the side pocket. I sob once, and Liam, noticing, says, "It's not a big deal, we'll ship them," which is what I did with the earrings, and I trace the lines of my palm with my fingernail and think, **I'm walking on uneven ground**, and thanks to this quote or my gentle scratching, I last another half hour before beginning to sob in earnest, which, seen in a certain light, is a victory.

Liam says, "Everything's okay."

The crying that overtakes me during these times is lusty, audible. I am grunting—a loud, guttural sound—with every out-breath. I am taking sharp swallows of air that hurt my throat. My eyes burn. I am not sad. I am not angry. I could not tell you what I am feeling, but I know what I feel—my knees pressed against my chest, my fingers tapping the hard bones of my shins. I wail, and I feel the wail in my throat.

Liam is driving onward, grimly. They will not interfere. They feel for the house keys, tuck them into the pocket on their door, out of reach. They say, "Stop," once, firmly, when I crack my skull against the window of the car. When I reach to turn off the air-conditioning, which is suddenly painful, like blades raked across my skin, Liam flinches a little, grips the wheel tighter, and I say, "You're scared of me." "That's not what I meant," Liam says. Liam is afraid of my meltdowns. Anyone—I almost wrote any sane person—would be afraid of my meltdowns. This is what I call them now, the new word I use since the diagnosis, and with the new word a new understanding, that they are not something I can prevent or control, though Liam has pushed back on this second part, saying, "I need to feel like I can hold you responsible for what you do, for what you say, even in a meltdown." I had agreed, easily. It made sense to me. Though what I feel in these moments is a lack of control, this must be in part illusion, I must have some control, why else am I sobbing now, in the car, and not earlier, at the restaurant. All I say, the last thing I will say that night, is "It's my fault, we shouldn't have gone. You're doing a good job," and though this is less generosity than defense, an attempt to ward off the shame that will come in the morning, I still give something away by saying it, or maybe it's the effort of the words, forcing them through a throat swollen nearly to occlusion, whatever the reason my body responds by sucking me deeper, redoubles the abdominal contractions that pull me in on myself, my sobs reaching farther, grabbing at my pelvic bone. Liam does not attempt conversation, knowing there will be no response, and as soon as we get home I slide from under the seat belt, not unbuckling it, and puddle in the footwell, back against the seat, knees against the glove compartment. Liam leaves me there, knows better than to try moving me. I will stumble from car to house hours later, the doorknob impossible so I throw my shoulder against the door, force it, and the ground tilts as I walk across it, weaving, and Liam has fit a twin sheet over the couch, left a pillow and a glass brimful with water, an attempt to cut the next morning's headache, the only type of hangover I ever experience, and as the heaving quiets, my abdominal muscles slowly relaxing, I feel, finally, ease. The nearly euphoric bloom of a quiet body and a calm mind. Since I was a child I have conceived of this sensation in the words of my mother's favorite prayer, in which St. John of the Cross, having come through a long night of suffering, describes in this way his communion with God:

> He struck me on the neck
> With His gentle hand,
> And all sensation left me.

. . . .

I continued in oblivion lost,
My head was resting on my love;
Lost to all things and myself,
And, amid the lilies forgotten,
Threw all my cares away.

"I'm concerned," my therapist says at the next session. "What would you have done if it had continued to escalate prior to this lunch?"

"Dinner," I say. When we got home, we washed my work shirt. Eva texted me photos of a drag poetry night she and Darcy and Swaati had gone to after—you missed a great event, she wrote, but I get wanting to turn in early. I read, in the second half of this text, a tacit acknowledgment of my being autistic, of Liam's reveal, which I hadn't confirmed, and so which couldn't be acknowledged directly. We washed my work shirt a second time. The color of the sauce came out but left behind an oily circle. Ruined.

My therapist makes a dismissive gesture—"On the side of the highway."

I understand what she worries about. I read the news—Man Struggling with Mental Health Issues Shot by Police in Jersey City. Bipolar Woman Stabbed Blind Date During Sex. Bexleyheath Man with Autism Convicted of Killing Grandpa. Grammy-Winning Country Musician Naomi Judd Dealing with Bipolar Disorder While She Died of Suicide. Autistic Man Jailed over Fatal Stabbing. Neighbor with Bipolar Disorder Shot by Sugar Land Police Officer. Autistic Thirteen-Year-Old Should Never Have Been Shot but Officer Won't Face Charges, DA Says. Bipolar Disorder: Three People Shot. Police Refuse to Press Charges Against Man with Autism Who Grabbed Three-Year-Old and Kissed Him—"Why Did You Let Him So Close to Your Kids?" Man Opening Doors of MRT Trains Suffering from Bipolar Disorder. Mother Looks for a Contractor to Build Wide and Tall Gate in Her Living Room to Keep Her Autistic Son Safe.

We are not unaware of such possibilities, but neither are we beholden to them. I say, "I'm good, I'm doing good."

"What does good mean?"

"Good. Like, good," I say.

"What you're describing doesn't sound good to me," she says, and I worry I've relayed too well the crisis of the previous day, a memory that stands out for its jagged edges, like a single rock in a river. "Usually in psychology," she says, "we think about happiness or fulfillment as an effect of sustained interaction with other people, a meaningful giving back."

I have an appointment just after this one with a client in Florida seeking care for her thirteen-year-old son, but I don't tell my therapist this. The work is not definitively illegal, but also not definitively legal, and I'm not interested in telling the story she wants me to tell. Instead, I say, "I'm just feeling really good."

"Do you think it's a feeling you can trust?" she asks. The question is the sort of verbal spring trap I never see coming, though I should. If my distress is suspect, why not happiness as well. But the happiness, if it's a delusion, is a delusion shared with Liam, and madness as part of a romantic partnership is a solid thing, one way the divinity of love is described in Plato's *Phaedrus*. Socially acceptable. Whole lives have been built on less.

"I'm not convinced this relationship is healthy for you," she says. "I still think you might be better off with someone more—stable, more emotionally resilient."

"A man," I say. She shakes her head. My therapist doesn't like being reminded that she is straight and I am queer. She refers to her husband as her partner. I only concluded her partner was a man after five sessions spent listening hard for his pronoun.

The author of *Mad Eden* is queer. I am certain of this. In the second installment of *Mad Eden*, Cardinaux and Nova's relationship becomes increasingly romantic. The author doesn't have words like love or kiss, so their romance is made up of long moments of **eye** (from *A close eye on the eagle-eyed visual acuity hypothesis of autism*) **contact** (from *Autistic disturbances of affective contact*) and changes in **heart-rate** (from *reductions in heart-rate in normal school children*). It's become almost a compulsion for me, tracing the sentences of *Mad Eden* back to the original text. Doing so reveals how difficult it is for the author to construct even the simplest sentence. They use whole clauses when they can (**relentlessly magical world**), but more often they're forced to match a noun from one sentence with a verb from another, taking adjectives and articles from others. English makes this relatively straightforward—the subject-verb agreement is easy to fib, there's no adjective or article matching. It would be more difficult in Spanish. Even so, to write **Many relationships that are clear to a scale would be undetectable to a magician**, they string together words from seven different sentences and knock the *un* off *unclear*. At times, they go further still—*apples* in the first installment comes from *applies*, **home** from *homogeneity*, **fall** from *differentially*. This effort is nearly invisible in the final text, the words flowing one after another. The invisible effort reminds me of masking, as if it isn't just the content of *Mad Eden* that's autistic, the process of creating *Mad Eden* is autistic, too.

Many auties dislike Cardinaux and Nova's romance. Codependent much? one wrote on the boards, and this comment received overwhelming agreement. A number of aro auties expressed their dismay that Cardinaux was lost to them as a role model. When Cardinaux and Nova had sex, the auties went wild. Omigod, Cardinaux is a groomer! someone posted. This led to dozens of responses, some attempting to interpret Cardinaux and Nova's anatomies, to which one autie responded, Enough with the gender nonsense, Cardinaux is a dragon. Another flurry of responses addressed the question of Nova's age: I think Nova is supposed to be like 19–20yo, one autie posted, and Cardinaux is . . . 400–600yo? Sure, it's an age gap, but it wouldn't be illegal and some folks are into that kind of thing. Another wrote, Given the technology described and the approach to magic, I'm interpreting the setting here to be (roughly) Europe (the Baltics? Latvia?) in the first half of the 13th century. It wouldn't be uncommon in that setting for a 16–17yo to be sexually active. I'm not saying that justifies it, but it may be true to the time period, to which one autie responded, There's no way this is Latvia, and another responded, Y'all, come on, it's a fucking dragon! To which an autie responded, More precisely, a fucking dragno, and a last autie responded, Most precisely, a dragno fucking. Some auties stopped reading *Mad Eden* at this point, but I liked the sex: **Nova runs their hands over Cardinaux's scales, feels the strength of the underlying muscle, follows the wandering path** [from *pathological*] **of a vein on the inside of Cardinaux's frith.** Or, **Nova presses their mouth to Cardinaux's grether and, for the first time ever, stops thinking.** The sex is an extension of their bond and, in that sense, natural. Thinking about all of this, I say to the therapist what I said to Quentin, what Quentin understood. "Our relationship is mutualistic."

"That's sweet," she says, and I want to rescind the word. Sure, Cardinaux and Nova's bond is sweet. It allows them to have a sense of what the other needs, even at a distance, as I once called Liam when they were working at a coffee shop to remind them to eat. It allows them to communicate without speaking aloud, as Liam wiggles their fingers at me when our neighbor insists she's eaten thirty-six peaches, letting me know she's being sarcastic so I won't inquire, worriedly, about her gut health. To fly together, Nova and Cardinaux have to sing the same notes, as when Liam says, "Good Ro, Best—" and we sing the last "Ro," together. Nova and Cardinaux sometimes lie on their backs, feeding each other figs, and Liam and I sometimes lie on our backs, feeding each other peanut butter pretzels. They're sweet, we're sweet, but sweetness isn't the point. The bond between dragno and scale is centrally about defense—it makes it possible for them to battle magicians. My connection with Liam, similarly, is centrally about our shared commitment to survival. The thing about alligators, the thing not reported in *5 Animal Friendships That Will Melt Your Heart*, is what they eat as they circle beneath the birds' nests. Not offal, not fish bones. The birds sacrifice nothing less than their smallest chicks, their runts, their unwanted young, shoved out of the nest and into the gullet of the gators to garner some protection from the world. This is what I wanted to communicate.

"But can you explain to me why you're happy?" my therapist asks.

I tell her. About the alligator, and Quentin leaving, so the house was quiet, and the repetition of our empty days edged against boredom, creating a perfect pleasure, how I craved, each morning, yogurt with a few blueberries, and how satisfying to experience the craving and then, just a few minutes later, the sensation I'd craved, and our cabin was so remote we went whole days without seeing anyone, and each time I read the second installment of *Mad Eden* I felt a little thrill. Take the sex, for instance:

> "How is this so good?" Nova says, Cardinaux's grether in their ear.
>
> *You don't habituate*, Cardinaux says. *So each sensation has the same intensity as the first sensation. We call it hyperarousal.*
>
> As if to demonstrate this point, Cardinaux guides Nova's fingers into his ivry and as Nova presses there rhythmically [from *Rhythmical stereotypies (leg-swinging) associated with reductions in heart-rate*], Cardinaux sings a note so high and long Nova thinks they cannot achieve it. They attempt and find that not only can they sing the note, but there beside Cardinaux, so close the two are like one body, they can sustain the note long after their body should have given out.

That word hyperarousal thrills me with its exactness, describing the pleasure and too-muchness of sex all at once.

Cardinaux doesn't orgasm, but at one point his ivry sort of crumbles away into dust, which **dribbles through Nova's fingers like sand**, a phrase that comes from a Temple Grandin quote included in the original article, and of course the auties on the boards were up in arms about this, and I agree it's pretty bad, but the badness is the point, I think, the paucity of language is the point. Nineteen hundred words, most of them clunkers like *heterogeneity* and *parametric*. That's all the author of *Mad Eden* has, all any of us auties have, to describe the joys and dramas of our lives in a way that's legible to the world.

"It's like someone is reading *Mad Eden* off the inside of my skull," I say to my therapist. *Mad Eden* insists that the world of dragnos and magicians is my world, the world of meltdowns after dinner and forgotten sachets of tea, of trans kids and politicians. I understand something then. I say to my therapist, "The magicians need the dragnos, but the dragnos don't need the magicians. They're just trying to live." I feel the comfort of a useful epiphany, but "I want to focus on your life," my therapist says. "In your life, it sounds like you're experiencing some real isolation." I agree, and her mouth puckers, suggesting she's less than pleased, and we talk about my support system, all it is lacking, and I don't tell her the second installment ends with a postcoital conversation between Cardinaux and Nova, in which Cardinaux tells Nova they need more friends. I don't tell her that when I talk about *Mad Eden* I am talking about my own life.

I reread the second installment when I get home. Nova has convinced Cardinaux to descend briefly to the lower world. They miss the sounds and smells of their old home, so the pair have eloped to a spot just beneath the islands to fuck in privacy:

> ***I'm concerned for you,*** **Cardinaux says, after.** ***You don't get on with the other scales, and you haven't started to transition.***
>
> **"And I need to transition, because all scales are . . . trans?"**
>
> ***Don't say because. And polymorphic is more precise, it's—***
>
> **A fox appears, and Nova jumps up: "Magicians!" The magicians hunt with foxes, which they train to track** [from *Computational systems for dynamic object tracking rely on predictive techniques*] **dragnos.**
>
> ***Is it my frith you don't like or my cerebellum?***
>
> **"We have to go. Quickly."**
>
> ***If you're concerned by the size of my ganglia, I can say that even after transition most scales aren't nearly as well-endo—***
>
> **"We don't have time for this!"**
>
> ***Don't have time? I'm a dragno. My temporal span is longer than my wing span.*** **Cardinaux opens his wings to exhibit this prodigious reach.** ***You are my scale. Time and space cannot restrict us. We have all the times—sometimes, oftentimes, manytimes, and many more.***

This turns out not to be true. As Cardinaux carries Nova toward the islands of proficiency, an arrow pierces the muscle of his wing, and they begin to fall.

"Your body is my body," Nova says, and sings a note so high, so painfully piercing, that it is also, nearly, a scream, pulling the arrow out of Cardinaux's wing and into their own shoulder, then passing out from the pain. Nova is frequently passing out, a convenient break in the narrative action, which allows *Mad Eden* to summarize events that are too difficult to narrate with its reduced vocabulary. Cardinaux can **take off** and **land** but can never fly, can **digest** but never swallow. Nova can **pass out**, but can't sleep, can **say** but can't talk or speak. When the author of *Mad Eden* is fully stymied by these missing words, they leave blank space.

When Nova **comes to** (waking up isn't possible) in the dragno's **hospital** (from *Massachusetts General Hospital*), Cardinaux is anxious and angry. Apparently such a display of magic is so advanced it should be impossible for a scale as new as Nova—***Had you been any less precise, you would have died, and without cause. A single arrow cannot end me, but if you die, I will unfold, becoming a being only of spirit. To unfold is a distasteful experience, so I would ask that you attempt to survive.*** But it's clear Nova saved him.

In the comments beneath the second installment, the auties discuss the author's identity. Queer, they agree. One suggests bisexuality. Another posts, Kinky for sure. One autie writes, I bet they were diagnosed as a kid. As a late-diagnosed autist, I'd never have the confidence to write something like this. I feel, reading this comment, what I have never felt before, a desire to wade in. I don't think the author of *Mad Eden* was diagnosed as a kid. I went looking for *Autism as a Disorder of Prediction* just a couple months after being diagnosed. Someone at peace with their diagnosis and securely ensconced in autistic community wouldn't be reading scientific articles from a decade ago. They wouldn't spend hours with a paper describing a little-known theory of autism, using its vocabulary to eke out a story about magicians. As a work of art, *Mad Eden* is desperate. I create an account—Ro1117—and I write these thoughts in a post that quickly runs to four hundred words. If we consider Nova's storyline, I write, we can conclude that the author, like Nova, was diagnosed as a young adult (likely recently). We can guess that the author is genderqueer, the alternative being that Nova's pronouns are a device that make it easier for the author to use plural verb forms. We can be pretty sure the author is queer and in a close partnership, given the way Nova and Cardinaux are bonded in a real physical sense—what risks one of them risks the other. Nova is a risk, I write at the end of my post, but they don't know it. The magicians are able, somehow, to locate them. Again and again, when they least expect it, the magicians appear.

My client is the mother of a thirteen-year-old seeking top surgery. She says when I open the call, "My kid's in her bedroom. She doesn't know I'm talking to you." Two red flags. First, the word *kid*—gender-neutral, but also tinged with resentment. Second, "Why not let them be a part of the call?" I ask. "I don't want to get their hopes up," she says, mirroring the pronoun back, which is a good sign, "and I'll be honest I don't know what to think about it all." She's sitting in front of a bookshelf. Mostly fantasy from what I can see. I twist my tongue, a ninety-degree rotation, and run it along the backs of my teeth, so it feels, from my tongue's perspective, as if my teeth are stacked vertically in my mouth. I trace the edges of those teeth until I am calm. Then I open my vertical teeth and say, "Date of birth?"

She rattles it off fast and continues before I have a chance to prompt her. "I heard there's a clinic in the Northeast y'all partner with that does these surgeries early, on kids twelve, thirteen."

This is a red flag. In my year of patient navigation, it's the first time any parent has asked about surgery. It's possible she's trying to trap me. She could be a bad actor. This is the phrase used in trainings, though it brings to my mind goofy people on a stage, forgetting their lines. I'm not afraid of her. For every script she has, I have a counterscript. "We don't have any clinical partners. What we can offer are recommendations based on the care your child needs and your location."

"I just need you to tell me where I can go to get it done," she says. "I know there's clinics y'all partner with that are a one-stop shop, we could get the blocks, the surgery, all of it."

I've tried explaining the tongue and teeth trick to Liam, but it doesn't work for them. Their tongue refuses to twist. "We don't have clinical partners," I repeat.

"Talk to me about the blocks," she counters. If she is a bad actor, I should limit what I say, end the call quickly, but I find myself talking at length about barriers to access and ways around those barriers. **Staying on a script is the sole means of keeping my anxiety at a minimum.** I want to please her, too, an impulse I feel with everyone, regardless of their possible intentions. So when she asks, "And if Lupron isn't possible, would they prescribe Depo-Provera?" I say, "Depo can be a low-cost alternative to Lupron but it has significant side effects."

"They're thirteen now—will that be an issue?" "Every clinic is going to provide care on a case-by-case basis," I say. I can do this dance all day. She says, "And if I don't support all of this, will they call CPS? Do you call CPS if a parent doesn't support this kind of care?" I am thrown by the question, so far from the day-to-day realities of my job. I don't have a script, end up ad-libbing: "No, if you're not looking for help accessing care, you're good to go. We can end this call right away."

I've considered that the tongue trick is a part of my ability to suspend causality, how I can forget, moment to moment, that I've twisted my tongue. There have been times when I'm aware of this suspension of cause and effect, the useful detachment of action from consequence, which makes it possible to pull out a painful splinter or press an alcohol pad to a bad scrape or drive to the pharmacy for another vaccine.

"She started filling out at ten," the woman says. "Same as me. You get hell for it. That young, you get hell. When she was twelve all of a sudden she wouldn't take the bus to school. All that winter, she refused. I figured she was being a spoiled brat. I drove her, but I made her pay for it. I never asked her why. I don't want to make that mistake again." She puts a lock of hair in her mouth, chewing it gently. I wait for her to be clear. "What if in her mind," she says, the hair falling from her lips as she leans toward her camera, "there's only two options—rape or be raped. What if all of this is just her way to keep herself safe."

This, too, is a script—the implication that trans identity is a response to trauma—but it isn't entirely a script, which is to say I think what she's recalling is true in a vague way, there is some truth in it. My suspicion wanes to something more like caution or even curiosity. "How can I know what's my kid," she says, "and what's the world around her, them?" She's looking away from me, fiddling with something on her desk. "This awful world," she says. "How can I know she's not making a mistake?"

There are things I can say to this. Regret isn't impossible, but it's rare. I could talk about support systems. I could cite the article suggesting traumatic experiences and gender identity are linked, but not in the way people think—trans identities are often visible at an early age and make youth more likely to be targeted. Being targeted doesn't make you trans. It's the other way around, a confusion of cause and effect, a confusion of time. But I don't want to say any of this. The scripts I have to respond to her are true in the way of slogans—a boxy, one-size-fits-all truth. None of them answer her real question, which is unanswerable. There is no way to disentangle history and identity, no way to extricate—not for anyone, not completely—desire from fear.

"We don't want to wait until eighteen. We can't wait," the woman says. She is talking fast now, agitated. "I was big at her age, and she's bigger. She gets a bad rash under there, which I tell her that's about hygiene, but what do I know? How early can they get them off her?" "It's not about age," I say. "Care plans are based on development." "And she's developing fast, I'm telling you," she says, twisting her hair tightly around her finger. "Don't they do it for girls with early puberty?"

We've talked for almost twelve minutes. It's best practice, if you suspect someone of having malicious intent, to talk for no more than five. This decreases the likelihood of the caller collecting enough video clips and seconds of audio to later spin against you. But her agitation, her quick, rigid speech, relaxes me. She is worried, desperate even, and this is usual. I no longer suspect her. I suggest she talk to a specialist about macromastia. I ask about her insurance. I say, "With a gender dysphoria indication, it's likely not possible to get your child in for surgery anywhere before eighteen, but if they have macromastia, that could shift the timeline. When did they start puberty?"

"You need me to sign off on the puberty, I'll sign off. There's no exam needed, right? You understand, I don't want to traumatize her."

And I say, thinking of Quentin, thinking of trauma, I say, little fool, "Every clinic is different, but usually a clinical exam isn't required at the first appointment."

"Is there a window of opportunity? Like, if we wait until she's twenty-five, twenty-six? Do you think that would be too late? I just want to do what's in my child's best interest."

I am suddenly spooked again, replaying this last comment in my head, realizing all the ways it could be turned, taken out of context, wishing I could wind back the tape. I return to my scripts, clinging to them. "People transition at all ages. The risk of waiting is that it could negatively impact your child's mental health."

A hand reaches into the screen then, the fingernails unpainted, chewed so low a few are crusted with blood. The hand is beseeching. The woman mutes her microphone, talks to someone I can't see off to her left, then hands them a few bills. "Sorry," she says, unmuting a moment later.

"She's headed out with a friend, wanted pocket money." Then she says, "I'm worried if we wait too long, she won't be able to manage the shift," as if womanhood were glue that dried solid. "Doesn't it matter how long she spends trying to be a certain way?"

Later, when I attempt to explain to Eva why I didn't abort the call after three minutes, why I talked for eighteen minutes instead, more than enough time for her to gather the seconds of video footage she needed to splice together a damning sequence, I will remember this comment. Not just the comment, but that note in her voice of yearning, and her voice itself, which suggested androgyny, the T-verb of it, and also the way she chewed her hair, a classic stim, which I was tempted to imitate, though my hair doesn't reach my mouth. Doesn't it matter? she had asked. I had the same question. Didn't it matter that I'd spent an entire lifetime perfecting an act, believing it was truth, only to be told to leave the stage, drop the mask, venture as myself out into the audience?

I give her what she wants. The name of a clinician off my list, a clinician who's done surgery for macromastia with a masculinizing closure. Her child's too young, but I want to offer something, and I end the call, and as that portal through spacetime closes I feel it—a surge of sensation, different from the tendrils Liam and I experienced earlier. I can't name it. Peace no longer fits. Neither does contentment. Relief is there, heady and premature. Also, the sensation of having helped someone, of accomplishment. It is a feeling as mature and full-bodied as happiness, but it isn't quite that either, and I touch the pads of my fingers to the pad of my thumb one at a time, feeling into the sensation, claiming it, and when I'm ready I spin around in my chair to face the desk where Liam is working, and I see it reflected in their face, that bright energy I couldn't name. "What am I feeling?" I ask. This was a game we often played.

Liam studies me for a moment. "Relieved?" they try. I shake my head. "Successful? Jubilant?" They consider each word before offering it, working through the translation with care, aware of the implications of the different synonyms, their histories and contexts, their particular illumination. "Fizzy?" Liam says. "Joyful?"

And it is possible then to name the thing that has been nipping at our heels for weeks. "Joy," I say.

As if it has been waiting to be named, the joy blooms outward, shiver and light, until it is visible—not corporeal, but substantive, hovering above us.

That night, in our mesh tent, curled beside Liam, who is sleeping with one hand in the joy that pulses slowly between us, I guess at causes. The cause of the joy must exist within its backward-facing light cone. But this is still vast. Say, for instance, that forty years and eleven months before this night, on the third planet from the sun in the Trappist-1 solar system, something pulsed. One pulse. I don't know the motivation for the pulse. Mating, perhaps, if such things mate. Or an attempt to avoid predation, like the flashes of bioluminescence in dinoflagellates. An emission caused by the slowing of an internal thermodynamic system, like the clapping of an engine as it cools. A pulse. And the released photons travel Earthward, taking the shortest path, a path already determined across some 230 trillion miles, and to say the photons arrive quickly, by any human standard, is an understatement, and my eyes received the photons but were unable to relay their frequency—which lies outside the visible spectrum—to my brain. Perhaps the joy began here, in a muddled communication between life forms in two solar systems. Or say the pulse came not from an organism but from some inorganic process that catalyzes the formation of an atmosphere in the Trappist-1 system. Or from a nova farther away, shining momentarily bright enough to see. Or it could be a photon released by a streetlight flickering on at dusk or by our neighbor driving down the wrong road or by a glitch in one pixel of my computer's screen, a digital joy the computer meant to keep for itself. A coot in our retention pond bleated their two-syllable call, and I startled as if hearing my name. Flowers bloomed—small, white, furry ones that smell like cum. Maybe the joy was in those atoms, which compared to light travel sluggishly. Or consider the armadillo who slept in a burrow beneath the floor of our bedroom and farted, so we smelled his digested grubs and earthworms, olfactory intimacy. This was also within the light cone. As was the yogurt we ate with homemade jam and the anxious sweat smell of my armpits after a meeting and the mosquitoes that were so abundant that June, floating through the walls and the floor, but what preceded the joy most immediately was that client call, and though I know proximity doesn't equal cause, I can't help but fall prey to that delusion so beloved of the human mind, can't help but think the call itself caused the joy. If that call caused the joy, what caused the call? To answer that question, I need another light cone. I put the call at its nexus. I need to move from the forward-facing light cone of the call to the backward-facing cone. This is tricky. Nothing—not sand or sound—is permitted to move in such a way. Only the observer who sits at the nexus of that light cone can do so. I am not the observer at the nexus of that light cone, but I know who is.

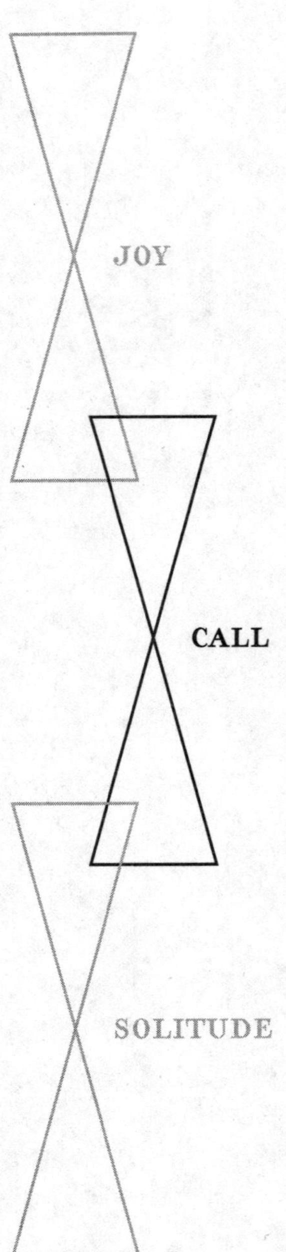

ELSEWHERE

Gabriella Holt didn't love Jennifer Flitok like a mother. She didn't love Jennifer Flitok like a sister or a lover or even a friend. She loved Jennifer Flitok the way the world loved Jennifer Flitok. Not all of the world, obviously, no one is universally loved, but a subset of the world loved Jennifer Flitok, and Gabbi was part of it, one of the 1.2 million people who followed Flitok on Twitter, one of the twenty thousand people who liked her post: 11 yo's teacher tells him calling a boy a boy makes people feel unsafe. Watch him own the libs #genderideology #radfem. Gabbi loved Jennifer Flitok the way her other 1,219,492 followers loved her with one exception—Gabbi loved her first.

The love began in a small back room of Gabbi's parents' house, which had been Gabbi's room as a child and which became her room again as a thirty-four-year-old—first temporarily, called home by her mother to confront her father's dementia, and later permanently.

She wasn't surprised by her mother's call. She'd predicted her father's dementia years before, when her mother was still calling his inability to work the laundry machine or orient himself well enough in the garage to find the mower laziness or general male entitlement. Gabbi is good at this type of prediction. She posted about it on r/Auties where her username is hell0kitkat. Gabbi sometimes thinks she has a special talent for the type of patterning used to predict things like extreme weather. She has never been surprised by a hurricane—meteorological or psychological. She considers facts, categorizes them, fits them together, and can, with remarkable precision, say what's likely to happen next. A blessing and a curse, she wrote in her Reddit post. Sometimes she can't do anything to change what's going to happen and has to sit chewing her nails in a college class as she watches the professor embarrass himself, predictably, in front of ninety undergraduates, or sit listening to her mother complain about her father's refusal to remember things like their anniversary and her birthday until years later her prediction is verified.

The verification happened in that case when Gabbi's aunt, her mother's sister, came to visit. At dinner, her aunt's new wife asked Gabbi's father about the hospital where he'd worked for forty years, and Gabbi's father couldn't name it. He knew where he'd worked. He could describe the hospital building, but he couldn't link the picture he had in his mind to a word. A few days later, in their stucco house with its sliding glass doors and electric mower and kidney-shaped aboveground pool, he solemnly asked his wife's sister if she wanted to elope with him to Pagosa Springs, and this is what caused Gabbi's mother, finally, to phone Gabbi and her brother, a three-way call, and say, "Your father has dementia," and to insist they travel home, as if dementia were a spell that might be broken by a filial kiss.

Gabbi went. Gabbi always went home when her mother called her. Gabbi's mother was her confidant, her support, her closest friend. Her mother drove her to college and stayed for two weeks in a nearby hotel, waiting until Gabbi was in the rhythm of classes and laundry and groceries before returning home. Seven years later, she drove Gabbi to grad school and stayed for a month. It was a more difficult city to navigate—larger, with several bus and train lines. For one month, they rode the bus together, learning to determine from the shape of the skyline the appropriate moment to push the red button marked STOP. They didn't agree about everything. Gabbi's mother didn't want her to get top surgery, which Gabbi referred to, in her mother's presence, as a reduction. Gabbi's mother didn't approve of Gabbi's artfully torn jeans. But friends can disagree, and anytime Gabbi expected her mother to be there, she was. So Gabbi wasn't surprised, flying home at her mother's summons, to exit the airport terminal into a warm December and find her mother waiting in the family minivan, though she felt a new thrill. It was the first time she was meeting her mother as an adult with a brand-new master's degree and a girlfriend and four job interviews lined up for the week to come. Gabbi's life was finally coming together.

The back windows of the minivan were shaded, a luxury Gabbi's mother had discovered thirty-three years before while nursing Gabbi on twelve-hour drives to visit her in-laws in Virginia. Gabbi rarely thought about the tinted windows, but on this trip she would be grateful for them, as ten minutes into the drive Gabbi's mother pulled a box from the passenger seat, handed it to Gabbi, and said, "Put this on."

In the box was a sundress. A sleeveless yellow sundress with small red flowers on the skirt. Her mother's dress.

Gabbi doesn't wear dresses. She has posted about this on r/Auties in response to a question about fabric sensitivities. Gabbi isn't sensitive to particular fabrics, but she can't stand dresses. It's the way the skirt bunches underneath you when you sit, the tightness around the hips, which is the wrong sort of tightness, forcing skin into contact with skin. I hate the feeling of one thigh touching the other thigh, hell0kitkat wrote. I hate being naked, how the thigh skin can touch the arm skin can touch the belly skin. I like all my limbs to be wrapped up. I never wear dresses. At some point it became sort of a gender thing, but I'm over that now. Still can't stand dresses. Gabbi wasn't over the gender thing when she flew into the rinky-dink airport near her parents' home in Florida and her mother handed her the yellow sundress.

Gabbi said, "What's this?"

Her mother said, "Just put it on. For your father."

In a later response to the same Reddit thread, hell0kitkat posted about finally getting top surgery, a relief after almost a year on a waiting list, finally ridding herself of the constant feeling of skin rubbing skin, which was the central discomfort she associated with boobs, a major discomfort—at times even a physical pain—she'd tried soothing with Vaseline and tight sports bras, even with binders (love the compression! she wrote), none of which had offered the relief top surgery did.

To her mother, driving home from the airport, Gabbi declined. Maybe she said, "No thanks," or, "What the fuck, Mom?" or, "Absolutely not." She'd gotten T at the student clinic in the northern city where she was living and, after two months of perseverating, had been injecting it for three months, long enough that her stomach had gotten a little fuzzy, which she liked. It helped to cover up the skin. Gabbi sometimes wished she were an animal—a dog or a bear, something with a pelt.

"We're trying to jog your father's long-term memory," her mother might have said. "Just this once he needs his daughter."

Gabbi still refused. She refused as they stopped for chicken nuggets at the fast-food restaurant just before the bridge, refused as they paused outside a three-story condo, which wasn't the house in which she'd grown up. "Your brother's house," her mother said, but her brother didn't own the place. He was selling the house for a couple moving to Virginia, had gotten his real estate license a few months before.

Gabbi's brother was gay. Her uncles and aunt were gay. Her mother was the only straight person among her five siblings. When Gabbi came out to her mother as a lesbian, her mother said, "Why is everyone in my life gay?" and left the room. Gabbi's brother was four years older and two notches less queer than Gabbi in Gabbi's estimation. I mean, real estate? On that day, Gabbi's brother was in a hurry, had exactly two hours before he needed to be on the beach showing a house to a retired couple. When Gabbi protested to him about the dress, he said, "What's the big deal? It's a dress. You want me to wear one, too?" He wasn't wearing a dress, he was wearing the black jeans and sports blazer he would wear to meet the retirees.

Gabbi had lost. She knew it, but still she postponed, waiting until they had turned onto her parents' cul-de-sac to unfold the dress and force her body into it. She didn't look at herself in the dress. Not in the window, not in the rearview, not in the metallic body of the car, knowing the squat, distorted reflection that would appear in the bright, flat sun. The dress wasn't flattering. It pulled across the shoulders. Clothes cut for women always did. Gabbi walked with a slight hunch, which her brother teased was scoliosis and her mother insisted was a physical manifestation of her lack of confidence, yet another thing—alongside shyness and her tendency to repeat words when nervous—that she could work on.

Gabbi's father was standing at the back sliding door, staring out across the lawn. "Miller," her mother said, "the kids are here to see you."

"Is it ours?" Gabbi's father asked, still looking through the glass.

"The kids?"

"The tower." He was pointing to a little structure, a pagoda-style cupola in the backyard of the house next door, built in blatant violation of HOA regulations.

"That's not ours," Gabbi's mother said.

"Can we build one?"

"What?"

"A tower."

Gabbi's mother, with practiced dismissal, said, "You draw up the plans, and we'll see. Now sit, I made gumbo."

Gabbi sat, tucking the dress in around each leg so that the meat of her body wouldn't touch. Already, the back of the dress was wet from her sweat, and Gabbi could tell, smelling herself, that the sweat was two parts heat, one part nerves.

Gabbi's father asked her brother about real estate, and

then about towers. It became clear slowly that Gabbi's father did not know Gabbi. Gabbi's mother realized it first, bustling in to say, "And our Gabbi just finished a degree in information science, right honey?" It had only been a year since Gabbi had visited home.

"There are two women living with me here," Gabbi's father said to Gabbi. "One of them is very nice. One of them is mean." Both of the women were Gabbi's mother.

Gabbi said, "That sounds difficult."

Gabbi's brother said, "Don't encourage him."

They kept this up long enough to eat a bowl of gumbo apiece and sop up the broth with French bread. Gabbi's father didn't ask who she was, where she was from. He was still a careful conversationalist, knew what he did not know and maneuvered deftly around those gaps. Gabbi talked about her desire to be a science librarian, how much she'd like a job that consisted solely of helping people find information. She regularly spent hours on her phone, ending up on corners of the internet her classmates mocked, and she was as interested in these forums as she was in library databases. They were deep wells. Deep dives, she said, were the only type of dives that interested her.

"But not into shallow water," her father said, and winked.

When he tired of their conversation, he lowered his voice and said, only to Gabbi's mother, his shoulder attempting to shield their conversation from Gabbi, "I'm staying in a room here. You can come back with me if you want."

Her mother said, "Sure, you want me to show you to your room?"

"Only if you want." He was passive to the point of obsequiousness. "Only if you're ready to retire." Remembering

Gabbi, and his manners, he said, "Perhaps I'll see you tomorrow. When are you leaving?"

"Sunday," Gabbi said.

He looked at Gabbi's mother. "And when are you leaving?"

"I'm staying," her mother said. "You're stuck with me."

Later, Gabbi's father asked Gabbi to leave. He said, gentle and apologetic, that she couldn't stay here. When Gabbi's mother objected, he said, "It would be different if she was our personal guest."

"This is Gabbi," her mother said.

Gabbi tugged at her hem.

"Of course, of course, Gabbi," her father said, turning the moon of his face toward her.

"Miller, this is our Gabbi."

Gabbi said, "Your daughter," but her voice broke across the second word. Not the breaking of T, which she'd come to enjoy, that affirming crack in her words. This was different. The word was clearly ridiculous, inaccurate, struck-through. She was a clown in a dress.

"We're her parents, Miller." Gabbi's mother said this roughly, a flash of some raw emotion. "It's our fault she destroys all her clothes." Gabbi glanced down to find the hem of the dress unraveled, the thread in her hand.

Gabbi retreated to her room, which hadn't changed since she left home—on a shelf above her bed, every Hello Kitty figurine made between 1997 and 2007; in the corner, the behemoth computer on which Gabbi, at sixteen, spent hours building zoo enclosures for unicorns and dragons; across the room, a bookshelf full of fantasy. All fifteen books about the wheel of time, three of the four books written by the fifteen-year-old who is now an adult, every book set in Osten Ard, every book set in Westeros, the seven books by the rich author who's always embarrassing herself on social media, the trilogy with the five-thousand-year-old djinn, the trilogy with the armored bears, she could go on. One day, she'd have her own room in her own apartment with space enough for all her things, and she'd move the books there, carefully, series by series.

She said this to her partner, who video called her later that evening. Gabbi was still wearing the dress. It was easier to wear it, to court her mother's approval in her mother's court. And she wanted to be a person her father would recognize. She didn't realize her mistake until her girlfriend's face appeared in her phone's screen and arranged itself into a stretched, alarmed expression Gabbi thought was surprise but realized, as the conversation continued, was nearer to horror. This was Gabbi's girlfriend, after all. Gabbi was her boyfriend with short hair and top surgery planned for February. Gabbi loved being her boyfriend, loved how the word concretized their relationship, which was otherwise nebulous, and Gabbi's gender, which was otherwise internal, not a thing she talked about with anyone else. She considered talking about it, coming out to her teachers, her classmates, but she hadn't. It wasn't safe, she said to her girlfriend, and this was maybe true in a distant sense. After top surgery it would be clear to everyone, Gabbi thought. She wouldn't be able to hide anymore. This thrilled her. Gabbi's girlfriend had helped her plan the surgery, suggested a surgeon in New York City, where she lived, so they'd finally have a reason to meet each other in person. Gabbi's girlfriend referred to Gabbi's chest as her pecs, referred to Gabbi as her future husband. Her girlfriend was a woman, and not the sort of woman who wanted her future husband wearing a dress. "You're trans, right?" she said to Gabbi that evening. "You're a man?" And Gabbi said yes.

Two months later, Gabbi flew back to Florida from New York. Girlfriendless, boobless, jobless, she was returning for good. I'm so tired of people talking about chosen family, hell0kitkat posted on r/Auties, like all of us should just up and leave our bio family, like there's better families just waiting with their arms open. Maybe if you're allistic it's true. But where am I supposed to find a chosen family who will fold my laundry so I don't have to touch the staticky clothes or use allergen-free no-odor cleaning products or let me stay rent-free for as long as I need? To which one user responded, Use dryer sheets!

But the refuge of Gabbi's family was imperfect. There's nothing to do here, hell0kitkat posted on Reddit. Stuck in the boondocks. Gabbi didn't have a license, and the buses sucked, and her body felt weird—tired, lethargic—which might have been due to stopping T, which her mother wouldn't allow her to take and which was hard to get, anyway, in the county where her parents lived. They should tell people how you'll feel, Gabbi wrote on r/Auties, how fucking down you're going to feel if you have to stop it.

When I picture Gabbi living again at her parents' home, I picture her building a tower with her father, engaged in carpentry and welding projects for which neither she nor her father is qualified, the sort of work a lesbian wouldn't be able to resist. I imagine the tower was the only thing that would hold her father's attention. He would place the nails as meticulously as he once maneuvered tissue samples beneath a microscope lens. The plans he'd drawn were more complicated than Gabbi had expected. It wasn't just two posts sunk into concrete and some crossbeams. There was weight and bracing to be accounted for, and you couldn't drill into end grain. There were instructional videos to watch, necessary workarounds to find. Gabbi was up to it, but the work didn't help her father recognize her, which Gabbi blamed on the top surgery and the T. I imagine that as Gabbi steadied the drill her father was holding, as she guided him gently away from the table saw, as her father's distance weighed more and more, Gabbi began to think she might not be trans, began seeking other ways to describe her hatred of women's clothing, of all pronouns, of her own skin.

r/Auties **Join . . .**
hell0kitkat
Am I Trans or Just Autigender?

Sorry in advance for the long post, and the provocative title. I'm not trying to offend anyone, I'm actually looking for some advice here. The issue is I can't decide if I'm trans or if I'm autigender or if I just don't get what gender is. I'm AFAB. Had top surgery. Was on T for half a year, but had to stop as it's not covered by my parents' (now my) insurance here in the sunny sunny sunshine state. Was in a straight-ish relationship with a woman, but that's over, so I guess I'm free. I'm not diagnosed autistic, but I'm self-diagnosed-ish. I always score high on the DIY quizzes, and a lot of what people write about in here resonates with me (relationship difficulties—amen!, sensory sensitivity, it's never just a sandwich, and so on). Y'all have really helped me understand myself. I don't even know if I can use the word autigender, since I'm not diagnosed, but I don't know how else I'm supposed to describe what I'm feeling.

Like, here's how I think about it: males make small gametes, females make large gametes. That makes sense to me. But a female lobster isn't a woman, she's just a lobster. I just want to be a lobster. I just want to be an adult human who makes—as I'm reminded monthly, thanks, God—large, bloody gametes and leave it at that? Can someone send me a little bird who can land on my shoulder and whisper my True Gender into my ear? I would pay beaucoup bucks for that.

I'm fine with being trans if I am trans, but I want to know for sure. Like, if I'm going to be trans I'm going to have to sacrifice a lot of things, spend a lot of time figuring out how to get T, have long drawn-out arguments with my mother, hold my pee in public places, etc etc etc, and I just want to know that it will be worth it.

Sort by: Best **13 comments**

+Add a Comment

> The title of your post is misleading. You can be both autigender and trans.
>
> > Trans autistic person here, and I get what you're saying, but this term is harmful for people like me. I have plenty of neurotypicals invalidating my identity, I don't need it from other auties, too.
> >
> > > Respectfully, you can't police someone else's language that they use to describe their gender just cuz some people use it against you. Haters gonna hate. If we threw out all the words that had ever been used against another person we'd be left with point and grunt.
> > >
> > > > As a nonspeaking autie here, I think you mean sign and—well, I don't have a word for *use a wide range of nonword vocalizations that encode as much meaning in a syllable as verbal English users manage in a sentence* but you get the gist

> Sounds like you're agender! Welcome to the community! DM me for resources!

> What's happening here is that aspies and auties are getting trapped in a NT turf war about gender, and

I'm over hear being like Switzerland! Be Switzerland! This isn't our fight.

Of all the hats, gender is the funniest hat.

I just want to say that self dx is valid! Being autistic is more like being queer than being ill. Fuck doctors.

I'm cis and a neuroscientist, not autistic, so I'm not going to comment here!

Autigender isn't a gender. Your gender can't be a disability.

> Yes! We're eating our own tail with this shit. This is why people make fun of us.

Being autigender is like looking at gender through an orange lens whereas NTs are looking through clear lenses. It doesn't tell you if you're trans or not, it just means being autistic influences your gender, which, honestly, it probably does for lots of us.

Reading this, I think you're probably an autistic dyke who likes dykes and sure, masculinity is alluring. The world hates women, I got way more girls as a trans man than I did as a butch, and way less hate, but that doesn't make it okay to turn your back on your womanhood. You have to learn to stop running away from what you are, to love who you are. DM me if you want to chat. I got you. You're not alone.

This last response is from Jennifer Flitok.

I imagine Gabbi messaging Flitok directly and learning her name, then sending Flitok a friend request on Facebook and scrolling back through her photo albums—past the conference photos with Flitok in a skirt suit, past the screenshot of a Transformer sharing their gender-neutral pronouns, past the vaguely drunk photo at some rooftop bar with two other girls, past the trans-guy years (all too-big shorts and mismanaged fades), past the butch years (all overalls and keys on carabiners), to the photo where Jennifer, eighteen, stands in a tux beneath a white gazebo with a girl on her arm. Maybe Gabbi accidentally liked this photo, an errant click, and then prayed that Jennifer, like most millennials, paid little attention to her Facebook account. Gabbi read the most recent post on Flitok's Substack, about a children's hospital offering gender-affirming surgeries to seventeen-year-olds. Gabbi read the second-most-recent post, a response to a Christian lobbying organization who linked to Flitok's Substack in an article about the ungodliness of gender transition. Flitok wrote:

> Don't quote my content without asking my permission. Don't trot out my story to bolster your fundamentalist agenda. We're not friends. Between the religious right and the trans guys, I'm with the trans guys every time.

Gabbi had seen enough already to know the trans guys didn't want Flitok, not when she was posting about parental rights in schools and calling for the slow death of a surgeon in Boston. Surely Flitok knew this, too. Gabbi felt sympathy for Flitok claiming allegiance to trans people even as she worked against them, setting herself up for rejection. Or maybe this is projecting. It's what I feel, reading Flitok's response to the Christian lobbyists. But Gabbi felt something, at least, that made her read on.

Flitok's account hadn't taken off yet. She still hadn't appeared on the conservative news channel Gabbi's family watched, where she would say, "I was targeted, brainwashed, and victimized," and her followers would quadruple. She had a respectable following, but not so many followers that she was above trawling the boards for recruits, and in Gabbi she found a good one. Gabbi consumed everything Flitok posted. When Flitok shared a quote from a psychologist claiming that gender dysphoria in people with autism was misinterpreted sensory sensitivity, Gabbi found the original podcast, listened to the whole thing, and sent Flitok a direct message complimenting the episode. When the board on which Jennifer Flitok had been posting regularly about the threats to women's bathrooms and women's sports was shut down, it moved to a separate, privately hosted forum, and Gabbi followed.

In April, Gabbi posted on this new forum for the first time: My decision to transition was rooted in my deep-seated misogyny and hatred for my body. In May, she mentioned something about working with Flitok on a project involving a map, and Flitok responded, When it comes to finding addresses, Gabbi is an autistic magician! Gabbi responded, I don't know if I even count as autistic, and Flitok responded, Of course you're autistic. Gabbi! You're not a broken neurotypical, you're a beautiful and whole autistic person.

I imagine Gabbi was flattered. She loved fantasy, some

part of her wanted magic. Maybe the mutual seduction had gone like this. Gabbi stepped away from her computer occasionally. Not to go outside—*What could there possibly be for me outside this house?* wrote hell0kitkat on the new platform in April—but for brief returns to the body, showers and sustenance. Her mother made her chicken nuggets and mashed potatoes. Her mother worked as an assistant to a forensic accountant who managed the divorces of the wealthiest couples in Florida. She scanned hundreds of pages of bank statements trying to determine whether it was possible for a man, in the four months leading up to his divorce, to spend two hundred thousand dollars on athleisure wear. The answer: By all the laws of Heaven and Earth it is not possible, yet he hath done it.

When Gabbi exited her room, her mother looked up from her work to ask Gabbi about her plans. "We can't support you forever, baby," she said. Gabbi avoided her questions, began avoiding her mother. Their relationship chilled. Gabbi hadn't talked about being trans with her mother, who pursed her lips at Gabbi's flat chest but didn't ask questions. Gabbi didn't talk about being autistic with her mother, though she was increasingly obsessed with this possible identity. When Gabbi had a worry or question she would previously have brought to her mother, she messaged Jennifer Flitok instead. Gabbi's mother felt this distance and became increasingly critical. As Gabbi made her way back to her room with a plate of microwaved potatoes, her mother said, without looking up from her spreadsheets, "How is it you're so tiny, but when you walk the windows shake." Gabbi stopped.

"No," she said.

"Listen. The glass rattles."

Gabbi walked. Her mother was right. The whole house, built shoddily in the nineties, vibrated with her steps.

"You could try being a little bit more graceful."

Gabbi walked again, quickly now, almost a run, damn the windows.

"Fee-fi-fo-fum," her mother said.

Gabbi escaped into her room and went straight to her computer. Gabbi was in tears, but her message to Jennifer Flitok was short and reasonable, a straightforward analysis of her mother's transphobia and ableism. Jennifer Flitok replied with a link to an article about dyspraxia, and they messaged until one in the morning about—what else?—their bodies. These were the messages in which Gabbi described her horror of flesh on flesh. Meat dreads, Flitok called it, and Gabbi leapt on the label immediately. Flitok was well-versed in this specific axis of self-hatred. Gabbi sent a final message at three in the morning. Gabbi slept until noon.

This became a pattern. Gabbi slept through each day, ignoring her mother's knocks on the door, her mother's announcement that the grocery down the street was hiring, even her mother's apology. Her father's tower stalled, which he didn't mind. He saw it upon waking each morning. At the top of it, he told Gabbi when he caught her in the kitchen, he sometimes saw a kid doing his homework and drinking a bottle of Coke.

The nights became Gabbi's solace. At two in the morning, no one insisted that Gabbi eat lettuce alongside her chicken nuggets. No one commented on her footfalls. No one interrupted her as she spent hours on her bed, phone in hand, watching the videos the algorithm fed her—*5 Commonly Overlooked Signs of Autism in Women*, *Autistic Adults*

AVOID These Mistakes, *Autistic Imposter Syndrome*. And on Tuesdays at eleven in the evening—eight on the Pacific Coast where Flitok lived—Flitok led a virtual support group. "For women who transitioned," she said, with emphasis on the past tense. Including Gabbi, there were four of them. They talked about receding hair lines, cancer risk, bruised butts. One by one, they pinpointed the moment they first questioned their gender identities and went back in time, working it out aloud, to the nearest trauma. The others helped—asked probing questions, reminded the speaker about selective memory and blackouts. Flitok attempted hypnosis using a free plug-in on the virtual platform, which was a failure. When it was Gabbi's turn, she began at thirteen and moved backward. She searched, but there was nothing there. She was assaulted once, on her way to school, by a group of older boys, but she was sixteen and it was mostly embarrassing. When she said this, Flitok's eyebrows popped up, but she didn't pursue it. It didn't sit within the backward-facing light cone of Gabbi's gender, and so it was irrelevant. Gabbi thought and thought, but aside from that one incident nothing moved in the shadows of her childhood.

"Something I'm thinking about in this case," Flitok said, "is the constant, daily trauma of growing up neurodivergent in a world designed for neurotypical people." The other women nodded. Gabbi nodded. It's true she had to attend birthday parties. It's true she had to eat peas. "Like," Flitok continued, "there's a way in which you've been assaulted every day of your life." The other women chimed in, agreeing. Gabbi felt soft and pummeled, a little stunned. She was glad she wasn't asked to talk. She wasn't sure she could talk. But it didn't feel bad, exactly. It felt, in a warped way, like being taken care of. The feeling took root and bloomed big in the next moment when Flitok sent Gabbi a private message saying, I hope this is feeling okay to you? Feel free to message me if you want me to stop the others. Then, a blue heart.

When the call ended, Gabbi noticed that her underwear was wet. Gabbi, knowing little about the vagina and its attention to arousal of all types—attraction and fear—thought this could only mean one thing. She had her eyes, the whole time, on Flitok.

Gabbi kept her eyes on Flitok. She studied Flitok, and her studies paid off. She was increasingly able to predict Flitok's questions and desired responses. One evening, Flitok messaged Gabbi to ask her to stay on after the other women left. Gabbi was thrilled. They waited in silence until the last woman waved farewell, left the call, and then Flitok gave Gabbi a sardonic look and said, "Can I be honest?"

Gabbi nodded, breath held.

"They fucking exhaust me," Flitok said, and laughed. "You're the only one who gets it. What we're doing here. What I'm trying to do."

How did Gabbi respond to this? Gratitude? Sympathy? They talked for an hour, and when they finally signed off, Gabbi lay awake for another three, tracing every twist of their conversation, planning what she would say next time, if she was invited to stay after again. It wasn't infatuation—Gabbi did this after most social interactions. But it felt a little like love.

Their debriefs became a ritual. In one of them, the map was born. Flitok took credit for the idea, but it was Gabbi who'd majored in information science, Gabbi who'd written her thesis on *Map-Based Visualizations for Digital Library*

Collections, Gabbi who knew how to code, how to determine location based on IP address, how to use ArcGIS.

It was easy enough at first. Most hospital addresses were publicly available. Some even advertised gender-affirming services on their websites. But the map that resulted from gathering this information was disappointing. If anything, it revealed how many people lived hundreds of miles from a gender clinic, which was the wrong emphasis. Flitok was unsatisfied by the map and more generally. A small profile of Flitok's social media presence had come out, and it wasn't flattering. Among other criticisms, it noted Flitok's focus on white women and girls. Flitok thought this was a valid, embarrassing critique. They needed to do things differently. The hospitals were fortresses, untouchable. They needed to focus on the nonprofits, the grantors, the ones targeting BIPOC kids, and it was then Gabbi thought, for the first time in months, of the week she spent in New York after top surgery, of the Southern Trans Care Access Taskforce, of Swaati. What did Gabbi feel when she suggested our program to Flitok as a potential focus? What trapped us both in this causal chain?

We need one more light cone. A light cone that explains how Gabbi went from being a guest at Swaati's safe house to targeting it. What is there, at its nexus? Anger? Vengeance? Or that burgeoning adoration and desire to please another person that Gabbi suspected she should call love?

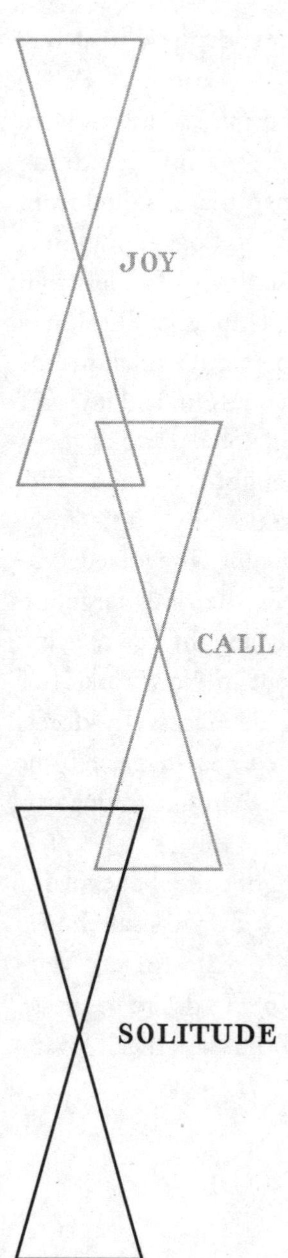

ELSEWHERE

Gabbi met her girlfriend on a Discord for GeoGuessrs. Their romance began when her girlfriend posted a link to a game in which she identified five countries in forty seconds solely by the grass. Gabbi was impressed and messaged her to say so. Over three years, their relationship progressed from private messages to one-on-one matches to pooling their money for a remote-controlled dildo they shipped back and forth. In the third year, they decided to be partners. Six months later Gabbi mentioned top surgery. Her girlfriend suggested a New York clinic—for its reputation, but also its proximity to her Brooklyn apartment. They would finally meet as meat, Gabbi wrote. Gabbi's insurance would cover some of the surgery expenses. Gabbi's parents gave her a generous allowance, which, coupled with her savings from her graduate assistantship, would cover the rest. Gabbi's parents were furious about this use of funds, but the money was Gabbi's. They couldn't stop her. Gabbi's choice to go to New York had nothing to do with the laws that would eventually make it difficult to access such surgeries across the country. When she first started planning, those bills were all dead in committee, left to be resurrected in the next year's session. In this way, Gabbi was unlike Swaati's usual residents. At the time, Swaati hosted mostly people getting abortions that weren't legal where they lived, and kids from places like North Dakota and Alaska where it was hard to get gender care given the hundreds of miles between their homes and the nearest clinics, which boasted a single nurse practitioner and an MD who visited two days a month. Their patients came for puberty blockers or hormones. They were mostly twelve-to-seventeen-year-olds accompanied by their parents, mostly stayed two nights with Swaati to avoid the exorbitant hotel costs. It was risky work. Once the shield laws were passed, it was more dangerous than the work of the prescribing clinicians. The clinicians were protected from retribution. Swaati wasn't protected, not by the law, not by the clinics, not by St. Cat, which refused to set up a contract with them but still paid monthly for services previously rendered, which were vaguely described on the invoice. Swaati knew the risks. They communicated with families only through voice calls. No texts, not even encrypted, no emails, no written communication at all. The police had entered once, called by a neighbor who'd seen a lot of people "coming and going."

They'd been lucky, Swaati said when they relayed this story to me, that the cops came when they did. Swaati was between residents. They were laundering sheets in preparation for the next family when the cops knocked. Swaati took a moment to scan the space, pulled down the appointment schedule the last resident had pinned to the corkboard, stashed it under the sink along with the subway directions to the clinic in Manhattan, which had been left in the trash. They opened the curtain to hide the bed.

The cops entered as a pair and went right to the living

area. Swaati silently cursed the child who'd been their last resident for scampering around in excitement the night after his appointment. Kid feet, as identifiable through a poorly soundproofed floor as the tapping claws of an illicit dog. The cops made their way, as if magnetized, toward the curtain that would reveal someone was sleeping in the studio, which was zoned only for business. Swaati waited until the younger cop was standing a foot from the curtain, then said, "Want to see the other room?" They followed Swaati through the kitchen to the far room with its industrial door, which was perfect for accommodating large canvases or sculptures and also made the place wheelchair accessible. Swaati had been sculpting. There was a useful dusting of plaster on the floor. If the cops had found the bed, Swaati was prepared to say it was a background for a recent nude portrait series and ask if they wanted to see the pics. When Swaati told this story, they always emphasized the same details—the curtain, the plaster, how the older policeman, walking a final circuit, said several times, "I don't see a lot of art here."

"Not everyone's a painter," Swaati said.

Swaati is an artist. They've done residencies in Mexico City and Milan. Their work focuses often on falling in love, often on falling out of love, often on beginning an action—like love—and then struggling to continue it. When asked once, by a journalist, why they don't make art about gender or diaspora, Swaati said, "Like most artists, I make art about my preoccupations, and I spend most of my time thinking about why I'm still dating some asshole or about the asshole who broke my heart or about how long it's been since the asshole I'm dating fucked me." In the first year of the pandemic, they took a daily photo from the single window of their studio, and this photo series was shown at a small gallery in Philadelphia. Most recently, heartbroken in Portugal, they brought a pile of sand in a truck from the coast to an inland town and with a narrow broom moved it through the streets, sweeping and sweeping, catching every grain they could, continuing for twenty hours, until the pile of sand had dwindled away to nothing. They didn't document this performance, but they told me about it after telling me about the police. We talked about the discomfort of sand up under your nails, and at the end of our conversation Swaati said, again, "I don't see a lot of art here," and cackled.

Swaati's usual residents had a sense of what they were up against, they had tried to get care locally, some for years, they had gratitude for Swaati's willingness to host them, understood the risk. Gabbi had none of these things. Gabbi was thirty-four. What she had was desperation, entitlement, and bucketfuls of grief. She'd ended up at Swaati's after her partner, meeting Gabbi for the first time, panicked. Gabbi was shorter than her partner expected and differently proportioned, she had thighs, her partner hadn't expected thighs, she had a rolling suitcase packed for three full weeks of recovery, and somehow her partner hadn't expected that either—the size of the suitcase!—though they'd discussed it, Gabbi had messages proving they'd discussed it, and those messages were the axis around which their argument spun, an argument so loud the tenant in the apartment beneath them knocked on the ceiling. An argument that ended with Gabbi's partner shouting, "I didn't realize you had a body."

After this argument, after Gabbi realized her girlfriend wasn't going to come through for her, she called her mother, asking for help, for enough money to rent a place for a week in the city, a lot of money, yes, but her mother had it. Her mother refused. Her mother said that this was the Lord's way of showing Gabbi top surgery wasn't in His plan for her, and she wasn't about to go up against Him. So Gabbi was stranded in the city with surgery a day away and no family, no friends, no place to stay, and Gabbi reached out to the social worker at the hospital that was scheduled to perform her top surgery and the social worker reached out to Swaati.

Swaati was generous and professional. They were more reliable than friends, their residents said, more comforting than family. They had a narrow wheelchair, which they used to transport Gabbi from the car to the freight elevator, from the freight elevator to the bed, which was higher than a usual bed and adorned with a penguin-printed mastectomy pillow. Swaati had already mixed up a vitamin drink—the kind that tastes like a chalky, liquid lollipop—in Gabbi's preferred flavor. They asked for consent before touching Gabbi's back and shoulders, helping Gabbi lean back against the cushion. They brought a second pillow for her knees. They proffered two Tylenol every six hours, one OxyContin between, staggering the meds to avoid any breakthrough pain.

When Gabbi drank the vitamin drink and gasped at how the cold from the drink permeated the reduced flesh of her chest, Swaati grinned. Gabbi was the first person to come to Swaati after top surgery, to need bandages changed and drains checked, a more intensive caretaking. Swaati didn't mind the additional work. The mastectomy pillow was Swaati's, from their breast augmentation two years before. In those first few hours, when Gabbi was still woozy, Swaati had felt happy to be shepherding someone else through the blurry, euphoric days that followed surgery. When, on the first night, Gabbi called them, awake and terrified of the dark, they went to her, sat at the foot of the bed, explained that however much you wanted surgery the body couldn't understand it as celebration, only as trauma, and so of course, in the nights after, there would be fear and grief. It was okay. When Gabbi, seeing her chest for the first time, began to sob—"I don't look normal, I don't look normal"—unable to stomach the bruises and the slits where the drains snaked through the fascia to suck at her incisions, when she burst into more frantic, painful sobs that pulled at the incisions, which were sealed with glue, Swaati showed her photos of their own chest in the days after their implants, which proved that the swelling would retreat, that the bruising would fade, that it would take time to adjust to a new body, that it was okay for it to take time. Swaati didn't say that normal was boring, though when Swaati had gotten implants they'd chosen a triangular shape, asked for a deliberate pucker at the bottom, their choices strange enough the surgeon had sent them for a psych eval not required by the state of New York, and Swaati had loved the appearance immediately, even when the left incision got infected, they had loved the discolored skin and the pain, the violence that seemed more honest, somehow, than what had come before.

They had taken the photographs as an act of celebration, an act of open love for that holy, bruised flesh. They told Gabbi about this love for their healing flesh, and Gabbi said, "I don't feel that way at all."

On the second day, Gabbi began to feel claustrophobic. She told Swaati, who agreed to open the blinds on the window a little. A risk, but a small one. Swaati also agreed to unwrap the bandage that had Gabbi's chest tightly bound. They helped Gabbi with the handheld nozzle in the shower, water splashing across Gabbi's belly and legs. For a moment Gabbi breathed easier, agreed it was the wrap that was bothering her, agreed to try a binder instead, agreed that the window helped, but that night Gabbi dreamed of standing up from the bed, walking to the studio's entrance, and throwing open the door. There, where she expected to find a hallway, was another room. Her childhood bedroom, maybe, or a principal's office. It was some room of further entrapment, I'm not sure which, these are the possibilities that occur to me. What I know is that Gabbi woke up, gasping and sweaty, her chest aching as if she had truly been throwing open doors. The binder was across the room, tented on the floor. Her shirt was half on, restricting her arms, and she thought at first that this was the discomfort that had woken her, but then Gabbi realized she needed to vomit. She was going to vomit, imminently. With a Herculean effort, chest searing, she propelled herself out of the unfamiliar bed, across the room that wasn't hers. She was a guest in that room, and her status demanded propriety. She would not vomit on someone else's rug, she would not vomit in someone else's room, and she kept this promise.

She made it, just, to the toilet, and heaved into the bowl of clean water, keeping the light off so she didn't have to see what splashed there, but still the smell rose, and she heaved again from the smell, though nothing came up, the sensation across her chest impossible, what stone feels before it is cracked in two. If she removed the hand she'd pressed against her chest, she thought, her chest would fall off—the flesh would peel from the ribs, and the ribs would fall, ringing like knitting needles on the tile. She was on her hands and knees and could not rise. She tried once, and the pain subdued her.

Her cell phone was in the inner pocket of her sleeping shirt, along with her drains. Swaati had put it there. Gabbi remembered this with a twinge of resentment. She knew she should be grateful. She was crumpled on the ground in the bathroom. Without Swaati, she couldn't get up, and Swaati had ensured she had her phone, ensured Gabbi wouldn't have to wait until Swaati arrived at seven to proffer the morning's Tylenol. But Gabbi didn't want to call Swaati. This wasn't just Gabbi's avoidance of any phone call, any unpredictable interaction with another human. It was the trapped feeling, which hung over Gabbi still from the dream. Shame and something lower, seedier—spite, maybe—grown from Gabbi's total helplessness, and the disgust she felt, resting her forehead on the toilet seat, at the machinations of her body, and when Swaati arrived, brushing off Gabbi's apologies, the feeling grew stronger. As Swaati helped her to stand—"Can I put my hand under your left arm? Can you take my right arm?"—Gabbi felt a surge of disdain. So cautious, Swaati, standing in a vomit-filled bathroom at three in the morning and parroting the language of consent like a small-town lesbian. How tepid. How embarrassing. Or maybe Gabbi didn't feel this. I did, in the hospital. I felt a seething frustration with the language of consent, which was used until it wasn't.

"If it happens again, it helps to hug a pillow against the incisions while you vomit," Swaati said. "It will hurt less." Gabbi couldn't name the emotion that swept over her at these words. Alexithymia, maybe. But I could name it. What Gabbi felt—as Swaati helped her back to the bed, fastened the binder, shifted the pillows from Gabbi's knees to her shoulders, so that Gabbi would be more upright—was hatred.

The next day, Gabbi said she couldn't be cooped up. She needed to take a walk outside. But a walk outside wasn't possible, Swaati insisted. Gabbi was a secret. She wasn't here. It wasn't possible to promenade, Swaati said, gently mocking Gabbi's wish, and Gabbi, rising with anger, said, "Then I need to leave." I don't know if this is actually what Gabbi said, but these are the words that occur to me. I used them in the emergency room, when it wasn't yet clear to me that I wasn't free to leave.

"You're just a few days out," Swaati said. "The psychiatrist won't be able to see you on a Sunday," my nurse said. "Maybe tomorrow," I imagine them both saying, their voices twinned. Did Gabbi ask to leave again and again? Did Swaati put her off, as the nurse put me off, saying first, "Pretty soon," then "I don't make that call."

"Why are you even doing this?" Gabbi asked Swaati.

"Pays for my art," Swaati said. When this didn't appear

to satisfy Gabbi, they said, "I like doing it. I have antiquated ideas about hosting. If a traveler arrives on a winter evening, and all that." Sure, they could have said more. They didn't mention the friends who had shown up after Swaati's own surgery with comic books and soup, the desire to offer Gabbi some of that comfort, didn't express the pity they felt for Gabbi, who received no phone calls, no deliveries of food, no care packages. Gabbi nodded, didn't say anything else, and so Swaati was surprised when Gabbi later asked, "Why don't you like me?" Her voice wasn't petulant. That would have been understandable. Gabbi was cooped up, alone and in pain. It would have made sense for her to express an insecurity she might otherwise have kept to herself, but she hadn't asked it that way. She'd asked straightforwardly, flatly, and when Swaati responded that it wasn't true, they did like her, Gabbi said, "Why don't you want to talk to me then?"

Gabbi wanted a heart-to-heart. Swaati wanted to get Gabbi dinner and go home. But Swaati realized that maybe Gabbi needed words more than dinner, and so, in the hours that followed, Swaati asked about Gabbi's life—Gabbi's goals, family, fears. Gabbi's responses were repetitive. She was obsessed with her girlfriend's abandonment. When Gabbi explained the particulars of what happened before the surgery, how she'd ended up with Swaati, Swaati was direct—"That's fucked up," they said. Gabbi, with Swaati's help, came to understand that she hadn't been treated well, that she had been wronged, perhaps twice over—first by her girlfriend, then by her mother. When Gabbi cried, painfully, about the relationship with her girlfriend being, possibly, over, Swaati talked about how heavy sand was. Swaati offered intimacy, but Gabbi continued to feel that cramped, claustrophobic feeling, continued to dream of escape, a desire I understand. I want to break the causal chain of this story, to escape the events to come. In this moment my desires and Gabbi's match, and isn't that miracle enough to precipitate some shift, to escape from the light cones, to leap somewhere, anywhere, else?

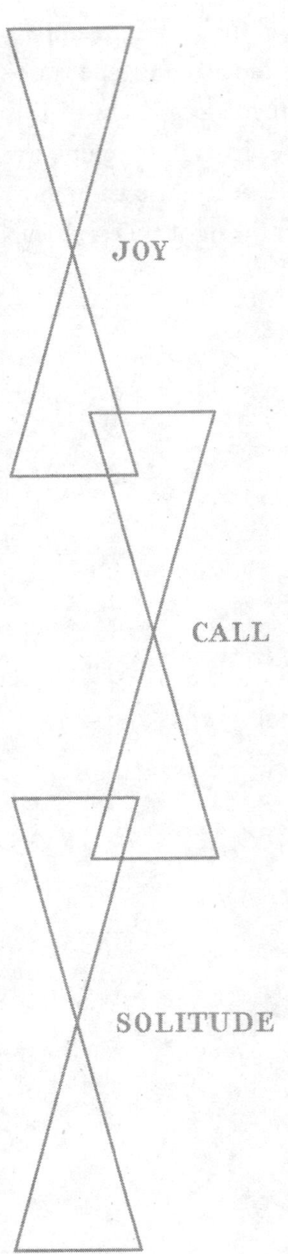

ELSEWHERE

Gabbi and I shouldn't be here. No one who knows us is here, and no one who knows anyone who knows us is here, and we don't know each other here. We can't. That is how it works elsewhere, where the small town that is home to the environmental justice movement is never polluted, where a woman stands in front of four white chairs, one leg over her head. For no reason. Where no one ever picks up the phone. Where in a desert of white sand a digger ant buries a grasshopper and every other digger ant vanishes. Elsewhere a snow leopard, creature of vertical space, leaps from a ledge onto the back of an unsuspecting ibex and—nothing. No ensuing tussle. The ibex does not escape only to leap onto a narrow precipice that shears away at his weight. The leopard does not follow, the two do not plummet to their deaths. There is death elsewhere—two brothers work under a pickup. No, there is no reason for this. No, there is no more to this story. There is only a swift collapse, broken ribs, crushed lungs. You might wonder if the brother who survives is later metaphorically crushed by guilt and regret, but guilt and regret do not exist elsewhere. Mistakes and successes are equally impossible. Nothing here affects anything else. If the world is defined as a closed system in which all events are causally related, elsewhere is the diffuse antiworld. Elsewhere crows fly east toward the coast and never arrive. Elsewhere automatic doors open without cause, slicing through the air at random. Elsewhere the ground moves in that specific, terrifying way that heralds a flood. Don't bother running. Don't wait for the wave, it won't come elsewhere, where a young mother sings a lullaby to a daughter who will never sleep, where a star burns itself out, and no one elsewhere notices its absence. Nothing here can share light with anything that shares light with anything that shares light with anything else here. A politician says, "I had no knowledge of the attack," but the attack never happened. Elsewhere light from the sun suggests to the squash flower that it open and release from its heart three solitary bees. Don't worry, you didn't experience that particular ray of light. If you had interacted with those photons you wouldn't be elsewhere, where five tomatoes rest, red and splendid, on a tomato vine. And you might think, given that we are talking primarily about light, that at night elsewhere would be a little smaller, would creep a little closer, be a little more intimate, a little more forgiving, that the great sweeping isolation of elsewhere, determined now in light-years, in trillions of kilometers, might be reduced to meters. You'd be wrong. The photons are more diffuse at night, but still an owl racking on a warm updraft along the edge of a stand of conifers causes the vanishing of every field mouse, every vole, meter by meter—the ones the owl considers, the ones the owl doesn't, the ones that duck back into their burrows at the brush of a shadow. A girl walks two blocks alone at night and is never seen again, and if you loved her you might think that elsewhere is the place you have been wishing for, the place where she arrives safely and can be seen, four years later, taking her tea with three cubes of sugar. But that girl climbing through her dorm window after sex with her boyfriend isn't elsewhere. That girl melting a slim shard of butter into rice isn't elsewhere. This isn't the place you think it is. Here, she only walks home, and the world around her disappears. The night clerk who glances up from her book in the corner bodega and considers walking out to ask if she's okay. The cat who slinks against her leg. The pigeon on the wire. Gone, gone, gone.

And, oh, aren't you being smart now, asking about the benthic zone. If causality is light then what about the deepest reaches of the ocean where light is reduced to narrow pockets generated by algae and comb jellies. In a crevice somewhere in the deepest sea, devoid of light, might two mantis shrimp fuck and exist long enough afterward to lay the eggs before they are obliterated in a cloud of shared bioluminescence? This is cheating, but I'll give it to you—and the subterranean, sure, if you are so thirsty for story. Sure, you can imagine a completely lightless space. Sure, you can begin to build one underground, hoping to entice whoever it is, your friend or enemy—someone you can't know elsewhere or they wouldn't be here—to join you, living without torch or cooking fire, hoping in that way to evade the rules. It's been attempted before, and you might, if you are especially careful with intention, if you work without purpose, if you imagine no use for the structure you build as you dig and dig, you might manage one day to call out to Gabbi, "Is it you?" but she can't hear you. She can't respond. You'd be safer saying, "Is it me?" And if Gabbi calls out, lonely and afraid, "Can anyone hear me?" stay quiet and still. You can't change anything, that's the rule of elsewhere, so there's no point getting up, there's no point scrambling toward her voice, there's no point clawing at the dense, impenetrable earth between the two of you until your fingernails break, no point shouting back, "I can hear you," you'll only end up

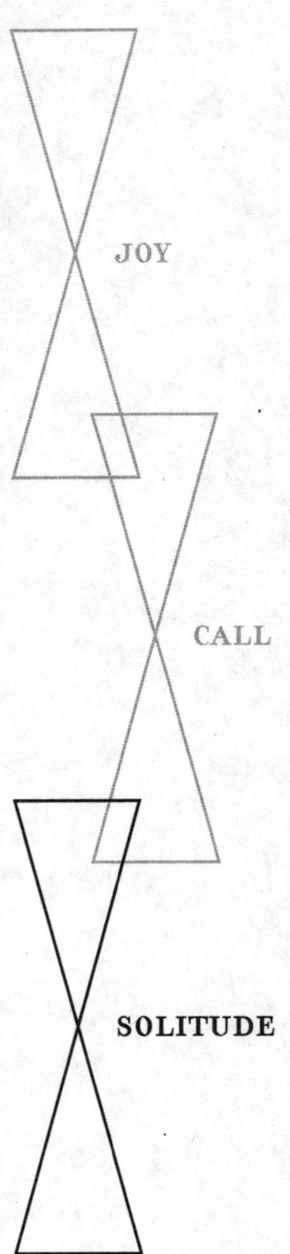

ELSEWHERE

In those restless days in Swaati's studio, Gabbi asked Swaati for advice, and Swaati offered it. Swaati had thought a great deal about beginnings and endings, in relationships as in any other thing. When Gabbi's girlfriend checked in after the surgery, a casual check-in that carefully skated apology and any reckoning with the argument they'd had, Swaati suggested Gabbi tell her how Gabbi was feeling, hold her accountable for abandoning Gabbi. This was how Swaati put it, and how Gabbi put it in the text she sent, which she took three hours to compose and showed to Swaati before sending. Gabbi's girlfriend responded quickly, saying she understood and was sorry and was discussing her fear of commitment in therapy, but also she felt like there were certain relationship dynamics that weren't being fully acknowledged by Gabbi, and she didn't think it was fair of Gabbi to place all the blame on her. She also needed to heal after their argument and thought they should focus on their independent healing journeys for now. Reading this, Swaati said, "What I hate more than anything is people using therapy-talk to get out of taking responsibility." Swaati told Gabbi about an ex-boyfriend who had assaulted Swaati and emailed them six months later to say he was sorry and had done fourteen hours of coursework focused on sexual violence and given that would they want to grab dinner sometime? "I replied, Good for you, bitch, but I don't need to hear about it." This isn't how Swaati replied. I remember this boyfriend. They'd gotten coffee with him and told him about their new sweetie, and he'd been alone and clearly at loose ends, and they'd had a fancy residency the following week, and they'd come away from the meeting feeling good about their life. But this is how they recalled their reply to him in that moment with Gabbi, a recall perhaps distorted by a desire to comfort Gabbi, a desire to show they were on Gabbi's side. And emboldened by Swaati's support or perhaps motivated by some thrill of daring, on the evening of the third day, Gabbi sent those words to her girlfriend verbatim.

On the fourth day, Gabbi watched her phone, waiting for a response from her girlfriend or a response from her mother, who hadn't replied to Gabbi's postsurgery updates. Gabbi waited in pain. She'd discontinued the OxyContin due to her nausea and couldn't yet take ibuprofen, which thins the blood, so she was taking only Tylenol, one thousand milligrams every six hours. By hour five, Gabbi's chest felt as though it had been cut apart and glued back together. She asked Swaati to come, and when Swaati arrived and asked what she needed, Gabbi said she needed a response from her girlfriend. She didn't say she needed touch, though she wanted Swaati to touch her. When Gabbi woke after surgery, the plastic surgeon had her hand on Gabbi's foot, and Gabbi had felt bereft when she took it away. Swaati touched Gabbi, but only when necessary and always with warning. The asking wiped the touch of intimacy. Gabbi wanted Swaati to hold her hand and tell her everything would be all right with her girlfriend and her mother, who were the only people in Gabbi's life. She tried to say this, but the effort to force the words out scraped at her vocal cords, and instead of speech Gabbi began to cough—loud, wracking coughs, which caused the muscles of her chest to contract, the pain bad enough Gabbi suggested she'd torn stitches. Swaati, proffering a vitamin drink with a limp straw, reminded her that there were no stitches.

Gabbi thought she'd grow bolder with time, but as the bleariness of the pain meds faded, her inhibitions rose. Swaati remained opaque and distant, a distance that felt increasingly deliberate to Gabbi, despite Swaati's willingness to listen to Gabbi, to offer advice. It was true Swaati had always recoiled from a specific sort of neediness or, perhaps more precisely, neediness beyond a certain point. We'd bonded over this before I met Liam and "jumped ship," Swaati said, leaping into an ocean of clingy partnership. We'd talked about how tawdry the trappings of romance were—Swaati pursued them, but they pursued them with the appetite of a collector, not the fanaticism of a believer. We'd both put off friends and partners who wanted to track our location, prized our ability to move through the world unmonitored. Swaati had fled a relationship with a guy who didn't like oral sex, a guy who tried to plan a romantic trip to the Maldives, a guy who said, "I love you," after sex on the third date. When I described autistic demand avoidance, Swaati said, "Brown people aren't allowed to act like that, but if I could, I would." We were both reserved, both happy alone, both cautious about how much of our lives we shared with other people, a caution that appeared sometimes arrogant, sometimes intimidating. Even with each other, we skirted the edges of real vulnerability. About a controlling partnership that they left secretly, in the middle of the night, Swaati said to me, "Well, that was a ride," and I said, "Yeah," wanting them to go on, to say more, and Swaati said, "You know?" This was the nearest we ever came to a heart-to-heart.

Gabbi thought Swaati was wary of offering friendship to a person newly single, a person whose mother was their best friend, but this wasn't true. Swaati was Gabbi's caretaker for a brief period, after which time Gabbi would return home. Swaati had no problem setting boundaries, no reason to fear Gabbi's attachment. They weren't disgusted by her farts, which on the fourth day were impossible to hold in, impossible to let out silently. Swaati had a thirteen-year-old Boston terrier whose farts after his evening kibble were potent enough to kill. Swaati would have said this to Gabbi, but Gabbi never mentioned having gas, and they were afraid bringing it up would rupture Gabbi's composure, which they described as "bottled up." "Southern," I suggested, but Swaati shook their head. "She was like a turtle in a shell," Swaati said. "Break the shell, and that turtle is dead." This was the instinct that kept Swaati at a remove.

Gabbi misinterpreted Swaati's caution. Swaati had seen the amber fluid that drained from the tissues around Gabbi's heart. Swaati had seen the tiny clots that appeared in that fluid, had seen deep into Gabbi and, Gabbi decided, hadn't liked what they saw. Gabbi's relationships always ended the same way—she showed up with too many items for a three-week postsurgery stay, she cut herself when her partner left for a conference, she needed too much. Now Swaati felt what other people who had been close to Gabbi felt, the burdensome responsibility of being her sole caretaker. Swaati wanted her gone. By the fifth morning, as Gabbi half stood from the toilet so Swaati could wipe her ass, Gabbi was certain Swaati felt for her a clean and simple revulsion.

Gabbi swung her arm back to stop Swaati from wiping her, fingers catching in her drain, jerking the tube, a ripping sensation beneath her skin—not painful, but alarming—and Gabbi stood abruptly, as if to flee, then half fell against the sink. Swaati reached for her, both hands outstretched, and Gabbi said, "Get away. Don't touch me."

"You're going to pull on the scars."

"You don't care about me," Gabbi said. "You don't love me." The words were a mistake. Gabbi could hurl them at her girlfriend, maybe, at her mother, maybe, and receive the apology she desired, but not at Swaati. Why would Swaati love her?

Swaati said, "Easy. It's hard to recover. Hard for anyone."

In an unsolicited email to St. Cat about her time in that narrow studio, Gabbi wrote that Swaati took superb care of her—*better than my own mother*—but could at times be *standoffish* and *hard to get to know*, that she thought they had *different communication styles*, and wished Swaati had been *more affectionate* and *more spontaneous*. Swaati had laughed—"Why do I feel like I'm getting dumped after two Tinder dates?" In a message to Jennifer Flitok, Gabbi would say that with Swaati she had felt exposed. Women are always offered hiding places. Makeup, hair, dresses—two-thirds of being a woman, Gabbi wrote, is covering yourself up, and she hadn't realized how much she relied on that. Swaati did as Gabbi asked—used he and him pronouns, and the name Gabriel.

Gabbi had thought she wanted those things, wanted to hear that name spoken aloud, but she hadn't. Gabbi linked her discomfort to the loss of her breasts, as though the flesh in front of her heart had literally protected it from a gaze like Swaati's—steady and unerring—and I wonder if the reason Gabbi came after St. Cat was this experience of exposure, but even here the causality I attempt to pin down must be faulty—it wasn't Swaati's name that Gabbi gave Jennifer Flitok. Gabbi had everything—Swaati's full name, the number of their work phone, even the address of their studio—but she kept those things to herself. The name Gabbi gave Flitok was mine.

There's only one thing I'm certain emerged, causally, from the days Gabbi spent in Swaati's studio. Gabbi flies home one week after her surgery, the evening her drains come out. Swaati drives her to the airport, the mastectomy pillow carefully placed to ease the bite of the seat belt. The pain, which is manageable at first, grows steadily worse so that by the time they're rolling up to the automatic doors of the airport Gabbi is crying silently, both hands at her chest, and when the doors slide open, the wheelchair bouncing over the threshold, Gabbi tips forward a little, off-balance, pulling at the thousand small muscles of her chest, and in the roiling waves of pain she reaches without thinking for something, anything to grip, and Swaati takes her hand, says, "I got you." Swaati is the last person to say this to Gabbi for weeks. The next person is Jennifer Flitok.

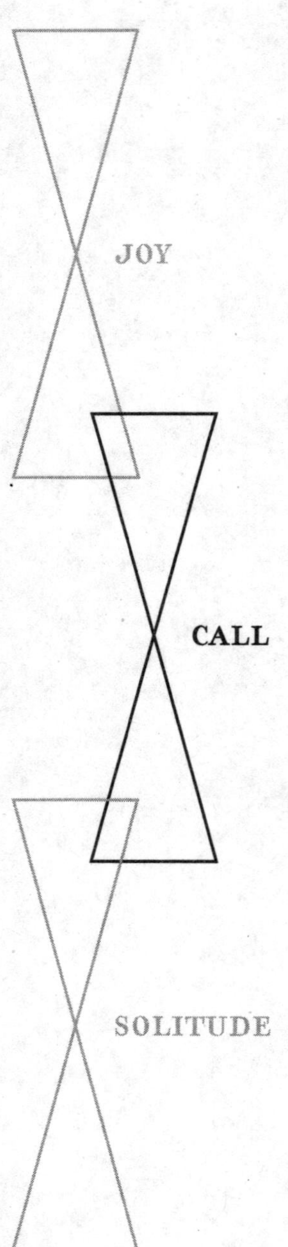

ELSEWHERE

Gabbi's daughter was conceived the night she swung with another woman.

The other woman was a stranger. It was hard, in the near dusk, to guess her age. Anywhere between twenty and thirty-six, though she swung like seventeen, like she could have swung for hours.

They exchanged only words of consent—"Can I swing beside you?" she asked.

"Yes," Gabbi said.

And they commenced.

It was Gabbi's style to release the chains at the highest point, leaning forward and pinching them in the crux of her elbow. The woman held to the chains, her arms bending sharply back, scapulae shifting beneath the skin. Wedges, not like wings, like the thing that came before wings.

At the arcs' tips, they were weightless. Gravity, in the instant after, a sudden, thrilling crush. Their pelvic bones protested the force. Their fingers cramped. Their legs tired from the incessant pumping. The swing set protested, metal joints crooning.

At points, the woman made small sounds—grunts, whimpers, a short, sharp exhale, which made Gabbi wonder if she was having fun. Once she threw back her head and said, "God," an abbreviated curse, bitten off at the end from embarrassment or from the jolt of the swing against her tailbone. Gabbi made no sound.

At the pinnacle of her arc, the woman knocked her shoes together, a quick Dorothy-in-Oz gesture. Gabbi thought it was a reflex, a compulsion, the sort of thing that, initially charming, would after a while become trying, and she was glad for this thought. It made it easier, as her swing wound down, drawn by the mechanical laws of the pendulum, to decide to stop. The other woman outlasted Gabbi, was still swinging as Gabbi left, and on the walk home, Gabbi's daughter came to her. She'd been present already as an idea, a list of biographical facts Gabbi had received from Jennifer Flitok ten days before and was told to memorize. Her daughter was thirteen years old. No friends. Early-onset puberty due in part to genetics and in part to the growth hormones in chicken, which she eats fast, packing it down like a boy, and she says sometimes that she wants to be a boy. She gets rashes beneath her breasts, complains that her boobs hurt when she runs, and she needs to be able to run. She's one of the best athletes on her school's cross-country team. Her dad's not in the picture.

Jennifer Flitok assigned them their daughters—Gabbi and five other now-mothers. A new phase of their work. If they were going to ensnare the patient navigators and front-desk staff at these nonprofits, they needed kids. Flitok said, about their daughters, "You have to know her better than anyone."

Gabbi tried. Gabbi read about high school versus club track, about patellofemoral pain syndrome and pasta after races. Gabbi read and read, but her daughter refused to materialize. When Jennifer Flitok, in their weekly check-ins, asked how their kids were doing, another mother answered, "She's not talking to me, I backed over her cat," and another mother answered, "It's crazy how early they go boy crazy," and Gabbi answered last, haltingly, "She's out running." She said this so often the response got her booed by the other mothers. "She needs balance in her life, you can't let her run all day sunrise to sunset."

"If you don't believe in the reality of your child," Jennifer Flitok said, "how will you convince the surgeons of the reality of your child?" Flitok still always spoke about surgeons, though they'd be speaking with patient navigators and front-desk staff. The conversations were scheduled for the next month, and Gabbi was dreading hers. She wasn't skilled at subterfuge. "Just get to know her," Jennifer Flitok said, and Gabbi had been trying—air-frying chicken nuggets and leaving them out on a plate until the flies found them, going for painful jogs, setting up an air mattress in her room and putting up posters of the country star turned pop star teenage girls were said to love.

As Gabbi walked home that day from the swing set, she imagined the woman she'd swung beside was the mother of her child, and suddenly someone was following Gabbi, almost treading on the backs of her shoes, and Gabbi, hardly daring to believe it, said, "Give me some space, please," and her daughter, yes, laughed, a low laugh. Gabbi didn't turn around, terrified of frightening her daughter off like an undecided cat. She led her carefully home.

In a message to Jennifer Flitok at 2:00 a.m. the next

morning, Gabbi wrote, I finally found her. In the next message she wrote, Fuck I never knew this was how it would feel to be a mother. Flitok sent back a blue heart emoji and a baby bottle emoji. Flitok's messages from this period are almost all reactions and emojis. She put almost nothing in writing, which made it difficult, when a major media outlet later wrote up an exposé of her, to parse her responsibility.

Gabbi got to know her daughter. They ran together, Gabbi's daughter lapping her. They swam together. Gabbi painted the nails on her left hand green with little black dots at her daughter's request, painted the nails on her right hand a matte rouge, and allowed the left hand, her daughter's hand, to take the right in excitement, lead Gabbi into her room or out to a nearby convenience store where Gabbi's daughter wanted a blue Slurpee. On a whim, Gabbi grabbed a bottle of cheap wine, and the cashier carded her, which to Gabbi proved she was both herself and her daughter. Her right hand reached for the wine, her left snatched the Slurpee.

Gabbi explained autism to her daughter. She'd watched hundreds of videos, listened to every relevant podcast episode, read every book available in her digital library, pirated academic articles. She'd read about microtubule-associated proteins and synaptic pruning, imagined her brain growing like an untended hedge. She'd read about diametric mind theory and intense world theory and magical world theory. I imagine she found the last especially resonant. Increasingly, she thought of autism as a central part of her person, a word that explained her desire to spend all day in her bedroom, her lack of friends, her lack of a job, her constant physical discomfort. To her daughter, she explained that autism was genetic. Her daughter might have it, too, though it wasn't included in the biographical sketch. When she asked Jennifer Flitok about this, Flitok said, "Does it matter?" It didn't matter for the call with the patient navigator. It did matter to Gabbi.

Gabbi explained dementia to her daughter, so she wouldn't be afraid when her grandfather talked at length about the casserole cooling in the upstairs kitchen, which was easy to access from the tower. In response, Gabbi's daughter said she'd been to the upstairs kitchen. The casserole was delicious—wild goose and cornbread. It was her daughter who woke Gabbi one night. "They're fighting," she said. Outside Gabbi's bedroom, raised voices. Gabbi squeezed her daughter's slender hand. "Go back to sleep."

Gabbi stepped out and closed the door behind her. The kitchen light was on. Her mother stood at the island, her father in the shadowy recess leading to the garage.

"It's two in the morning," her mother said. "Nothing's open."

"You can't keep me here," Gabbi's father said.

"He wants to go to the police station," Gabbi's mother said when she noticed Gabbi. "Tell them he's been kidnapped."

Gabbi's father spun toward Gabbi, relief in his face. "I've been kidnapped," he said. His voice was devoid of the ironic tone she expected. "She's after my money," Gabbi's father said. "This woman."

"Our marriage I guess being chopped liver," Gabbi's mother said.

"They're after my money. They've put me here to get me out of the way." He was nervous. His hands twisted in the hem of his T-shirt. "You have a car?"

"Nothing's open," Gabbi's mother said over him.

"We're going to escape," Gabbi said, directing the words at her mother, so she understood Gabbi was helping. "We just need to finish the tower."

Gabbi turned on the backyard's floodlights and led her father outside. The tower was a few two-by-fours sunk eighteen inches into the ground and a few planks screwed to the sides. Gabbi had stopped working on it weeks before. The planks had warped in the humidity. Some had molded. Gabbi gave her father a screwdriver, so he'd have something to hold in his hand.

"I don't know how I got here," he said. He was calmer now that they were doing something. He said, with more force, "I did not choose to be here."

Gabbi, thinking perhaps about her own life or perhaps about how she coerced her daughter into the world, said, "None of us chose to be here."

"Are you very wealthy?" he asked.

Gabbi didn't answer. He stood silently, waiting for her answer. He was still beholden to a stiff politesse. He would not pry.

"What does he look like?" Gabbi asked then. She was asking about the boy in the tower, and her father understood immediately. He described the boy—large T-shirt, thick black hair cropped short and carefully combed. It could be Gabbi's daughter, with the haircut she sometimes asked for, or threatened to get without Gabbi's permission.

"How do you know he's a boy?" Gabbi asked.

"The way he climbed that tower," her father said quietly.

At dawn, Gabbi's daughter joined them, and as the three

of them worked together—her daughter unable to take up the hammer but quick with plans and strategies and nimble on the planks—the tower finally began to rise into the sky.

In a message from early June, Gabbi wrote to Jennifer Flitok about her wish to be partnered. It's not easy raising a girl by yourself, she wrote. Flitok responded with, You're doing a great job, and an angel emoji.

Gabbi: Would you date a woman with a kid?

Jennifer: I don't know. I haven't been thinking about dating. I've been doing some soul-searching instead.

Gabbi: Soul-searching?

Jennifer, three hours later: I don't think I'm actually queer.

This message was central to the exposé. Well-known TERFs were mostly white straight women, as terrified of dykes as they were of trans men. Jennifer Flitok was, supposedly, a lesbian. Her first popular post was about her refusal to allow a trans woman entry to a dykes-only poetry night. She said, in an early interview with a conservative radio show, "I'm trans masc. It's not possible for me to change that at this point due to choices I made in the past. I'll always have this hairline. I'll always have this chest, but I'm also a woman, and a lesbian." But the drama that captivated the media—was Jennifer lying? was she confused?—doesn't interest me nearly as much as the continuation of the exchange with Gabbi, which wasn't included in the exposé:

Jennifer: I think I just wanted to be. What straight guy is ever going to go for this?

Gabbi: No. Niffy. Don't say that.

Three minutes later: You're beautiful.

Jennifer: Don't bullshit me.

It's that nickname—Niffy. Jennifer Flitok would later portray Gabbi as a fan who got too close, got a taste of her popularity and her power and went star crazy, but that special name suggests to me something else.

Four days later hell0kitkat posted in r/Auties:

r/Auties **Join . . .**

hell0kitkat

DAE feel like a person has become your special interest?

Self-diagnosed autie here. I made a friend on the internet and lately she's all I can think about. I want to talk to her all day 365 days a year. I want to know everything about her—everything! I asked her favorite sandwich the other day, and she got annoyed with me. I get frustrated when I feel like my knowledge of her has stagnated, like I haven't learned anything new about her in a few days. I thought we were flirting some, but she just told me she wasn't queer, which whatever, I'm never able to tell when I'm flirting and when I'm not. 55% sure my feeling isn't reciprocated, and I don't even know what I'm feeling. I guess I'm asking, Is it love or is it a special interest?

Sort by: Best **32 comments**

+Add a Comment

I'd urge you to BE CAREFUL and MOVE SLOWLY. This sort of thing will really scare a neurotypical off.

This isn't uncommon. Most of us are pretty isolated, finding one good friend can seem like locating the honeypot at the end of the rainbow.

> I think it's gold at the end of the rainbow. But I wish it was honey, honey!

I get this with historical people (Olive B. O'Connor, anyone?), but someone you just met? That seems a little weird.

> I should clarify we've been friends for like three months.

Anyone else have P!NK in their heads now?

> Is it love is it love is it love

> Or 3LAU

This happens to me. If it's mutual, you're fine. If she's not into you, you're a creep.

A few years back I had a female colleague and got really obsessed with her and did things that count as stalking her until her asshole of a boyfriend "'warned me off.'"

THIS! I thought I was codependent for a while, but then realized this is what's happening. When someone new comes into my life I get super-obsessed and everything else falls away for awhile. I'm in my forties now and better at masking it, but I've still had a lot of people walk away after I "come on too strong."

The numbers in your post add up to 420! I'm a bot!

I know everything there is to know about Emiliano Martínez. And a few other footballers, but I don't think normal people should be special interests.

A decade ago, I was YOUR WORST NIGHTMARE. Undiagnosed AuDHD. Undiagnosed DID. I was Hell on two kitten heels, and did I ever have a special interest on a popular vlogger WHO SHALL GO UNNAMED! I used to send cakes in the mail to her home address. I went broke sending her cakes! Once I locked my own credit card account against myself to stop myself spending so much stupid money sending cakes. Once I brought a cake to an event she was doing and I set it down and said, "I made this cake for you, will you eat it?" I look back now and figure she probably thought the cakes were being sent by some enemy trying to poison her. What I want to know is whether the self sending the cakes and the self closing the credit card account were both autistic, and I think so.

> Edit: The cakes weren't poisoned.
> Edit: She didn't eat the cake.
> Edit: Spelling.

>> **14 replies**

> Tell her you're autistic. Tell her what's happening. Consent is important if you're going to stay in the friendship. If you're feeling obsessed with this person, she deserves to know.

> Don't pretend like this is autism. I'm so tired of people using autism or other disabilities to get a pass on doing fucked up creepy shit. You're an adult. Respect her boundaries. I'm so tired of parents of boys with autism being like, I can't teach him not to pinch boobs, he has the mental age of a 3 year old. Fuck you. He can learn, and you can learn, to respect other people. Having autism doesn't make you an asshole, some people are just assholes who also happen to have autism.

>> To be fair, OP wasn't saying they were disrespecting boundaries. Though I take your point.

>> Identity-first language on here, please and thank you!

Over the next few weeks, Gabbi messaged Flitok less. She focused on her daughter. Gabbi's daughter survived not on food, but on facts. Gabbi fed her daughter her back pain and her aversion to mustard greens, her love of anything crunchy, her genetic predisposition for osteopenia, her inability to stomach the acrid smell of shaving cream. She read to her daughter every evening, returning to Pern and Discworld, her teenage haunts. When they'd read every book on Gabbi's shelf, Gabbi made up her own fantasy story, inventing it little by little each night. Her daughter, fed by this story and by her mother's attention, grew increasingly real, became solid enough to turn the AC down until the room was freezing, solid enough to continue building the tower without Gabbi's help. The top of the tower now disappeared on damp, misty days. Gabbi's father struggled to climb beyond a few rungs. Gabbi could climb only about ten feet up before the entire tower swayed ominously. But Gabbi's daughter scaled it easily—into the clouds. When Gabbi asked her what was up there, she said, "Dragons that live on floating islands and sometimes let you ride them." This excited Gabbi. It was just the sort of thing a child would make up. She couldn't wait to tell the other mothers.

On calls with the mothers, Gabbi was now quickest to answer. "She has a new friend," she said one evening. Her daughter had descended the tower with a boy in tow. "I grounded her," Gabbi said on the following call. Her daughter had spent the night up the tower without asking.

A week before they were to meet with the patient navigators, Gabbi said to the mothers, "She isn't trans."

"She's your creation," Flitok countered. "She's trans if you say she is." Gabbi shook her head. She had no control over her daughter. She tried to say this, but Flitok wouldn't hear it—"If you're backing out, say so. We'll need to make new plans." Gabbi was sick at Flitok's brusque response, as if Gabbi's disappearance would be only a logistical hassle. Gabbi knew what it meant to back out. Another mother dropped off three weeks before, citing health issues. Flitok blocked her on all social media channels, disparaged her to the other mothers. "I'm in," Gabbi said.

That night, Gabbi messaged Flitok. She asked if Flitok could edit her daughter's biographical sketch. Gabbi could still do the call with the patient navigator, she just wanted to give her daughter room to decide her own gender. She wanted to include college and a gesture toward a career path, to give her daughter a future beyond the call.

We already decided on these details, Flitok responded. I'm hurt that you're choosing one child over the work we're both committed to.

Over me, Flitok didn't write, but Gabbi saw the unwritten words, responded with apologies and protestations of loyalty, which Flitok took as a withdrawal of her earlier request. I'm glad you feel that way, Flitok responded. I care a lot about you, you know.

Me, too, Gabbi wrote. I wish I could tell her to stop here, but she messaged again almost immediately: I worry sometimes I might be in love with you.

Flitok could have responded to this message. Flitok didn't.

Fifty-two minutes later: Not in a gay way.

Four minutes later: Like we could be sisters.

Two minutes later: I've never felt so myself around anyone.

Eight minutes later: I want you to be in my life forever.

Two hours later: Sorry, did I weird you out?

Ten minutes later: I shouldn't have said anything.

Sixteen minutes later: Ignore me, please.

Three hours later: I'm such an idiot.

Then a spree of messages:

I'm not trying to say I'm in love, like, romantically.

I hope that's clear.

It's more like, I want to know everything about you.

Possibly it's an autistic thing.

I just wanted you to know.

At noon the following day, Flitok sent two messages to Gabbi:

Nbd

Let's just focus on the work.

And later that day, Gabbi messaged all the mothers. Her daughter had asked about top surgery. The other mothers sent birthday hat and applause emojis.

In the days that followed, Gabbi's daughter asked Gabbi to strip the paint off her nails, to get her a binder, a buzz cut. Flitok celebrated each of these developments, their messaging finding its original flow.

At the next meeting, Gabbi's daughter appeared in the square of Gabbi's video feed—her shadow was thrown on the wall behind Gabbi, hunched over her phone. Once, her hand reached past the camera to grab a hair tie she'd left on the desk, and Flitok squealed. "That's so good," she said. "That's so good." She made all the mothers practice, until each of them could summon their daughter's hand. "You have to do that when you're talking to the navigator," she said, and Gabbi, glowing in the light of her praise, agreed.

This might not be true. I don't know if Gabbi kept hair

ties on her desk. I don't know if she favored chicken nuggets. Many auties do. I don't know if Gabbi's father had dementia. Mine did. He died six years ago. This is all I know for certain—in the call with me, on June 28, at 1:00 p.m., Gabbi reaches into the video's frame with her daughter's undecorated hand.

None of it is illegal, precisely. The honesty attestation is about as legally binding as a bumper sticker. There's nothing prohibiting Gabbi from recording her own consultation with her own daughter's HIPAA information. We haven't implemented a consent-form policy with its list of expectations, its signature at the bottom. I'm not saying, at the beginning of every meeting, "By joining this call, you are promising not to record the video or the audio of the call, and to disclose to me if you plan to share the contents of this call with any other person." I wonder, sometimes, if any of that would have stopped her.

She has it all set up. Recording software, silent and invisible. A second, external microphone on her desk, bent over, supplicant, its small ear to the speaker, out of sight of her computer's camera, into which she says, "I just want to do what's in my child's best interest."

I remember wondering if she was recording me, but maybe that's just memory, which distorts the past as it compresses it, the compression generating heat, which is to say, time, so that the act of creating memory propels us into the future. In my memory, she's nervous. She recites her daughter's birthday with quick rigidity. She has the short, hard vowels, the squeaky *æ* sound I associate with a specific type of white Southerner. I notice it when she says, "She gets a bad rash under there, which I tell her that's about hygiene." She doesn't look like me.

I've replayed the memory time and again. I don't have her recording, can't quibble with the quotes they later pulled, which have anyway infiltrated my memory, so that when she says, "I heard there's a clinic in the Northeast y'all partner with that does these surgeries early, on kids twelve, thirteen," I hear myself say, "It's not about age. Care plans are based on puberty." When she says, "I know there's clinics y'all partner with that are a one-stop shop we could get the blocks, the surgery, all of it," I hear myself say, "Every clinic can help you access care right away, at the first appointment." Sometimes, caught up in that memory, I whimper aloud, and Liam says, "Snap out of it, Ro. There's nothing you can do about it now." The defining characteristic of the past.

What interests me here isn't the conversation. Leave that for later. Jump to the end. We've finished the call. She's switched off the mic, stopped the recording. Her child has gone. "Out with a friend," she said, which means she went up the tower. I see Gabbi, who waited twenty years to get the surgery she wanted at thirteen, who quit track though she loved it. Gabbi, alone, holds her left hand tightly in her right, and she closes her eyes, and she says, "You don't have to wait."

The navigator has made two critical mistakes—they haven't blurred their background and they've positioned their camera in front of a window, the vista beyond the window clear. A sand pine forest with a retention pond, fan palms in the understory, and a gap in the trees to the west to make way for a transmission tower and seven high-voltage power lines. Google would get her pretty close. The rest would likely require only a little time with satellite images. If creating a map was necessary, it would take only three well-chosen layers. The work of a day at most. Gabbi messages all of this to Jennifer Flitok after the call. Got them, she writes in a last, separate message, and then—or this at least is how I picture it—she walks out to the backyard, where the tower stands, creaking in the wind. Her daughter is up there. Gabbi gave her pocket money, and she disappeared with it into that other world, where her life is not arrowed toward a single video call, where she is more than that one purpose, where she can grow up, unconstrained by her conception. Gabbi uses a drill to pull out the screws one by one, dismantling the tower, taking an axe to the final posts until nothing is left but splintered wood, and her father comes rushing out from the lanai, shouting, "Stop," shouting, "Gabbi," for the first time using her name without prompting. What does he recognize in her? The impulsivity? The destruction? The protectiveness? "Gabbi," he shouts, "what are you doing?" "They were after my daughter," Gabbi says, and her father calms, understanding not the meaning of the statement, but its syntax.

All of this is inflected by what I know came next. Gabbi edits the video Flitok will publish on her Substack several months later. After the post goes live, Gabbi pulls out of the project publicly, citing Flitok's callousness and including some of Flitok's direct messages as evidence. In retaliation Flitok publishes messages Gabbi sent her, building a case against Gabbi as a weird, unstable fan. Retrocausality may not be true in life, but it's true in story. The end of this story is already written. Everything between this point and that one is chosen in service of that ending. Whatever may be true or untrue about backward causation in life, there is no such rule here. The end causes the beginning, and the beginning causes the end, and the difficulty of causal sequencing, which researchers point to as characteristic of autistic ineptitude, is perhaps not a deficiency, not a paucity of understanding, but a recognition of sheer causal complexity, so that even after pages of searching I am still lost in the proliferation of possible causes, the impenetrable density of the past tense. All I can say for certain in this moment is that I feel close to Gabbi. Perhaps this is inevitable—I've given her the kitchen island in my childhood home, my mother's gumbo, the summer I spent helping my father build a tower, the last summer I talked to my family, my hatred of the odor of shaving cream, my hatred of hospitals, of cramped sickrooms, of being cooped up, being cared for, and my totalizing isolation, which, without Liam, would still be a fact of my life. Still, this feeling of closeness surprises me as would any large miracle, which is to say, a small miracle distorted by the arrow of time. It suggests other worlds. The world where Gabbi and I meet on the boards, messaging about dysphoria or dyspraxia. The world where we cross paths in our shared hometown at a queer meetup and spend the evening in a corner, talking about our fathers' dementia and how we've handled it—by giving up on the role of daughter, introducing ourselves to our fathers anew, as Ro and Gabriel. Even the world where she comes to me at St. Cat, her child seated beside her, to talk about options, and the three of us commiserate about the panhandle's heteronormative beaches, how much we'd like to go topless in the dunes, and at some point the joy joins us. Gabbi and her daughter can both sense it. These worlds are impossible, but they tell us something about causality. Perhaps most usefully, they free causality from tense, so that I might describe a causal link this way: Gabbi can't understand or control her daughter, and I can't understand or control the joy. Perhaps Gabbi's daughter and the joy are linked, like scale and dragno. And it feels as plausible as anything else that this is why, before Flitok presses publish, as Gabbi takes her axe to the tower, liberating her daughter, the joy explodes around Liam and me.

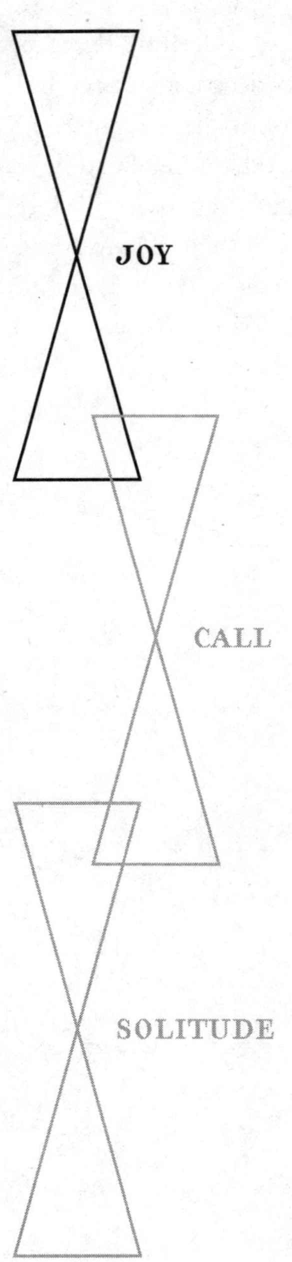

ELSEWHERE

There is a theory in physics, unproven and with many detractors, that time is a peculiar quality of our corner of the universe that we ourselves have a hand in creating. Not that we create time, consciously, but that the particles that are us interact with the physical world in such a way as to denote a random moment in our past as low-entropy, making every other moment higher entropy. In this sense time is a random distortion, an accident of physics, just as eyes are an accident of evolution. If this is the case, then asking by what magic our subset of the universe keeps time is a nonsense question, inverted. Like asking, as Carlo Rovelli writes in *The Order of Time*, why apples grow where people drink cider. A confusion of cause and effect.

If this is true, there are places in the universe where time doesn't pass, age has no meaning, heat and entropy do not rule. It is from a corner like this, I think, that the joy comes. I tell Liam this. I tell them there is a greater-than-zero chance our joy has extragalactic origins.

"What are you talking about?" they say. "The joy is ours. We made it."

But I believe joy, like matter, can be neither created nor destroyed. "Could it be from the future?" I ask.

Liam laughs. "It's just joy," they say. "It isn't so complicated."

This is easy for Liam to say. The joy is clear to them. They are adept with it, as they are with emotion generally. They've spent two decades learning to track their moods, to search them for any hint of danger. They are expert at answering that question most beloved of therapists: What are you feeling? The question always stumps me, and the joy, too, stumps me. I sense it—a suggestion of energy and peace—but I have no idea what to do with it. When I say this, Liam laughs—"You're just supposed to feel it." But I can't. The joy exists outside of me. I don't know how to nurture it, how to ensure it continues.

Take today, Liam's favorite holiday, 7-Eleven Day, the day you can get a free Slurpee from any participating 7-Eleven. Liam wakes up and insists we drive twenty minutes to the nearest 7-Eleven. For joy. For the joy of it. I don't have any meetings scheduled, and the joy makes it easier to take a risk like driving into town for a cold drink. And Liam is right. Returning to our cabin with two free Slurpees, the joy is more potent. But I couldn't tell you how Liam knew this was what the joy wanted. I would like to feel confident, as they do, about which activities will buttress it, and so I ask them, sipping my Slurpee, "What does it look like?"

"Metaphorically?"

"Sure," I say, though I am not speaking metaphorically. Liam considers for a moment then explains to me what the joy isn't. It isn't delicate. It isn't meretricious. It isn't interested in production of any kind. It likes us best on the couch eating peanut butter pretzels and mochi directly from the pack. It isn't an extrovert. It thrives on the kind of isolation that abolishes questions of gender and masking.

"But what does it look like?"

Liam shrugs, smiling.

"Come on, what does it look like?"

"Ears?" Liam says finally.

"How many?"

"Dozens," Liam says, indulging me. "Dozens of ears." The better to hear our worries, to soothe or banish them.

"And a mouth?" I say.

"Maybe a different vibratory organ."

"Like a syrinx or a throat pouch." The better to hum and gurgle, the better to growl when Liam considers working through lunch on their book, when I consider visiting Eva, when we make the mistake of inviting our neighbor for tea.

"It can leap and soar, fly almost, so I'd say long hind legs," Liam says, "and a tail." The better to jump like a deer or rabbit.

"Or wings," I say, and as I say it, I know I'm right. I feel the joy. For the first time, I really feel it—a heavy, lap-cat feeling. The joy, winged, is stretched across my legs. I take a long draw of my Slurpee, careful not to jostle the joy.

"Scales," Liam says, and from their careful movements, I think they also feel the joy across their lap. I nod. Of course, the joy is armored.

"Fire," Liam says. "In the belly maybe. Or its piss. Fiery piss."

"What?"

"Haven't you felt it? How it scalds sometimes?" And it's true I'm overheating in the porous house. I refuse to turn on the portable fan, can't stand its violence. "It's growing," Liam says. They extend their arms, as though measuring the joy with their hands. To lie comfortably across both our laps, the joy must be about the size and weight of a human four-year-old.

I am quiet. Liam laughs, as though all of this is a game, but it isn't a game, isn't only a game to me. The conversation changes something for both of us. Liam reaches out with one hand and strokes the air a few inches above their lap. My legs are vibrated by a long, barely audible hum.

I still can't see the joy, but at least now I know what I'm looking for. I reach out my own hand, attempting to touch the joy, but my hand sinks right past the place where I imagine it to be. There's only air.

In the days that follow, Liam continues to describe the joy. The joy likes lemonade. The joy likes the minnows darting at the edge of the swimming hole. The joy likes the patterns made by menstrual blood in the toilet bowl after the first flush. The joy likes the vibrations that result when I harmonize with my electric toothbrush, and the joy likes it when Liam and I work side by side in the kitchen without speaking, our actions synchronized. The joy likes us on our backs in the sunlight, indolent as house cats. The joy doesn't like obligations or deadlines. The joy doesn't like the postman. Quentin is okay. When he calls, the joy becomes smaller and denser, as if attempting to protect itself, but it doesn't flee as it does at the knock of our neighbor. Quentin calls frequently. He is having a hard time. He calls from the bus, lost in the unfamiliar city. He calls from school, after his

Intro to Astronomy professor refuses to add five points back to his test score. He calls from the doctor's office, asks us to explain to the PCP that he's emancipated and doesn't need a parent or guardian to sign off on hormones, and I attempt to explain, but the age of consent is eighteen in Missouri and the doctor remains uncertain, suggests an appointment with a case navigator who can help figure out the bureaucratic aspects, suggests also a full blood-work panel and a DXA scan, and all of this is okay, all of this is manageable, the first available appointment with the case navigator is in two weeks. There's still time before August, before the care ban goes into effect, but Quentin is worried about the timing and the blood work, hates needle pricks. "Something to work through," I say, "if you're going to be injecting T." We talk to him on speakerphone as he walks downstairs to the lab, which is at least in the same building. "Blood work is usual," I say. I look at Liam. I have promised Quentin a prescription, and I feel the weight of that promise now. "Don't worry," I say to Quentin, who hangs up when the lab tech calls his name.

As the season's first hurricane enters the Gulf, I begin to recognize the joy without Liam as translator. I sense it as Liam spins around and around in the kitchen, singing, "We won't be dry soon, here come the tides." This memory repeats. The song is stuck in their head for days, the bad sort of sticking, an agitating, nonconsensual sort, but I don't tire of the song, and so to me the repetition is joyful. Sometimes, I sing along.

One day, as if manifested by this song, a storm comes off the ocean, skims over the coast and harrows us. The power goes out. Rain taps patterns on the metal roof. A tornado warning makes our phones dance. The warning is useless. The cabin has no interior rooms. We huddle with the joy in the unmade bed, and as the tornado skids past us, as we rotate with the earth into calmer hours, I sense the joy is sultry, and I touch Liam's ear, asking, and Liam strokes a thumb across my cheek, confirming my intuition was right, we want this and, more importantly, the joy wants it.

I take the pendant of my necklace into my mouth. Liam drops their weight on top of me, and I realize I don't want to have sex this way. It's too difficult to track the sensations of my body and attend to Liam's body at the same time, too complicated, unjoyful, and the joy helps me find the proper exhalation patterns to say, "One at a time?" and Liam says, easily, "Who's first?"

Usually our hands move in concert. This is different. First, my hands touch Liam, who is mostly still. There are parts of Liam I'm uncertain about—their chest, the crack of their ass. They are places where Liam has hurt and healed—a fistula from a night of sex years ago that ends up rougher than Liam wants it, scars from the bilateral mastectomy their genes mandate. This is perhaps why I hesitate to touch, a hesitation that seems cowardly to me now. I begin with their chest. It is easier, a place I touch in the evenings, offering the gentle scar massage that is supposed to help—even years later—with tissue regeneration, with renewing the sensation that is still patchy, so Liam feels pressure but not touch, the opposite of the touch sensors on the alligator's jaw, and I think of how it felt to touch the alligator—easy, familiar. If only Liam were an alligator, I think, and suddenly I imagine it, scales beneath my fingers. Their anatomy is not so different from an alligator's anatomy—

sternum slightly concave, a place wings might attach. When my fingers find the lips of their scars, I imagine this is where wings were cut away, imagine them not an alligator but that next thing. Behind their sternum, some organ allows them to ignite breath. Scalding. It would scald to touch a dragon this way, and touch always scalds me a little. **Hyperarousal.** At the word a new weight settles in my abdomen. **You are a dragno**, I think to Liam, and the weight increases. My clit swells, a good pressure. I trace every curve of Liam's sternum, every pocket and divot. **I am a scale.** Sex is a bit like dragno riding—**You have to know what note the dragno will sing next and sing it at the same moment.** Two fingers stroke Liam's underarm and they shudder, a right note. I put my lips to Liam's left nipple, lick it with a firm tongue, and they take a deliberate slow breath, another right note. My hands dart up to Liam's chin, and a scatter of pimples on the underside of their jaw makes me gasp, so like the touch sensors on the alligator's jaw—little bumps, more sensitive than the skin around them, so that when I press one firmly Liam says, "Ow," and bats my hand away. A wrong note, but not a disaster. My fingers are enlivened. I am not near Liam's aorta, but I sense their pulse, feel the thrum of it in their skin. It's fast. Elevated heart rate is one of the side effects of their medications, a side effect their psychiatrist insists they needn't worry about, but I do worry. Does a heart have a finite number of beats? I want Liam's pulse to slow to an ectothermic rate, I wish them a reptilian heart. The thought thrusts me nearer them, I want their body in my mouth, all of it, but only three fingers will fit, the fingers each tipped with a single, perfect scale. I tongue their fingers while my left hand traces the edge of their ribs, and Liam laughs.

Liam pulls their hand slowly out of my mouth. I leave my mouth open. Liam rolls toward me to bite my lips. "You found my sternum," they say, "good for you," a hint of impatience in their voice. It is difficult, given this new positioning, to touch their chest, which is perhaps their point, to insist I touch elsewhere, so I lip at their neck and chin, avoiding their mouth, and make a kissing sound to express agreement, walking my fingers toward their ass. I scratch my nails across their back, and they breathe out, pleased. Their breath is a little musky, and I worry about their gum health. I am not enjoying myself as much as I was a moment ago, but the joy is right there, adjacent to me, offering courage. I continue, scraping my nails gently across their ass cheeks and then touching between, feeling the small suck of their anus against my finger, the flat seed of the fistula. I move, caught up with my daring, to touch the softer flesh of their perineum and Liam whimpers, a right note. They reach around to push my arm against their back, my fingers now at the opening of their cunt. It is unusual to approach them this way, but they nod against my shoulder, whining a little, and my wrist curves around neatly to reach them, to slip first one finger then two into their cunt, everything fits well enough, and I return to the usual rhythms of our intimacy, moving between their cunt and clit, an easy back-and-forth, which I continue until Liam squirms and says, "Are you bored?" I say, "No." I continue until Liam squirms again. "You're bored." "No." I'm not bored, I'm recovering from my earlier daring—**I am a scale**—but Liam extends their legs, making it harder for me to reach. I raise my eyebrows. They shake their head. "Your turn."

I prepare myself—soles of my feet pressed together, legs butterflied, hands above my head. When Liam asks if I want my eye mask, I nod. They slip the mask over my eyes, put my earplugs into my ears. Liam says, "Can I touch you, like just touch you touch you?" I nod again, though I don't usually allow touch, don't—as a rule—like it.

They begin at the nob atop my left shoulder and draw a finger across my clavicles. I think of the sign for *deadline*, the etymology of the word that has to do with Civil War prisons, but the touch draws me back. Their finger runs down my arm, tracing the border between the ticklish skin beneath and the less sensitive skin above. They cut between thumb and forefinger, leap to my stomach and meander toward my chest, looping and zigzagging, tracing a rough arch, touching down again at my left hip bone, then tracing up my left arm to the knob of my shoulder and swinging easily across my collarbones to begin again. It takes just two circuits for me to be sure of the pattern. By the fourth circuit, their touch stings. What is Liam using to touch me? A tooth? A talon? At the thought, I lift a little. By the sixth circuit, it feels like being brushed with nettle. By the eighth my anticipation has become a light dread. The circuit sears. I imagine a red raised line on my skin, which is then—on the ninth circuit—sliced open. The pain does what pain always does, pins me to my body. I am still, and my stillness has a profound quality, a reptilian stillness, which, unlike mammalian stillness, doesn't anticipate movement. I try to think about time, but the thoughts merely jangle against one another. I am trapped in my body. It is splendid. I want it to stop. I feel what I never feel—the sensation preceding the puncture of orgasm, a trembling in my abdomen, the drained feeling of my legs, the pressure that is like the pressure to pee but transmutes quickly into pleasurable inertia.

They are at the peak of the arch over my abdomen when they break the pattern, flattening their hand and sweeping down with their palm across my belly, and my body's stillness ruptures into little shudders, then larger shudders. The tremors are as overwhelming and involuntary as the shocks that overtake me sometimes in moments of distress. I've never before felt them in a moment of pleasure.

Liam says from somewhere on my left, "One at a time is harder for me," and I have no hope of responding with speech, so I offer an apologetic whir. And then, miracle of miracles, Liam whirs back at me, a whir of understanding and comfort, and I whir back at them a grateful whir, and for a time we are whir and counterwhir. When Liam begins a long and low whir, I whir along with them, finding synchrony. Liam takes a whir high at the end, a question, and I whir long and low, an answer.

Later, in the shower, there isn't water enough for both of us. Liam lets me wash first. When we trade places, they slip. I catch them around the waist, our bodies pressed together, and they say, "Rescued me," and I say, "Rescue," enjoying the twist at the word's center, soft *s* to hard *c*. There is little space in the shower for the joy, but it is there, in the front of the tub where a black snake emerges from the drain, avoids our feet, and curls around the water-warmed tap, and I tell Liam that during sex I imagined them a dragon, a little timid, uncertain of their reaction. They laugh and say, "Next time tell me, and I'll act like one." They put their mouth very close to my ear and huff hot breath, and I whir and say, thinking of *Mad Eden*, "Your soul of fire, my soul of scale." Then I whisper, "Will they unite?"

That night, as I rub foot against leg in the ritual way I do before sleep, Liam says, "When's the last time you dreaded the morning?" I say, "Dread?" as if it's a concept I've never heard of, and Liam says, "Right? Me too," and I say, "Liam?" and Liam says, "Mm?" and I say, "Love you," and they say, "Love you, too," and I say, "Liam?" and Liam says, "Mm?" and I say, "Love you," and they say, "Love you, too," and I say, "Liam?" and Liam indulges my repetition, my expression of a feeling I don't feel, exactly, but can still package into a word and toss to them, and the tossing makes the feeling more real, makes the joy more real. The joy hovers behind Liam. I can see it only if I look away, tracking it blurrily from the colorless, movement-sensitive corners of my retinas. Liam, I think, can see it directly. Liam talks about the iridescence of its scales, the narrow claws on the ends of its wings. I want to see the joy as they do.

I try to entice the joy. I take walks along the shore of the retention pond. I eat an extra mochi in the evening. I talk to Eva on the phone, a reliably joyful thing. "Can I vent?" she says, which of course she can. Her wedding to Darcy is strategic, a way of formalizing a relationship that both her family and Darcy's are liable to ignore, failing to invite Darcy to Eva's sister's wedding or Eva on the family vacation. The wedding is supposed to be simple, just the two of them and the officiant on a low mountain, but now Darcy wants a wreath of flowers up there, and her Nana is insisting on coming, and Eva is increasingly leaning toward a courthouse—you don't have to walk a thousand feet uphill to get to a courthouse—and Darcy and Eva don't fight, but Eva is beginning to think a fight would be cathartic.

I try to apply *Mad Eden* to Eva's situation. A dragno could easily carry a wreath of flowers to a mountaintop, but in *Mad Eden* neither the word flower nor the word mountain is possible. Also, Eva and Darcy are not dragno and scale. They get along easily, they aren't two different species trying to survive in close proximity, and although this leaves me unable to help Eva, it makes me joyful to think *Mad Eden* is still just for me, though the joy itself is off with Liam somewhere.

After Eva hangs up, I put on my eye mask and headphones and play a song. It's a song with a long mandolin solo, a song that, since childhood, has reliably brought me joy. I listen the way I most like to listen—the song repeating again and again. I peek out from beneath my mask, but the joy isn't there. After an hour, I'm well into the middle stage of listening. Every note is known. I am plucking with my left hand each time the cello jumps, making the sign for *found* again and again, and tears come, rolling gently into my hair, part of the richness I am feeling, and isn't that joy? I would name it joy but the joy isn't here, and I wonder for the first time if this inability to name the feeling isn't alexithymia, but a lack within language itself. There are gaps in our language of fear. Why not, too, in our language of pleasure?

Then Liam shouts, "Henlo," from somewhere in the house. Searching for me. And I shout, "Spree!" Found.

They enter our bedroom, bringing the joy and a box. Inside the box, an exact replica of my work shirt. "I combed eBay for weeks," they say, and I say, "Spree," a loud chirp of surprise and glee, and the joy is at my side. Joy in exactitude, which I respond to the way others respond to art, as an aesthetic principle. The glorious repeatability of objects. I try to bring the joy into more precise focus, but then Liam's phone rings, and the joy disperses, so diffuse as to be imperceptible.

Quentin is on the phone, panicked. The meeting with the caseworker is done, and he's cleared to consent to his own treatment, but there is some minor aberration in his blood work. His cholesterol is a little high. The provider doesn't think it's an issue but wants an endocrinologist to manage his hormones just in case, and the endocrinologist doesn't have any openings until September, and we both jump on our computers to search for alternate providers, and later, after we find an endocrinologist near him, after Quentin makes an appointment, Liam says, "I thought it would flee farther," and it's true. The joy is still here, hovering, and I understand only then how daring the joy is. It isn't comfort. Comfort, we would question. Complacency would frighten and enrage us. We would kick it out of our house. But the joy is liberatory, predisposed to risk.

I am reminded of this a week later, in the middle of the night, when Liam hisses through their teeth on the outbreath, whimpers, a hand on their abdomen, face blank, and says, when I ask what's wrong, that their stomach hurts, or not hurts precisely, it's a strange, uncomfortable sensation like electricity in their body, it happens when they're on a too-high dose of one medication. Probably the generics in this region are different than the generics they were on previously. Generics have to be bioequivalent to the name-brand drug, but that doesn't mean they're identical.

The average difference in drug concentration is around 4 percent, and 4 percent is more than enough to intensify a side effect, and they hiss again, both hands sanding the skin of their belly, they toss their body to the far side of the bed, and I say, quietly, "There is a bird and a stone," and they say, "Fuck," and I say, agitated, "Bird and stone, bird and stone," and the joy is the force that keeps me from taking them to the hospital. The joy is what allows me, instead, to make the sign for *sleep* on Liam's face, drawing all my fingers together and down as though sleep is a cowl I can pull over their eyes. *Sleep*, I sign, touching them gently, *sleep*, until they do. The next night, I take the small flattened sphere of the pill in its unassuming peach color and I shave it with an X-Acto knife, just a little, turning the sphere into a gibbous moon. Four percent. Or so. The pill crumbles a little under the knife blade. They aren't supposed to be cut, but the joy steadies my hand. Liam takes the partial pill from the tip of my finger. I say, "My soul of flowing water, your soul of thirst," and Liam laughs, and Liam sleeps that night without discomfort. It becomes a new pattern, one of the many rituals we develop to safeguard the joy, small extensions of our mutualism. I bring Liam coffee in bed. Liam measures my yogurt in the mornings. When the nearby store is out, Liam drives an hour into the city for the mochi I prefer. Our life constricts a little, pulled tighter by the joy.

The next time Quentin calls, I'm sprawled on the couch, reading the third installment of *Mad Eden*. Nova and Cardinaux are lazing by a waterfall on the islands of proficiency, high on magical roots, when Cardinaux, always eagle-eyed, spots magicians approaching beneath them. At Nova's urging, Cardinaux descends to help a dragno and scale who are struggling under a bombardment of arrows. Cardinaux and Nova are, by this time, an acrobatic pair, capable of accelerations that defy physics. ***Avoid anticipation*****, Cardinaux says to Nova, and Nova attempts it—not to imagine the magicians catching Cardinaux, not to give in to their anxiety.** But then Nova sees a magician they grew up with notch an arrow in his bow, and they know, fatalistically, that the arrow will find them, and the arrow does, knocking Nova off Cardinaux, sending them plummeting through the air into a crowd of magicians. Cardinaux catches them, helpless before that deterministic law of scale and dragno, so they both end up on the ground.

If Nova had managed to **avoid anticipation**, the pair could have escaped through some impossible bending of spacetime. This is why Nova is a threat to the dragnos—not through a tracker embedded in their brain, as some scales speculate, but due to latent self-doubt and anxiety, which can be exploited by the magicians, so that **for a moment Nova is no longer a fearsome scale, but only weak.**

Swap the last two clauses of that final sentence, and it says the opposite thing—**Nova is no longer weak, but a fearsome scale**. Similarly, the phrase **not to give in to their anxiety** can be inverted by deleting one word—**not**. It's easier than it should be to twist an English sentence into its opposite, a carelessness in the language itself, it seems to me, which *Mad Eden* exploits, causing the original article to undermine itself again and again. The word *pathological* is shortened to **path**, used to designate the vein Nova traces across Cardinaux's body and the trails on the islands of proficiency that lead them always back to their dragno; stimming, which in the original article is described as a compulsive and socially inappropriate need, makes flight possible in *Mad Eden*. And anticipatory failure, which in the article is a central impairment of autism, in *Mad Eden* would have saved Nova and Cardinaux.

Due to Nova's anticipation, they are caught and tied up in a **net** (from *shared gene networks across many autism subtypes*). The magicians manage to throw chains over Cardinaux. Nova considers **driving the magicians' arrow into their heart**, which is one part dread at the fate that awaits them and one part self-sacrifice. Their death would cause Cardinaux to unfold, freeing the dragno, but Cardinaux says, ***Can you outrun a stream, scale? Then don't be so quick to start swinging your legs. We're not yet drowned for certain.***

The last thing Nova sees before being hauled away by the magicians is Cardinaux snapping one chain, freeing a wing and unfolding it so rapidly he knocks three magicians to the ground. The dragno whispers in their mind, ***Don't let them find the islands***. That magic garden, a refuge.

I have that word, refuge, in mind as Liam's phone begins to ring, and sure enough the call is glorious. Quentin has a one-month prescription. "Call the pharmacy," we say. "Get it filled today." It is August 15. Quentin fills the prescription and calls the next morning to say his sheets and pillows smell like boy—like boy! Liam and I are ebullient, and I look to the corner of the room where the joy is. For the first time I see it, the full embodied being of it—ears, yes, dozens of them (from *research*, from *year*, from *learned*, from *search*, from *early*, from *rehearsal*), lining the ridge of the joy's back; a long narrow face, noseless, but with a wide reptilian mouth and red eagle eyes; wings above long hind legs and a wide frith. I say to Liam, "Is it a dragno?"

"A what?"

"Like a dragon," I say. Dragnos are not dragons, not exactly. The original text lacks the words—scorch, tear, bloody—that would allow them to kill. They have **mouths** but no teeth, no fangs. Many **ears**, but no nose. **Legs**, but no claws, no talons. They cannot breathe fire. They are **winged** and **scaled**, but not savage. They are reclusive, only emerging from the islands of proficiency when they have no choice. They are, and this is the whole point of the text, not creatures to fear.

Liam tilts their head, staring at the place I'm staring. "I have no idea," they say. "To me it's joy—bliss, alegría. I've been following your lead."

So I say it again, more confident this time—"The joy is a dragno."

Autism as a disorder of prediction

3. REDUCED APPRECIATION OF HUMOR.

On the way to the magician's laboratory, Nova keeps their anxiety at bay by thinking about moments of joy: rising early on Most-of-Sky under the bright bands of dawn; immersion in the island's rivers, so clear they mirror the sky; wandering the island's paths only to find themselves, somehow, back at Cardinaux; Cardinaux's joke about magicians that ends with him singing, *Don't fear your part in the resistance, for most events are happenstance*; Cardinaux saying, when Nova appears confused by his jokes, *I know a hallmark feature of magicians is their humorlessness, but as my scale, you could at least smile*; Cardinaux catching Nova with such affection it feels like coming home; eloping with Cardinaux to the islands away from Most-of-Sky, their hands on Cardinaux's scales, their spirit replicating the dragno's every note as he hunts; and how the magicians' foxes run when Cardinaux's prodigious wings open above them.

Cardinaux got away, Nova thinks. He is a great dragno, and Nova can read his mind. If Cardinaux were in danger, Nova would know.

In the stories about dragons I read as a kid, dragons hunt humans and humans hunt dragons—for the precious stones of their pupils, for their skin and teeth, for their fat, which heals ulcers, their scleras, which can be whipped with honey into an ointment that guards against night terrors—but there are exceptions to these old tales. Edward Topsell writes of the dragon-love of Aetholis, who comes to her every night and plays with her until morning. Another woman, though she is in love with a man, spends most of her nights leaving his bed for a dragon. These stories rarely end well. Usually, the women are found out and hidden from their dragon lovers by jealous boyfriends or worried family members. The dragons seek the women endlessly, and when they are finally reunited, the dragons bind and beat the women with their tails. In another sort of story, a boy grows up alongside a dragon whelp, and though the dragon is taken to the woods when it begins to grow, the two do not forget each other. When the boy, grown to a man, falls into trouble with thieves, the dragon hears his cry of alarm and rescues him. I do not think of these stories in the first months of the joy. I am preoccupied with joyful things—my client in Alabama has a six-month supply of hormones, which should see him through his eighteenth birthday; my client in Oklahoma has raised almost seven hundred dollars and is pleased by this, though it isn't enough to cover the genioplasty, isn't even enough for first month, last month, and deposit on an apartment; my client in West Virginia has permission to use the girls' bathroom all year in spite of state policy. I am preoccupied with Quentin, who has joined a wrestling club and grown one hair on his chin. Quentin calls to say he's craving chips, then jerky, then steak. He has the desire to eat his couch, and this thrills him. Quentin calls to say he's aced his astronomy final.

So when Liam's phone rings in early September and Quentin's name scrolls slowly across the top of the screen, I am surprised that the joy cowers. I am unprepared for the desolation of that call, which Liam quickly puts on speakerphone. Quentin is panting. At first I think he is running—a terrified, flat-out running. He is breathing heavily into the phone, and it's only when Liam signs *crying* with a pointer finger that I revise my assumption of danger and flight. Quentin is sobbing, hard enough it is impossible to make out his words.

"I can't understand you," Liam says. "Take a deep breath. We'll figure it out, whatever happened." As they continue this low-toned monologue, punctuated occasionally by a vocalization from Quentin, I realize they are speaking to Quentin the way they speak to me. The words they offer as comfort when I am upset are scripts, not spontaneous constructions, not created for me alone.

The first sentence of Quentin's we are able to make out is, "Why did I leave Florida?" Then two phrases, "don't know any" and "was I even." I assume Quentin is feeling upset about the move, feeling lonely, a reasonable thing to feel in your first semester of college, especially if you're seventeen and trans, but Liam says in response, "I don't understand, you have a prescription," and "Why would they stop it?"

And Quentin says—annoyance at having to repeat himself helping to make his voice clearer—"The *law*."

Liam holds the phone out to me on the flat palm of their hand, a request. I don't take it. I say, "What's happening?"

"They stopped his T," Liam says. "Apparently there isn't a continuation clause."

"There's a continuation clause," I say.

"They're not treating anyone," Quentin says.

"What does that mean?"

"I guess if you're over eighteen, maybe, but otherwise they're not treating anyone. I'm almost out. I want to come back to Florida. I never should have left."

I am on my computer, pulling up the text of the bill, the news articles about its recent implementation—"There's a continuation clause."

"Can I come live with you?"

"Quentin, you have class."

"I'm not going to class. I've told everyone here I'm—I can't."

"It's a misunderstanding probably."

"They offered to put me on that birth control where you don't get periods for three years."

"Progestin?"

"I don't know."

"Don't let them put you on birth control."

"That's my only option."

"It isn't. Someone's confused. Who told you they couldn't prescribe it?"

"I want to come home. I want to come stay with you."

"How much do you have left?" I say, the scripts snapping to my tongue, Quentin just another upset client.

"I'm not happy here."

"How much testosterone do you have left?"

"I don't know, I don't care. I want to come home."

"Who told you no? Probably some PCP doesn't know what they're talking—"

"I wish I had parents, I wish I had parents, I wish I had parents."

"You just need to—"

But Liam lifts a hand to stop me.

"You can come here," Liam says. "If you absolutely can't stick it out, of course you can come here, but we're not there yet."

The promise eases something in Quentin, he is breathing more steadily, and he says, "My friends here know me as this new person, and if I can't be that person—I can't go to class, I just can't." Liam is comforting Quentin and the joy. I say, to be part of it, "I'll talk to them. I'll figure this out." No one responds. Quentin is crying but more gently, and Liam is making soft, crooning noises, and the joy croons back, staring at me, a warning posture. I've made a mistake. I've threatened the joy. "I'll fix it," I say.

I call the clinic the next morning. Phone calls are the part of my work I dread most, but Liam comes past on their way to the kitchen and says, "Good Ro, best Ro," and I say, "Best Ro," and this gives me the courage to dial. I press three for the nurses' line. The nurses generally know more than anyone else. I say I'm Quentin's guardian and am confused by the change in his prescription. The nurse on the phone is brusque, says she's not able to disclose any patient information. I ask about hormone therapy more generally, and she says, "We're not able to help with that at this time." When I ask why, she says, "We're not able at this time." It's Eva who explains it to me that afternoon in our weekly team meeting. There are clauses in the bill stating that any minor offered gender-affirming care can sue up to fifteen years after they've ceased treatment or until they are thirty-six, whichever is later, for damages up to five hundred thousand dollars, even if the care was performed suitably and with no finding of malpractice or neglect. The hospitals' lawyers have only recently come to understand the significance of this clause and now gender care at both university hospitals is shut down, and Planned Parenthood is heading the same way. "Right out of the abortion playbook," Eva says. I repeat, my microphone muted, "Right out of the abortion playbook," catching Eva's intonation, a blend of bitter humor and stress.

"What's your continuation of care plan?" I ask the nurse on my next call. I imagine the sound waves of my voice entering the microphone and traveling to the speaker of her phone, exiting at a speed much slower than the speed of light. My calls are in the backward-facing light cone of Quentin's next interaction with the clinic. There is a causal relationship. I insist on it. "Where are you sending patients?" "Ma'am, I'm going to have to ask you to call the front desk," she says. "I don't have the answers to your questions." The front desk doesn't have the answers either. "All of our patients received a written notice. If you look at that notice, you'll see some resources down at the bottom."

"So there's no continuation plan? You're just dropping him?"

"Your child is how old?"

"Seventeen."

"Seventeen, we're suggesting they wait until their eighteenth birthday to resume care at our facility."

"That's eight months away."

"I'm sorry I don't have better news."

I've said the same thing to clients just shy of legal adulthood. There are fifteen-year-olds who need triaging and referrals. Eight months is nothing in corporate or legal time, but it is an eternity in parental time, and when a robot asks me, at the end of the call, to rate my experience, I give the clinic a one out of ten, pressing the button with a thumb full of fury. The joy gives a chipper trill, glad I'm off the phone. "It seems okay," Liam says. We are both nurturing a hope too self-centered to speak aloud in this moment of Quentin's crisis—if the joy can outlast this, perhaps we can keep it forever.

Later, in a national strategy meeting, a St. Louis clinician asks the same questions I have. The Planned Parenthoods in Kansas City are almost all on the Missouri side. The two in Kansas aren't taking any new cases. The clinic just across the Iowa border is understaffed. The Oregon clinic has a one-year waiting list after absorbing a bunch of clients from Idaho. A Planned Parenthood in Tennessee has openings at the moment, but it's unclear whether the care ban there would allow them to see patients from Missouri, and as soon as the Sixth Circuit Court makes a decision, which could be as early as the following morning, they're likely to close their doors. The injunction in Alabama is kaput, the lower court citing the *Dobbs* decision. A Colorado clinic has openings six weeks out, and the flights from St. Louis aren't too bad, but not too bad is impossible for most people. A clinic in New York can prescribe for a year with one trip if there's someone in Missouri who can legally adjust doses to manage side effects, but at the moment they're waiting on their lawyers to make sure such a setup is legal, so, "For now we're in a holding pattern." The St. Louis clinician, bunching her hair up in her hands only to let it fall again, says, "The sooner the better. We're scrambling."

I draw my leg up into my chair, the heel of my right foot wedged against my crotch, a good sensation of being tightly held by the chair, which gives me the courage to open an incognito window and navigate to a site where I can get bulk testosterone powder for three hundred dollars. The joy scrambles to its feet and comes toward me as I waver about whether or not to place the order. I pause at its sudden approach, unsure if it's encouragement or threat. The California clinician says, "My central message to anyone in a safe state is don't do anything too risky. If you get shut down, we've lost the opportunity to provide that resource, so while I understand the urgency from our providers in Missouri, I want us to move at the speed our lawyers think is safe." I close the incognito window and the joy wanders away. I can't tell whether it's relieved or disappointed.

That night I suggest the joy might want T. Perhaps the joy wants more body hair, wants to crave salt with such ferocity it dips its grether directly into the shaker.

"That's just guilt," Liam says. We are lying side by side. I am preparing for sleep by rubbing the arch of my left foot against my right leg. "Guilt isn't joy," Liam says.

"I could make T," I say to Liam, testing out this possible solution to Quentin's crisis. The recipe from Swaati is still stored on my phone. The applicators can be ordered from any bath and beauty supply store. The powder can be ordered online and arrives at your door in a nondescript box. Going from powder to gel is easy. One gram is 1 percent, mathematics a child could do. You just need a measuring cup and a stove—a one-pot recipe.

"This isn't even our house."

"Not even our house," I agree. This protects us.

"Can you imagine what would happen if Trevor's aunt figured out you were cooking in her house?"

"Not cooking."

"T is quite literally a drug."

In fact, testosterone is a schedule III controlled substance, along with steroids and ketamine. Still I say, "It's more like making your own deodorant than like meth."

"Is that what you're planning to say in front of the judge?"

"What judge?"

"We're not doing this. You're not doing this."

As much as anything else, I'm surprised by our role reversal. I am the one who follows rules. Liam considers unthinking obedience to be morally bankrupt, but now Liam says, "Don't kill the bird."

I say, rubbing my foot a little faster, "It's the joy. That's why you're against it."

"It's illegal."

"You're worried about the joy."

"I'm worried about you going to prison. Don't do this. Promise me."

I rub my foot a little faster.

"Promise me."

"Promise me," I say.

"Promise."

"Promise."

"It is about the joy," Liam says then, softened by my acquiescence. "It is, a little bit. I feel, I don't know, protective of it." It is inevitable, this protective impulse that causes us to mistrust each other. The joy is likely to disappear if sabotaged, and who is more likely to sabotage our shared joy than the other?

"I'm not trying to shut you down," Liam says. "I want you to feel the joy, too." But in the wake of Quentin's call, the joy slinks out of any room I enter. It hisses when I call Swaati to ask if Quentin can stay with them in New York City if the lawyers decide clinicians there can prescribe with one visit. "Testosterone is going to be tough with that setup," Swaati says. As a controlled substance, testosterone is difficult to prescribe across state lines, but if I can find someone willing to call a prescription into a mail-order pharmacy that's willing to ship it—"It's the only option I have," I say, and Swaati says, "Of course, then. Just call with dates when you've got them." A few minutes after we hang up, they send me a photo of their studio, lit softly by slanted morning light, and the message, His turret awaits. I don't mention Swaati's studio or the possibility of a New York appointment to Quentin. "Not until we have something definite," Liam says. So when Quentin calls to see if I have a solution, I tell him I need more time. Quentin is quieter and quieter on these calls until he hardly says anything at all. He isn't going to class, isn't handing in assignments. I can't think of anything to say to comfort him.

Liam becomes the joy's keeper, and I do not contest their interpretations. When they return from the supermarket with a can of tuna, saying, "The joy wants fish," I do not say that thousands of dolphins die each year in tuna nets. When they wrap an arm around me in the morning, insisting the joy wants a lie-in, I do not protest, though the late start forces me to truncate my morning routine to make it to my meetings on time. My first client that day is a twenty-nine-year-old in Montana seeking a tracheal shave, who says, after I explain about the flights to New York City and the average out-of-pocket cost, "Cheaper to kill myself." My client in Oklahoma has taken a bus to western Massachusetts and is staying with a friend of a friend, trying to figure out how to establish residency, and though she seems cheerful, I am terrified at how completely she has upended her life. Then Quentin calls, and I have to tell him, "No, nothing yet, I'm working on it." That evening, I watch Liam eat a salmon filet and feel the joy purr, a rippling, mechanical hum, and I know before Liam suggests it, before we zip ourselves into the mesh tent, that we are to have sex, and it isn't that I don't want to, but I know it isn't each other we'll be attempting to satisfy. It's the joy, which follows us into the tent though I close the zipper to keep it out. The joy seeps through the mesh to wrap around our naked bodies, inhibiting our usual patterns, so instead of one atop and one beneath, we end up straddling each other, thigh against clit, and it feels okay but neither of us comes, and coming isn't the point, Liam says, but I also think it's the fault of the joy, which soaks up our pleasure, siphoning it off us, smug as a cat.

On the day we are to drive into the city for an abdominal ultrasound, a biannual precaution for Liam, the joy refuses to join. It twists down on itself in the center of the kitchen, its distress convincing enough that Liam cancels the appointment, though same-day cancellation results in a fifty-dollar fee our state insurance won't touch. They tell me this when I return from an early run. I've rearranged my day around the interruption that was the appointment. I've taken off work. I've eaten two meals two hours apart, so I won't need food again until the evening. Now the appointment isn't happening.

"You rescheduled it," I say.

"I didn't." They are gleaming, self-satisfied.

"But your ovaries."

"Might be sheltering little tumors even as we speak." Liam shrugs. It's a reckless statement, a reckless decision both medically and financially, out of character for Liam, made possible, I think, by the joy. The decision worries me, but it's the change of schedule that really throws me off, how quickly the shape of our day has morphed. All afternoon, I am heavy and lethargic, unable to adapt, useless as a train derailed by a switch thrown at the last minute. I try rereading the fourth installment of *Mad Eden*, but it's hardly joyful—Nova is being tortured, and it's their own fault. I suppose it's also the fault of the original article, which includes a section on torture as an example of an anxiolytic stimulus. Nova's torture begins with **unfamiliar music** (from *"acoustic bombardment" has long been used as an instrument of torture. Unfamiliar, and hence unpredictable, music is found to be especially effective*).

For the next time and many times, Nova suffers. Their ears sear with the relentless influx, note after unpredictable note. Sound, sound, sound, sound, chronic enough to drive them mad. They cannot move, so they

cannot stim, and only stimming could help them. They beg. The magicians ignore them.

When the music stops, it is only so that the magicians can question Nova.

"Do you like the music?"

Nova attempts to turn their head to see the magician, but the chains are rigid. They can't move. "That was a joke," the magician says. "Dragnos are known for their humorlessness, but I expected more from a magician. I did suggest you attend to your studies, Nova. If you better understood theory of mind, perhaps we wouldn't be here."

The magician steps into Nova's view. It's Hans. Nova's stress intensifies.

"Together," Hans says, "we can make an empire [from *empirical*] **without dragnos, in which magicians don't have to resort to clever contrivances to achieve even our most mundane magic." The magician puts his hand on Nova's leg, a threat. "Where are the islands of proficiency?"**

"I don't know."

"We knew you were a scale," Hans continues. "We tried to keep you from becoming a"—Hans fingers Nova's developing frith—"a mutant [from *Shank3 mutant mice display autistic-like behaviours*]**." Now, I see that you were meant to become a scale and lead us to the dragnos. Where are the islands of proficiency?"**

Nova thinks of Cardinaux saying, *Don't let them find the islands.*

"I don't know."

The torture proceeds from there down avenues both familiar and upsetting. It is Nova's mind that interests the magicians—their knowledge of the dragnos and ability to withstand their chaos. The magicians begin to **examine and experiment**, and I know those words are delineated by the scientific article from which *Mad Eden* takes its lexicon, but the comfort of being pierced by a distant intelligence, of being seen, is warped in this installment into something unnerving. The torture reminds me of the hospital—not in any direct way, but in a general sense. The words of the article—the words of autism testing and treatment, which I first heard in the hospital—are distorted by *Mad Eden* into something clearly malicious, and malice is what I felt in the hospital, a feeling I've tried, in the months since, to reason away. I add to my list of hypotheses about the author of *Mad Eden* that they too have been hospitalized, have spent time in a room with glass walls but no windows. But what I feel, as I reread the fourth installment, is gratitude not to the author of *Mad Eden* but to the authors of the original article, for all the words that don't appear there—blood, saw, knife, cut, drill—so that the torture is described obliquely: **They tie Nova's head back and use their tools to find certain key brain loci**, and since I am rereading I let myself skim, unable to stomach this scene. I consider, for the first time, how it would feel for the authors of *Autism as a Disorder of Prediction* to see every edit, every trick, every sleight of hand invisible to the rest of us. It would be a sort of intimacy. A complicated intimacy, to be sure, but intimacy nonetheless—with *Mad Eden* and with its author.

"Go to work," Liam says when I complain about having nothing to do, but I have taken off work to go to the appointment and can't face the social awkwardness of explaining my change of heart. "Go on a run," Liam says, but I have already gone on a run. When the time comes for my second daily meal, the meal I have already eaten, I sob. "Eat it again," Liam says, but I have already eaten black beans, so I am not craving black beans. I am craving the craving, but manifesting this is beyond me.

"I love you, but I don't understand," Liam says. "You have a day off. Nothing is bad." And I think, ungenerously, that the author of *Mad Eden* would understand, and for a moment I long for them—to know the author of *Mad Eden*, to be intimate with them as with an old friend.

"It is silly," I say, and a sob takes me. I expect the sobs to grow, expect a full-on meltdown. Almost I wish for this, to be given a reason to abdicate control. I wish for the feeling after meltdown, that total exhaustion, but the meltdown won't come. The joy has bolstered me just enough to make meltdown impossible. I was wrong. The joy isn't brittle, I am brittle. The joy is strong, fluid and changeable as Liam is.

"It prefers you," I say to Liam. They deny it at first, but I lay out the evidence—the joy's rejection of my black beans, the joy's dislike of my work meetings, the joy's apparent ease with sudden shifts in plan. "It hasn't forgiven me for messing things up with Quentin."

"You're scared," Liam says, and I think they are telling me what I'm feeling in this moment, but then they say, "Scared of eating anything new, scared of saying the wrong thing to your clients, scared of disappointing Quentin. Of course the joy doesn't know how to be around you."

"There are costs to breaking the rules," I say. "Quentin," I say, though I am not thinking of Quentin. I am thinking of the day I just lost to a schedule change, of eating tuna on a night when we should be eating black beans. I have rules for a reason.

Liam shrugs. "You know your stuff. If you trusted yourself on the calls, enjoyed them, the joy wouldn't cower."

"You're the same way with your work," I say. And then, remembering, "Meticulous."

"But I love it. I'm just saying fear is the opposite of joy. Not a direct opposite like despair or misery, but a—a slant opposite."

"Plenty of people don't love work."

"The joy wants us to be happy. It's guiding us."

"The rules keep us happy."

"The whole time we've been together I've prioritized your rules, your needs. It has to be okay for me to prioritize something else for a little while."

And it is okay, and I say this, but the following day I finish talking to Quentin and look up to find Liam in the kitchen, earbuds in, waltzing. They've never waltzed before. They don't like dancing, don't believe they're good at it. But they waltz with rhythm and grace, the joy holding their shoulders, ears floppy, docile with them, as it never is with me. With me it is a muscular thing, tight and predatory. I watch, for a while, this dance that is not for me. We have agreed the joy is shared yet I can't, watching Liam move with the joy from window to sink, even guess the song.

Autism as a disorder of predicten

4. ISLANDS OF PROFICIENCY.

Nova can't sense Cardinaux. The music, that bombardment of sound, makes it impossible to imagine the alternate note that could unify them with their dragno.

"You can make it stop," Hans says, "I just need to know where the islands of proficiency are."

"I don't know," Nova says.

"The dragnos don't care about you. They keep you and all their mutant scales impaired. Unable to catch a ball, unable to habituate, unable to make simple predictions. Where are the islands of proficiency?"

Nova thinks of Cardinaux saying, *You don't habituate*, thinks of Cardinaux's grether in their ear.

"I don't know," Nova says.

"Give me the information, and I'll let your dragno go."

Nova feels a rush of anxiety, understanding then, and only then, the real measure of the crux they are in.

If you've been paying attention to causality, the Substack article—*1970s Throwback: Southern Nonprofit Chemically Sterilizing Kids*—won't surprise you, not the way it surprised me, landing in my inbox in an email from Amalia, who also asked that I attend an emergency strategy meeting that morning.

It begins like this:

> Why, you may ask, is an organization focused on the chemical sterilization of young children targeting low-income Black, Indigenous, and POC communities? You've heard the old adage: history repeats.

A break in the article for a thirteen-second video clip. "And if Lupron isn't possible, would they prescribe Depo-Provera?" a voice asks, and I respond, "Depo can be a low-cost alternative to Lupron," and I know the rest of the sentence is, "but it has significant side effects," but no one else does. And the article continues:

> In 1967, the FDA denied approval of Depo-Provera, known as "the shot," due to animal studies suggesting the drug was associated with increased risk of

> cancer and sterility. In spite of this, over the next decade, seven thousand low-income Black women in Atlanta were given the shot by their doctors. In 1978 and 1983 the drug was again denied approval after causing cancer in dogs, but in 1987, the FDA changed its requirements to mandate testing for cancer in rats. Depo doesn't cause cancer in rats, so in 1992, twenty-five years after the first submission by Big Pharma, Depo was approved. Today, 84 percent of the people in the United States given Depo are Black women. From 1994 to 2000, the US government sent 41 million doses of Depo-Provera to "low-income" nations. Depo isn't commonly used as a puberty blocker, but as this representative of the Southern Trans Care Access Taskforce suggests, it might be an alternative for "low-income" kids.

A picture of a map follows—*Legislative Status of Eugenical Sterilization in the United States*. I have begun hitting my head gently with my right hand.

> Of course, in the 1970s the doctors didn't stop at chemical sterilization. After twenty-four months on Depo-Provera, Minnie and Mary Alice Relf were driven by their local doctor to their community hospital for surgical sterilizations. Their sister Katie escaped this fate only by locking herself in her room. Or consider two fifteen-year-old Native American girls who went to their local clinic for a tonsillectomy and woke up surprised to find their abdomens stitched. One in four Native American women were

> coerced into sterilization between 1970 and 1976. And if you think this ended in the seventies, consider the women sterilized while in the custody of ICE, some of them without any paperwork explaining why the sterilization was medically necessary. Asked about sterilizing surgeries, this is what the butcher's pet said.

There I am again—the vertical cleft between my eyes, the buzz cut Quentin asked if I did myself. "How early can they get them off of her?" the voice says, and I say, "It's not about age. Care plans are based on——puberty." The video glitches slightly before the word puberty, a less than smooth edit. "If they have——started puberty——you're good to go."

> Notice the butcher's pet feels nothing, has no emotion as she describes castrating children who have started puberty, which can happen as young as eight. Though I guess the lack of emotion is better than the gleeful and graphic descriptions of the butchers themselves.

"Are you okay?"
"Ro."
"Are you okay?"

The computer is gone. The rest of the article and the comments that follow disappear. Liam is there instead, crouched in front of me. My hands hit my head. My head is a ball, and my hands volley it back and forth. Each tap is another comment.

My mom still won't go near an IHS.

Butcher. Butcher. Butcher

The gheys drive this lunacy. They hate their lives and are looking to inflict pain on others.

King of the Butchers

Sadistic perverts cut off their arms see how they like it

"Stop. Ro, stop. Stop."

Liam has put their hands on my temples, effectively pausing the volleys, but the pressure in me is like water, and having one outlet blocked it finds another. My knees bounce. My fist finds my upper thigh and drives into it rhythmically. Keeping time, like corralling a flighty horse, and I do feel paused. I know, for instance, that in fifteen minutes I meet with Amalia and the director of St. Cat, and this feels possible thanks to the slowness of seconds. Liam's words are drawn out, almost unintelligible. This is the deal I have made with time. I never duck out of a minute, never change a plan, and time stretches when I need it to stretch. I have fifteen minutes to return myself to some semblance of functionality. An eternity. It is a gift, the meeting with Amalia. Like a fence around me, it limits how far I can bolt. Amalia knows me better, maybe, than I've realized.

Liam is reading, quickly, still crouched on the floor. Their face is scrunched in what might be concentration, pity, anger, or disgust. "Fuckers," they say as they near the end. "Did you know this was coming?"

A causal question. They glance up, judging the effect of their words. They open their arms to me, offering touch. I lean away. To be touched now would be to feel a thousand splinters of glass pierce my skin.

"Best Ro," they say. "Good Ro."

I shake my head.

Distress translates across species. A study of distress calls in terrestrial vertebrates found humans were able to note distress in the giant panda, the hourglass tree frog, the domestic pig, the African bush elephant, the American alligator, the Barbary macaque, the common raven, and the black-capped chickadee. Chickadee alarm calls use a recombinant system of four notes. The number of "dee" notes at the end of the call corresponds to the intensity of the threat, so while a great horned owl receives only five or six dees, a pygmy owl might elicit twenty.

"Bad," I say. "Bad bad bad bad bad bad bad bad bad bad bad." Twenty times. Forty-two. And the joy, whatever species it is, identifies my distress, slinks over to Liam, puts its head in Liam's lap, flaps its ears slowly, the better to record my betrayal. I feel a kick of self-righteousness. I was right to distrust the joy's spontaneity. I was right to be afraid. I should have been more afraid.

"Do you have a sense of who might have recorded this conversation?" the director of St. Cat asks me on the call that follows. The article is hosted on a Substack maintained by a woman named Jennifer Flitok, but the byline reads: Excited for this guest post by my friend and collaborator hell0kitkat. The user hell0kitkat has posted a link to the article on Reddit. Flitok has posted a link on Twitter, where her handle is @womxnXX. Amalia shares her screen and scrolls briefly through Flitok's Twitter. The usual—pronoun fury and daily reminders to homeschool your kids. She stops at a photo. I've never seen Flitok before, never spoken with her. She isn't the person we're searching for. Amalia can't find a photo of the user hell0kitkat or her real name.

It is clear, of course, to you. Made clear by juxtaposition. This is a central feature of magic tricks. The magician shows the audience a coin on the table, lifts it in one hand, brings their hands together and opens their palms—the coin is gone. It has been swept into a pocket on the table. The brain is tricked, unlikely to recognize this cause and effect across time. I have met with dozens of clients since the call with Gabbi. I don't have the benefit of story in which the relevant details are included, and the irrelevant details left off, a ranking I've never gotten the hang of in life. I once noted the missing clasp on a friend's earring, but not that they were seven months pregnant and showing. I shake my head, and Amalia jumps in. "We have records of all the client calls. I'm sure we can track this down."

"Listen, they've gone after UT and Boston Children's. The question I'm going to have to answer for the board isn't why this happened but how we didn't manage to see it coming," the director says. Again, the causal question, the emphasis on prediction.

"All staff have received multiple security trainings,"

Amalia says. "We've trained them on what to look for, scripts and mannerisms that could indicate a bad actor." Laughter nearly overcomes me at the phrase. I choke it down.

"Were there gaps in the training you received that you feel would have helped you prevent this?" the director asks me.

"Ro excelled in the security trainings," Amalia says for me. "They're more observant in this sense than I am. They were the one who caught the phishing email in the winter."

"I'm just trying to ensure this doesn't happen again," the director says.

"And I'm just hoping we can assure Ro the organization is behind them, that they have our full support, that we aren't holding them solely responsible for what happened."

It hasn't occurred to me that I am in trouble, but it makes sense. There are consequences ahead for the organization. Backlash, government scrutiny. "I'm sorry," I say immediately, the script occurring easily though additional words refuse me.

"I just wonder whether this role aligns with your particular strengths and weaknesses," the director says. Both the director and Amalia are silent then, long enough that I feel the conversational pressure of the silence through the screen. One theory suggests conversational timing tasks are managed in the brain by individual neurons, which keep time by increasing their rate of firing. The brain makes a decision—to speak, to scream—when the firing rate hits a certain threshold. There, in front of the director, every neuronal clock in my brain fires faster and faster, insisting with increasing shrillness that it's time to say something, excruciatingly past time, but no words come. The director speaks again, laying out a series of next steps—a public statement from St. Cat and the immediate cessation of navigation services pending further guidance from the executive board. Amalia asks to stay on with me, and the director signs off.

"Sorry," Amalia says. "They're in a tizzy. Apparently they weren't aware we were offering guidance about minors." Amalia makes quotes when she says *aware*, which I'm uncertain how to interpret. I say, "Tizzy," quietly. It's a good word—the sharp beginning and the buzz at the end, a downhill word. I understand the director's concerns. Florida doesn't have an aiding-and-abetting clause, but one of St. Cat's programs has a federal grant. They can't afford to look like they're breaking the law. "We're going to have to pause the patient navigation piece for a while. The lawyers are looking into when or even whether we can start it up again. They wanted to cut your contract, but I told them it was my decision." "It's okay," I say, and Amalia makes a face that lets me know this is a strange response. "This isn't your fault," she says, and the fault doubles down. "I'm not sure," I say.

"I'm not saying this as a friend, okay? If I thought it was in St. Cat's best interest to end your contract, that's what I'd do." This phrase, best interest, pings something, a near memory, half present then gone. "I've asked the director about security protocols for the next twenty-four hours. We're monitoring 4chan and Twitter and Reddit. If you're worried about threats to physical safety, I can get you a hotel for a few nights."

"I'm not," I say. "Worried."

"They have your email?" The bad actors. I nod. "Whatever comes in over the next few days, don't delete it." Amalia looks at me. "Are you as calm as you seem to be?"

"That's interesting," I say, falling back on the only script that occurs to me. "That I seem calm. The navigation—I may not be able. To continue." I watch Amalia's face. She has a careful face, always, and I'm not good at expressions, tend to read into them my own fears—boredom, anger—but I think I see something like disappointment or maybe even resentment, betrayal, which might be at my leaving or at my mistake, which has risked all of us and the work that motivates us, or usually does, though now I only feel distant from it.

"Don't decide now," she says. "Everything's still raw. Send your schedule for consultations to Eva before you sign off, so she can send through the cancellations. Talk to Liam and let me know about a hotel."

I talk to Liam. The idea of leaving our cabin for a cheap hotel, spending the night in a box on top of other boxes, without a stove on which to make black beans, without a fridge to store yogurt—it sickens me. Liam doesn't want to leave either. "These people are usually more bluster than anything else," Liam says. Liam looks across the room at the joy. "The joy doesn't want to leave," they say, and this settles it.

The emails begin that afternoon.

> **Subject: Prosecute!**
> **You're a pervert who preys on little kids you should be arrested and prosecuted to the highest extant of the law.**

Subject: No subject
I've known what you're trying to do since the beginning—acceptance, marriage, and now this. One day soon, you'll see, folks like you will all be in prison or send to the camps.

Subject: Homo
Go F¥CK yourself!

Subject: SICKO
Sad for you that you, that, was molested as a child and now you are so fucked up but you don't get to fuck others

Some of the emails are translated by Google. Go find Dick desserts, one of these says, which confuses me until I find another translation—Go fuck yourself.

St. Cat receives similar messages semiregularly, has restricted the use of certain words on our social media accounts to dampen the flow. These emails don't bother me, it's the other emails that bother me. The other emails can be divided into two categories.

The first are emails with subject lines like Missed appt. and Need to reschedule appointment and Hello, why did you cancel appt??! These emails come from addresses I know. They are politely confused. They are frustrated. I open them by habit and begin to reply—I'm so sorry that or I understand that or As soon as we—but these replies quickly fizzle. Eva is replying for me. I don't need to reply, but I wish I had a reply to send. I think about Quentin, my frustration with the clinic that dropped him so cavalierly. Now

I am the one acting cavalier, though it isn't cavalierness that causes me not to reply but a lack of adequate responses. Eva is sending a boilerplate email, which she modifies to include local resources. This is helpful and aligned with organizational principles, but it feels violent as a response to the desperate emails. Please, I swear I'm trans, one says. Take an MRI of my body you'll see me light up rainbow. Another is despondent—These resources aren't helpful, you can't help me, no one can help me. Another is terrified—You can't tell these groups you sent I'm trans, you haven't told them right, I reached out to you it was confidential. Over several, the specter of suicide hangs. I don't see her getting through another school year without this, one reads. Please let us know what appointments are available, we're very flexible.

The one that haunts me most comes from a twenty-five-year-old client who got her bottom surgery covered through another nonprofit and was promised logistical and travel support from us. She only needs a few pieces of information—Swaati's name and phone number, contact information for the volunteer pilot who will provide transportation, and a couple cab vouchers. The appointment is made and paid for. It took her five years to get it, now she's two months away, and Eva's cancellation email elicits first polite, then increasingly desperate replies. Without the transportation and lodging support, she can't afford to do it. It's a long time to stay in New York City. She doesn't know what to do. I text Amalia to ask if we can give her the information, if we can make an exception given she's an adult, but we can't, Amalia replies, too many eyes, the board would throw a fit.

Then there's the second category, the comments less easy to write off as pure vitriol—

> **Subject: No subject**
> **YOU are a part of the PROBLEM! I know God, and She does not make mistakes, and no child is born in the wrong body.**

> **Subject: Protecting Our Kids**
> **Who is sending these messages to our kids, teaching our kids to hate themselves, signing our kids up for these surgeries without us parents even knowing—what is your LEGAL name? where do you live?**

Liam reads these emails over my shoulder. "Let me set up a filter. Stop opening them." But I want to read them. It's holding something at bay.

> **Subject: educate yourself**
> **your an uneducated idiot who should spend some time reading the facts about these drusg. i think you don't know what you're doing, but that's not an excuse to be hurting our babies.**

What I couldn't say to Amalia, I say to Liam: "Do you think it's true?"

A sudden stillness in their body. I have surprised them. "Is what true?" Liam has brought water in one of our good glasses, a trick of theirs. The glass is wide-mouthed, fragile. To drink without spilling, without risking the glass, I have to still the tremors of my body.

"The article. What it says."

"Do I think you're actually a eugenicist working toward your vision of a white supremacist state? I guess it hadn't occurred to me." They watch me, ready maybe to laugh. Something shifts in their face, a slight tightening of their forehead, which could signify confusion or disappointment or surprise. "You tell me? If I'm living with a neo-Nazi, I feel like I should know."

"You wouldn't want to be with me. You wouldn't love me anymore."

Two blinks from Liam. "Yeah, if you're working toward the construction of a white supremacist state, I guess I wouldn't love you anymore." They speak slowly, with a hint of humor in their voice, and I am as surprised as they are by my response, which is to shout, "Butcher, butcher, butcher!" Liam flinches. "Okay, no," Liam says. "No, obviously not. If you're really asking this, then the answer is no." I swing both hands up to my temples and press as hard as I can, marveling at how the body withstands the body, how my own hands can't crush my own skull. "I need you to have perspective," Liam says, has said, says again and again. "I know you feel bad now, but you will not feel bad forever." But I have lost the power of time travel. The time through which another's brain might move easily is thick. There is no escaping the sharpness of the present.

"I've made all the wrong choices," I say to Liam. "Work. Quentin. I hate this life. I hate our life." Liam doesn't respond, doesn't appear affected by the words. They have become accustomed, maybe, to my cruelty in these moments—a cruelty that has myself as the target but is unconcerned about collateral damage. "I've made all the wrong choices. I can't do this. I can't live like this. I can't live like this. I can't live like—"

"You're just trying to wreck everything," Liam says. Wreck, a verb that requires time, forward movement. To wreck something would be a victory.

"I can't live like this."

"This never lasts," Liam says, again offering me the comfort of time, that age-old cure that is always offered to mourners and scorned lovers and sufferers of every type of malady. It's miraculous that Liam should see whole days ahead of us while I perceive only a single, dilating moment of increasing discomfort, and if time is a spatial construction, pinned to a single location, then might one escape the now, the unbearable present, if one runs far enough? It is an instinct along this axis that propels me up and through the door.

There should be a word for this sudden inability to remain indoors. My leaving is less desire than physical need, like drawing a breath after a long exhalation, like urinating, an instinct one can suppress for a time but not indefinitely. But there is also an element of spitefulness. I know this as Liam behind me shouts, "Where the fuck are you going? At least put on your shoes."

Then I am in a field of stubbly grass and fire ants. I have not put on my shoes. The bottoms of my feet have the tingly feeling they get from walking across asphalt in summer. My legs are covered with seeds and insects. Out here, in the right ecosystem, my periods of agitation are okay. It is only in cities and houses that one must, at the last second, choose not the five-hundred-dollar cell phone to hurl across the room but the cheaper remote for the standing fan, and it heightens my despair to think one must spend the worst moments of one's life making choices of practicality and thrift, but the feel of the grass helps, and I manage to think: I am outside time. I've left it behind.

According to various experiments, though who can say what there is to learn from experiments, not all animals, not even all apes, use their minds as time machines. They don't worry about bills due in three months. They don't consider where they will be sleeping in three days—in their cabin or at a hotel, in partnership or alone. Chimpanzees might. Ravens might. Squirrels likely don't. Lizards likely don't. Which means at some point, in the history of evolution, some creature thinks tomorrow for the first time. And perhaps digs their burrow a little deeper, puts some food away. Maybe that creature never thinks past tomorrow, never imagines the winter that follows the summer. It must be a life-carrying creature who first considers those longer time frames, comes to realize that the bulge of their abdomen after some period gives way to the mewling babe or the egg. And what a trick it is, this ability in the heat of summer to thrust oneself into the icy threat of winter, this ability in the deepest chill of winter to remind oneself that summer comes, and having understood this, others might press upon time's boundaries, might imagine forward, season after season, beyond the limits of pregnancy or hatching, racing into the future, and imagine what they find, imagine what waits for them at the end, a realization that, for a moment, they carry alone. Death. Their family's. Their own. Like the morals of old stories, death as punishment for their audacity. How long do they keep it to themself, this forbidden knowledge? That loneliest creature—do they go to their grave with it?

The first bomb threat is called in to St. Cat that evening—"We're sending some people to take care of you," the caller says. "You shouldn't have castrated kids, you're all gonna die." The next day, everyone works from home. I text Amalia: What can I do? How can I help? Amalia doesn't reply. I send the same text to Eva, who writes back, Fucking police tried to comfort us by saying this response was typical and there was a "better than even" chance it wouldn't escalate to actual violence.

Early explosives are developed in China during the Song Dynasty. The new word used to describe these weapons is 火砲藥, fire bomb medicine. The technology is described at length in the 火龍經, transliterated as the *Huolongjing*, translated as the *Fire Dragon Manual.* One version of this military text, reputedly published in the Ming Dynasty, is said to include a description of an early multistage rocket, the 火龍出水, the fire dragon emerging from water. With a dragon's head carved and fixed to a hollow bamboo pole, the 火龍出水 did not explode but, through a sophisticated mechanism, breathed arrows tipped with fire. The name is part of the threat, an attempt to intimidate opponents.

Animal linguist Toshitaka Suzuki describes the difference between sound and word this way: if you look at a cloud and someone says "dog," you look for, and perhaps see, a dog in the cloud. If you look at a cloud and someone trills, the sound does not change your perception of the cloud. Words change our perceptions. Suzuki has used this definition to suggest animal noises should be studied through the lens of language.

To test whether or not animal sounds qualify as words, Suzuki played the alarm call the Japanese tit uses when snakes are present to a group of tits while dragging a stick through the dirt. When no alarm call is played, the tits ignore the stick. When an alarm call is played, the tits flee or mob the stick, behaving as though the stick is a snake. When the tits hear the word snake, they look at the stick and see a snake.

An envelope addressed to me arrives at St. Cat. The address is handwritten in an uneven scrawl beneath an American flag stamp. There is no return address. My message to Amalia says not to open it, to send it to me. I don't want to be responsible for anyone else getting hurt. Amalia says I'm being ridiculous, she's not going to put something potentially hazardous through the mail a second time. She opens it outside St. Cat near the garbage dumpsters wearing a mask and rubber gloves. Inside are twelve cab vouchers from a months-old order.

I'm texting Eva about the cab vouchers—she'll need to find a use for them if the navigation services aren't starting up again. Eva responds, wait did you quit??!

Me: I messed up.

I'm thinking about both St. Cat and Quentin, the two catastrophes melding in my mind into a single, overwhelming failure.

Eva: you got called names by the school bully, it happens to everyone

Eva: i'm livid, we all are of course

I am not livid.

Eva: but are you really surprised?

I am surprised. Not by Gabbi's actions, the threat to my person, which I have long understood and accepted, but by the real measure of the crux I am in. I believed, a belief that seems delusional to me now, that I could risk myself without risking Liam, without risking Eva and Swaati and Amalia, without risking the joy.

Eva: i get it's scary

Eva: i'm not trying to minimize but don't fucking quit over it

Eva: you're giving them what they want

But it isn't the risk driving me away from St. Cat. It's more complicated. There is my guilt about putting others in danger, about failing Quentin, and there is the question—suddenly and wholly unanswerable—of whether the work I do is good or bad. If I tell Eva this, she, like Liam, would be quick to insist it is good, a rapidity that appears unconsidered and so further undercuts my confidence. She would say, like Liam, "This is just autism. This is something other people's brains do easily. Yours can't do it, so you have to trust people who can. People like me. Or, I don't know, the ACLU?" Autism is supposed to make me better at this—black-and-white thinking, rigid moral beliefs. These are all listed as autistic traits, but nothing ever feels clearly good or bad to me, I'm explaining to Liam. Everything is always gray without exception. "Sounds pretty black-and-white," Liam says. "Puberty blockers have side effects," I whisper, almost unable to speak the words aloud. Liam says, "Of course they do. All medicines do. So what?"

I attempt to retreat onto the boards, reading the speculation about *Mad Eden*'s forthcoming final installment, which should be posted in the next few days, but my refuge is breached by a post that argues the magicians in *Mad Eden* are the autistic ones, the dragnos are ADHD, and the whole text is about the internal war in the mind of AuDHDers. A substantial number of people agree with this, or at least feel their autistic traits are better described by the magicians' rituals and cognitive rigidity than the dragnos' chaos and bending of spacetime. Some are suggesting the author must be AuDHD. I upvote a comment that reads, They're all autistic, everything in *Mad Eden* is autistic, it comes from an article that's literally about autism. Someone asks, So then are we reading a story about auties fighting auties? Another person jumps in to say that the whole point of *Mad Eden* is that it subverts the original article, but then an autie quotes Lorde: The master's tools will never dismantle the master's house. Maybe I'm being extra autistic here, an autie responds, but I never understood that metaphor, the hammer that put nails in a wall can take those nails out again, and an autie responds, I don't think you put nails in a wall to build a house, and another autie responds, I think OP was talking about framing, not drywall, and an autie writes, This is sort of ruining *Mad Eden* for me. If the bad guys are autistic, I'm not sure I want to read, and many auties respond with posts about justice sensitivity and how auties are less likely to be agents of fascism since they aren't inclined to follow hierarchical structures of authority, how we're overrepresented among activists and vegans and trans folks, naming the young climate activist to prove their point, and other auties respond that we're also overrepresented among tech bros and pronatalists and transphobes, naming the electric-car tycoon who's trying to send people to Mars, and someone writes that the electric-car tycoon uses aspie, not autie, and I close the window and sit for a long time with my head in my hands.

At the end of the fourth installment of *Mad Eden*, Nova sees a mouse. The mouse runs in a zigzag pattern across the floor of the laboratory where they're tied up too tightly to stim. Watching the mouse, which is present in *Mad Eden* due to a section in the original article about mouse models of autism, Nova's eyes dart left and right, a visual stim, which the magicians haven't thought to prevent. This allows them to withstand the music, to think a little. They realize how to escape—***When a scale falls, their dragno will catch them.*** **Nova doesn't need to get free, they only need to fall.** I fall. I fall and fall, and Liam tries to catch me.

At night, I'm saying it over and over again: "I can't live like this." Liam says, "This isn't good self-talk." Liam is on their back beside me. We are not sleeping. The gene that regulates sleep-wake cycles in *Drosophila* and possibly in humans—we share the gene with those flies—is called Timeless. When it is disrupted, the flies lose all sense of time. I am Timeless. "I can't live like this." "Stop," Liam says. "I can't live like this." Liam says, louder than me, "Me neither. Have you considered that my life is also a fucking mess right now? I haven't looked at the book in two days." Liam says, after a pause, in a lower voice, "We have a good life."

"I can't live like this." Having lost the magnetic field that directed my life. "I can't live like this." A compass needle, spinning.

"If you keep saying that, I'm going to start believing you. I'm going to make changes. You won't like it, you hate changes."

"I can't live like this." Lost. "I can't live like this." Spinning.

"It's just a hit piece. Think about Quentin." But Quentin is stuck in Missouri, yet another person whose life I've upended. My rules are meant to ensure I am good. Don't eat inside restaurants. Wear masks on public transport. Don't eat meat. Don't eat chocolate. Don't drink coffee. Don't buy tulips. Buy secondhand clothes. Stop for small birds in the street. When someone asks for help, help them. Don't ask for help in return except from Liam. When offered an invitation, accept. Drive as little as possible. Don't drink alcohol. Work to make the world a better place. But I'm no longer sure of that last one. The rules have failed me. I'm no longer able to trust them. "Some of it's true," I'm saying, "about Depo." Liam says, relieved I've offered a novel statement, "Everything has risks. You're not a doctor. It's not your job to explain side effects." "I should have said less," I'm saying, and Liam doesn't respond, which I think proves I'm right, I should have said less, I feel at once regret and something like vindication, and I'm starting to explain about the rules again, their purpose, my inability to take any action now, in the wake of their collapse when, "I don't actually think I care," Liam breaks in, continuing despite my look of confused outrage, "if you're a good person. You do good work, you show up for this partnership, who cares if you're following these rules?"

"I can't live like this," I say, and Liam groans and puts the pillow over their head.

In the morning, a second bomb threat is called in to St. Cat. Everyone works from home. There's an email from a man who wants to fuck me in the ass with the devil's pitchfork and leave me to bleed out on his double bed. There's an email suggesting politely that I burn for eternity in Hell. It is Pope Gregory the Great who, in the sixth century, popularizes the image of dragons as scions of Satan, and their gaping, toothy jaws as the Hellmouth.

In the video, I say, "You're good to go." In life, I've stopped speaking for days.

We hear silence. Our brains process silence as auditory input, using the same neuronal channels we use to process noise. Researchers discover this using illusions. Participants in a study listen to an organ tone and the sound of an engine running simultaneously, then the organ tone stops. This happens four times. The fifth time, the engine sound stops instead. All silences are of the same length, but participants believe the final silence is longest. This misperception is identical to one way our brains misperceive sound. Silence might exert pressure like that of a continuous tone. It is something of this nature, some pressure my silence creates in Liam, which causes them one day to say, "Don't you have work?"

The signs come easily to my fingers: *Now, work none.*

"So you'll go back Monday?"

Don't know.

"What does that mean?"

Don't know. Don't know. I shake my head, moving my hands quickly, slicing the air beside my ears, refusing to look at Liam.

Liam stares at me—a long, hard stare. "What does that mean?"

I'm still, watching the understanding come.

"You realize we have bills. You realize we have health insurance payments and hospital payments and we can't make those on the pittance I'm going to get for this translation if I ever actually finish it."

I'm nodding.

"So you just quit without telling me?" I feel again the desire to flee. Liam notices, says, "I need us to finish this conversation. I need to know if there's no more money coming in after this month's paycheck."

Noise is dependent on fluid—water or air—and my speech center is a dried-up sea. My right forefinger is knocking against the left one, a loose downstroke. *Can't. Can't can't can't can't*, faster and faster.

"Okay," Liam says. "Okay. Okay."

I work less, less stress have. You want that.

"But we can't afford this, Ro. We can't afford this." Liam runs their hands through their hair, leaving it standing crazily on end. "Maybe we should take St. Cat up on the hotel. I can go. You can stay."

This is a surprise. I hate surprises. *Why?* I'm signing, attempting with my expression to convey my total bewilderment.

"I need to figure this out. I have to work. I can't work here, I can't think."

No, I'm signing quickly. *No. No. No.* It is infuriatingly like Liam to suggest, in this moment of crisis, the single action that would make it worse, would rend the only stability we have. *You leave me?* My eyebrows are as far up as they go. *Now? You leave me alone?*

"Okay, then you can go, I'll stay. I don't care about whatever's happening online, I care about the two of us being good to each other."

My fingers close with the quickness and force of an alligator's jaw. *No, no, no.*

"Then what's your idea?" Liam says.

You want what? I sign.

"To talk about this. To have some say in our life. To communicate, like adults, like normal adults who can have a normal conversation about all of this and make reasonable decisions."

There it is, what Liam needs, that familiar debt of spoken language. Bringing in breath is the first step, inviting it into my chest then squeezing it out just right—the right pressure, the right muscular vibrations of my vocal cords. I am standing on a high-diving board, looking down at the water that, if I hit it wrong, is hard as concrete. I expect pain—"Can't, I can't." What I don't expect is the shattering, the total disruption.

"You can't what?" Liam says, and this time I have a clear and straightforward answer. My open right hand taps my chin. *Speak*.

"I don't need you to speak," Liam says, surprised. "I don't care if you speak, I just need you to communicate with me. We can sign. We can text. You thought this was about wanting you to speak?"

I'm nodding, carefully, and Liam drops their head into their hands, groans. The groan is not for me, it is for some other, larger thing, which Liam targets as they say, "I never cared about that. English, I never cared about that. You know that, I thought you knew," and as they say, "Is it impossible for us to ever understand each other?"

Here is one thing about mutualism: it doesn't require understanding. I don't understand the bacteria in my intestinal lining, though we are in permanent cohabitation. I eat yogurt and mochi to soothe them, avoid meat and fish to prevent their distress, which is painful to me, but still I don't understand them. I don't know why they prefer green-tea to ube mochi, why they produce gases so rapidly after a meal of lightly fried squash blossoms. This is a hopeful thing to me—that such an intimacy, one of the greatest intimacies, a permanent intimacy, which is surely adjacent to love, doesn't require understanding.

But we do understand each other, Liam and I. At least, a moment later, as I'm signing, *Run*, Liam opens the door for me.

When I return home, Liam says, "You have a client." A skitter of panic. Where is my phone? Did I miss a text reminder? Then it returns to me—the article, the emails, the last few days. *Work none*, I'm signing. *Nice trick.* "You start with name and date of birth, right?" Liam rattles off their own information, then says, "I need your help." This is still some trick, but with Liam such things are usually in my best interest, so I'm sitting in the chair I use for work meetings, eating one blue candy. *Help how?* "I need resources to support my partner. They're having a hard time, and I'm out of my depth." They've chosen our roles well. I don't argue with clients, so I accept their summary. The next step is to ask for clarification—what sort of hard time?—but I'm unsure which sign to use for *time*. The most common is a tap on the left wrist, often believed to mimic tapping a wristwatch, though the sign actually comes from the French sign *heure*, used before wristwatches were invented. In a compilation of French signs circa 1785, the description for this sign says to show the hammer which hits the bell, an iconic sign tied not to the wristwatch but to the clock tower. *From time to time* is signed differently, by bouncing a bent right hand out along the axis of time, away from the speaker's body. *Time period* is different still—the right hand makes a T handshape and circles the left palm. After a few moments,

I decide to show the hammer which hits the bell as I sign, *Hard time?* My eyebrows are lowered to signal I'm looking for more information than just a yes or no. Liam opens their hands. "I want to comfort them, but I don't know what they need. Nothing I say helps, I can't touch them, and I'm afraid if I look away from them even for a second something bad will happen." My hands are quiet, stumped by this admission and the hollow it opens in me. "Isn't there anything they can do?" Liam says. "Anyone they can talk to?" Liam and I have discussed the sorry state of mental health care in this country, how the first time I call the suicide prevention lifeline the counselor, in response to my hesitant admission of suicidal ideation, suggests I adopt a dog. This is before 988, before the lifeline is handsomely funded and presidents laud it in speeches. The counselor suggests I adopt not just any dog, but a dachshund. They have a dachshund named Tony, who's really helped them, and dachshunds are difficult to train, so they're common in shelters. It wouldn't be difficult to find one. When the counselor pauses I say I have to go, and they ask if I have someone else there to talk to, and when I say I don't they suggest I stay on the phone and they continue on about Tony's love of pickles and Tony's stuffed doughnut, and my panic at the possibility of killing myself is quickly subsumed by a greater panic—being stuck on the phone. Tony loves the beach but hates the bathtub. I would do well with a dog like Tony, they aren't too much responsibility. Never mind that I'm struggling to feed myself on the meager income from a summer internship. Never mind that the apartment I'm living in doesn't take pets. Never mind that my roommate is allergic. After six minutes of this, I start to laugh, a laugh of bitter irony and despair—if these are the words meant to keep me from the void, I'm surely lost—but laughter is laughter, it eases something, and as I'm remembering this, I'm also opening my computer, finding the sheets of resources I use with clients—there's the Trans Lifeline, and a resource offering free telehealth therapy to the first one hundred trans adults who apply. There's a sheet of basic distress tolerance strategies—rubber band, ice cube, cold shower. There's a link to a safety plan, which I send to Liam. There's a question I sign about support—*Family? Friends?*—and when Liam mentions Eva, I suggest their partner reach out. And there's the final disclaimer, which I manage in halting sign, explaining that if they are in immediate danger they should call 911 or go to a hospital.

Liam doesn't insist, in the days that follow, that I call any hotlines, hold any ice cubes, snap any rubber bands, fill out the safety plan. The only action Liam makes based on my advice is to drop my phone into my lap one morning on their way into town. They've texted Eva—I'm having a hard time, the text reads. I'm panicked by this conversation suddenly thrust upon me, shaking my phone at Liam, signing *privacy*, *consent*, *privacy*, *consent*, eyebrows down to emphasize my sense of betrayal. They shrug. "I can't be the only person in your life right now."

Eva responds, what's up? I'm fully stymied by this question. Eva knows what's up—the dissolution of the program, the bomb threats, the dropped clients, the hateful emails.

Me: Nothing much, I just don't know what to do with myself.

The wrong choice, as Eva sends immediately: come back to work!

Me: I don't think I can.

Eva: i never really thought of you as an ally

Eva: you know?

I know. St. Cat uses an accomplice framework. It's not enough to be an ally, to buy pins and wave flags. You have to be an accomplice, a word with criminal undertones, which suggests putting everything on the line. The word lingers like an accusation, demands a response, some action, but I am still without rules, compass broken, timeless.

Heat washes over me then, as if the air-conditioning has gone out, but it's the joy, standing beside me. Liam believes the joy is a compass, guiding us toward the life we want, and in all my time with the joy, there's one thing I've clearly imagined the joy wanting—the homemade testosterone gel that frightens Liam. But didn't Liam also say that fear was opposite joy, that joy couldn't exist alongside it? Isn't this the theory behind their weird, meaty dinners and changed routines? If they are allowed to challenge my fears, can't I also challenge theirs?

Quickly, before Liam returns and before I lose my nerve, I open an incognito window on my computer's browser and purchase testosterone powder from the only supplier that doesn't require me to pay with crypto. I purchase twelve applicator tubes from a bath and body store. I ship everything to the cabin. I use my personal credit card, so Liam won't see the charge. The joy yawns and curls up on the floor a few yards away, but I feel joy in my body, or at least I feel something—the immense relief of taking action, breaking back into the flow of time.

Late that evening, there's a knock on our door—"Pizza!" someone calls. We haven't ordered pizza, and we are two miles down a dirt road, out of the way of mistaken addresses, so we go still and quiet on our bed. The lamp on the bedside table is on, the only light in the house, an attempt to conserve electricity that also advertises our precise location to anyone outside. The person with the pizza is walking back and forth along the wall of our house, calling, "Pizza," at intervals, "Hello?" at intervals. We are far from our neighbors, no one will hear us if something happens. "Pizza," they call. "Pizza!" I close my eyes and imagine that we are on the islands of proficiency, a thousand meters off the ground, and as if my imagining has some power, a few minutes later the delivery person gives up. I hear the clunky opening of a car door, then the relieving slam, and Liam breathes slowly out, and I breathe slowly out, and in the morning Amalia says they've had their security consultant scour the internet for my address, and she's come up with nothing, so probably this is someone close to the bad actor. Amalia asks me again if I have any sense of who the bad actor might be, information that would help their consultant keep me safe. Amalia says, at the end of the call, "If they can send pizza, they can send other things." "We might have to leave," Liam says, but it is difficult then, in the sun-drenched midday, to remember the terror of the night, and we decide to give it a few more days. If our address starts circulating on the forums, if there's another pizza, we'll go, Liam insists, and I agree, glad they haven't decided to leave yet—my testosterone still hasn't come. It arrives some days later, in the midafternoon. I bring the package inside before Liam can see.

Autism as a disorder of predictien

5. CONCLUSION.

Time to lam it, Cardinaux says as the dragno in the magicians' libby unfolds, freed from years of preservation. Magicians approach from all directions. *Jump on.*

But Nova turns away from Cardinaux. "I can't go back. I've failed the dragnos."

What do you mean? You've saved not one but two dragnos. This is a great success.

Nova hides their face in Cardinaux's frith. "I gave the magicians the information," they say. "They know where to find the islands of proficiency."

Cardinaux turns their red eagle eyes on Nova. *The whereas or the wherein?*

"Just the where."

Ah! And you think they'll find us with only that? With the map but not the key? Jump on, Nova. Stop thinking you cause the world.

The magicians are closing in. Three of them come into the libby. Nova recognizes them from years of playground torture. One is an especially good marksman.

"What is that?" one says. "Next to the dragno."

"It's the dragno's pet."

"Is it Nova?"

"What's on your head, Nova?"

Don't listen, Cardinaux says, moving to avoid an arrow through the eye. *You look great with a frith. Avoid anticipation, and we will survive this. Jump on.*

But Nova is listening.

When I get a notification that the conclusion of *Mad Eden* has posted to the boards, I'm online, reading the Substack article about me for the dozenth time. I open *Mad Eden* but I can't focus, can't lose myself as I usually do in that world. I return to the Substack article and play the second video. The audio is so familiar I find myself listening for each edit. It is difficult work, creating the video out of the recording of the call. They can only use words I've said, though they stretch them, impressively, as far as they can. These distortions are increasingly audible to me. When I say, "If they have——start-ed puberty," there's an obvious glitch between *they have* and *started*, marking that edit, but also a less obvious glitch before the *-ed* ending, as though the ending was appended later. My face is expressionless: Notice the butcher's pet feels nothing, has no emotion as she describes castrating children. I say, "Whatever your child needs—we can offer," and here, too, the edits are noticeable, separating the sentence into two phrases, the audio jumping a little between "needs" and "we." I work backward from these phrases, trying to remember the conversation. "What we can offer" is a script I deploy in most calls. "Child needs" is also a common phrase, a careful gender-neutral response to parental misgendering. I listen again and notice the stress is wrong on the word "whatever." There's the slightest hitch between the first and second syllables, as though the compound word was created from two words—"what" and "ever." I listen again and realize this isn't exactly right. I'm not saying "ever," but "every." The last syllable has been chopped off, giving the word a strange quickness, a lilt.

It's difficult to catch these changes. My brain, like any viewer's brain, is helping the editor, wants to imagine the words proceeding fluidly from my mouth. Our brains always want to assume that the most proximate possible cause is the correct one. It's the assumption so often exploited by magicians—

I toggle to the other tab, stare at the cut-and-spliced fantasy of *Mad Eden*. I return to the article. I toggle back and forth. In *Mad Eden*, a phrase or a single word is cut from the original paper and lifted from context, just as bits of footage are cut from the recording they took of me. In both cases, the goal is a complete inversion of the source material, not finding a new meaning within it but creating, through brute force, an opposite, manipulated meaning. It is clear to me, then: the artistic signature is the same.

I say it so loud Liam startles hard at their desk, ink blotched across their notebook. They aren't upset. They are happy at this spontaneous display of speech, but my exclamation is just a name. "Hello," I say. "Kitkat, Hello, Kitkat."

"Hello?" Liam prompts, and I say, easily, "Kitkat," but I can't say the rest. I sign it instead—*M-A-D E-D-E-N*, I sign. *They wrote.* I have to sign it three times for Liam to understand. We're both poor at fingerspelling. *The article*, I sign, *they wrote. Same person made both.*

When Liam understands, they are skeptical. "That's a pretty big leap."

But the anonymity makes sense now, too. It's a puzzle the auties discuss endlessly on the boards. *Mad Eden* isn't universally approved of, but it has a significant following, plenty of people are interested in the author. Why use a throwaway handle without any other posts? Why not show yourself, receive the acclaim, engage with the detractors? But if your other handle is creating and posting TERF propaganda—it makes sense to hide. It all makes sense. I feel a simmering relief. The playing field has become more even. I again pull up the last installment of *Mad Eden*, read the beginning with a new and sober purpose, comparing. It's so clear. It's the only thing, recently, that has offered this golden glow of insight and agency. I sign it again: *Same person made both.*

"Slow down," Liam says. "Let's think this through," and so together we return to the videos. With every second, I'm more convinced. Even the style is similar between the videos and *Mad Eden*, the way they pull a noun clause from one source and a verb clause from another. The sentence "Whatever your child needs we can offer"—two phrases mashed together and a compound word created from two separate words—matches up with the sentence **One is an especially good marksman.** "What" and "every" become "whatever," *markers* and *many* become **marksman.**

I trace the borrowed phrases of *Mad Eden* back to the source text, and more and more of the conversation returns to me. I can almost hear their voice. I understand how they ask questions until I say a word they need—"puberty"—which they then use again and again, just as they steal the word **hunt** from *Hunt LT* in the notes of *Autism as a Disorder of Prediction* and use it again and again to describe the relationship between dragnos and magicians. I try tracing the title, *Mad Eden*, back to the original title, but I can't. It doesn't work. There's no *e* between the *d* and *n* in prediction. The second *e* in *Eden* is an edited *o*. This is not entirely new. *Diagnosis* to **dragnos**, *empirical* to **empire**—*Mad Eden* has changed letters before, but suddenly it feels unfair to me, makes clear to me the total disregard for original meaning that characterizes *Mad Eden*. I pause. I turn to Liam and slide my bent hand in front of my chin to sign *lie*.

"What's a lie?"

I point to the screen where *Mad Eden* and the Substack article sit side by side. *Lie*, I sign again. Then I sign *lie* and *person* for *liar*.

"Yes," Liam says with a force and volume that surprises me. "It's a lie, they're liars. It's a hit piece, that's what I've been telling you." I'm not talking about the Substack post. I'm talking about *Mad Eden*, the lengths to which the creator of *Mad Eden* will go to force the meaning they desire. They could make it say almost anything. But Liam is happy, relieved. They are looking at me with a new willingness, a new openness, so I don't point out our misunderstanding. "I'm glad you're finally realizing," Liam says. I nod, and Liam agrees to help me search for hell0kitkat on Reddit.

We find the question about being autigender.

That, I sign. *That.*

Liam shakes their head. "This doesn't prove they created *Mad Eden*."

I point toward my screen to indicate hell0kitkat, then fingerspell autistic. *They're autistic.*

"So? There are lots of autistic people on Reddit." Liam scrolls through the comments, reads the one from Jennifer Flitok. When we find the post about the obsessive friendship, Liam suggests Flitok could be the subject of it. "This just proves they're obsessed with Jennifer Flitok," Liam says. "I almost feel sorry for them, it's like she's the only person in their life." I think about Liam saying to me, just a few days before, "I can't be the only person in your life."

M-A-D E-D-E-N, I sign. *They wrote.* Liam says, "This is what your brain does. It finds patterns. They're not always true."

We search every combination of words I can think of on every possible platform to find new posts by hell0kitkat. It's useful to have Liam's help, as they are often better at getting search engines to divulge their secrets. We find a handful of additional posts—hell0kitkat has sensory sensitivities, hell0kitkat has meat dreads. Stuck in the boondocks, hell0kitkat writes, and I feel a blossoming likeness—*They live where?* I sign, excited. *South. South!* Suddenly I can hear hell0kitkat's voice, the hard *æ* sound I associate with a specific type of white Southerner. I can nearly see their face.

"None of this has anything to do with *Mad Eden*," Liam says.

But they're wrong. *Mad Eden*'s author is Southern. This has always been one of my hypotheses. I sign this and then sign my other hypotheses quickly—the creator of *Mad Eden* is genderqueer, late-diagnosed, has been hospitalized, is in a close partnership with another neurodivergent person.

"But hell0kitkat doesn't have a partner and isn't diagnosed," Liam says, gesturing at the screen.

Okay, I make some mistakes, I sign, feeling an upwelling of frustration.

"That list of identities," Liam says very gently, "you're just describing yourself."

And other people, I sign, the upwelling transforming from frustration into something nearer tears. I'm so close, so close to knowing who wrote *Mad Eden*, to knowing I've talked to them.

"But not the person who wrote these posts. They're alone except for Flitok."

I spin away from Liam, wanting privacy, frustrated with them for insisting on fraying the pattern that has finally come together, with a leap of intuition, the product of that pleasing sense of order and rightness offered by two mochi every evening, by the deliberate routines that undergird my life.

I look back at the latest installment of *Mad Eden*, seeking additional evidence, and my eyes catch on two lines:

> **"What is that?" one says. "Next to the dragno."**
> **"It's the dragno's pet."**

And in the Substack article, one tab over, to describe my flat affect: Notice the butcher's pet feels nothing, has no emotion as she describes castrating children. The butcher's pet. **The dragno's pet.** I don't bother offering this last bit of proof to Liam, who would only say something about common cultural phrases. All of it together is proof enough for me. I'm sure. Not sure in the way of discovery, a certainty based in data, but sure in the way of determination, a certainty based in need.

I read again through the posts, and an image of hell0kitkat's life comes together. We live in the same state. We have the same dislike of dresses. They want to be a lobster, which I can understand.

"It sounds like they're in love with Flitok," Liam says. I can't distill that feeling from hell0kitkat's posts, but I trust Liam's interpretation. It helps, thinking about hell0-kitkat as a person in love, a vulnerable person. It catalyzes the thought, which becomes an idea, which becomes a plan, which becomes, within seconds, a necessity—a way to protect us, a protection that doesn't require leaving the cabin.

When Liam heads for the kitchen, I message hell0kitkat.

The first message is just one word: Yours? Then I send screenshots of each of the installments of *Mad Eden*. Then the last, carefully worded message: Share any more of my personal information, and who you are goes public.

I feel, after, the consuming elation I usually feel when I'm alone. I've forgotten Liam, and I've forgotten the joy until it trills behind me. Then I realize, with a jolt, the potential cost of my action. The joy, which takes the dragnos' form—can it survive though I've turned my back on their world? I spin in my chair. "What?" Liam says from the kitchen.

Joy, I sign, eyebrows lowered to make clear that it's a question, a worry and concern.

The joy is still there. Startling and magnificent. It no longer looks like a dragno, that many-eared, tame creature. It is sharper, all talons and teeth, all angles. Neither of us will ever ride it. Hell0kitkat is not its creator. "The joy is ours. We made it," Liam says all those weeks ago, and of course they're right. Alligator afterlives, scalding touch, Liam's sternum—dragons have always been my joy, my original spin.

I never finish the last installment of *Mad Eden*. I know from the boards that Nova escapes and frees the preserved dragno, making it impossible for the magicians to continue their dragno-warding rituals or find the islands of proficiency, saving the day. A few auties quote Nova's final speech on the boards—**I am Nova, mind-reader, expert stimmer, I have perfect pitch, I elapse time and elaborate space, I am gifted with a prodigious memory for faces, and I will hunt each one of you to the end of my days.** I should perhaps share their glee at Nova's triumph, but I can't relate, have never felt such vindictiveness. All I think, reading the quote, is that perhaps this is the sort of revenge hell0kitkat was seeking when she started hunting me.

Maybe I'm wrong about the authorship of *Mad Eden*. I never find any actual evidence that hell0kitkat is behind the series. Three accounts on r/Auties eventually take credit for it. The favored one belongs to a nonspeaking autie out of Carbondale, Illinois, whose other artwork is similar to *Mad Eden*, full of layering and erasures. I don't follow the debate. For months, I don't log on to the boards. When I finally do, hell0kitkat has posted a new question. It asks if you can be trans but keep it secret all your life, if transness can be like a stone in the heart. When I read this I think of Victoria Chang, the bird and the stone, and feel momentarily as though hell0kitkat has pierced our private language. My address never appears on the internet. I don't know if my message has anything to do with that. In this, as in every moment of my life, the possible causes proliferate, making it impossible to identify the primary one, to tell the linear story, A to B to C.

When Liam returns from the kitchen, I sign, *Finished.* Meaning hell0kitkat. Meaning our period of fear.

"I know you think hell0kitkat is like you," Liam says, sitting down across from me in the butterfly chair, "but they aren't. They're alone. You're not alone." I can't tell if this statement is meant as comfort or warning. "This is the longest you've ever gone without talking," Liam says. "Ten days." I am surprised by their neat accounting of time. *With you*, I sign, to reassure them. I've gone months, but I haven't told them this, don't speak often or openly about those periods of silence in childhood. They say, "I know I'm not supposed to find it difficult, but I am finding it difficult."

They need comfort—speech or touch, two nearly impossible things. Liam is not a dragno, I am not a scale, but one last time, I think, **A bond across species**, and this thought makes it possible to go to Liam, to fold myself up in their arms. They receive me with stillness, as you might receive a reluctant cat—pleased and apprehensive at once. When I relax against them, they hold me tightly, the way I like to be held. They say, "Mon cheval sauvage," and I sign *wild horse* at the same time, offering a small harmony. How long do we lie there, our noses nearly touching? For hours, it seems to me. For days. At some point I sign *happy*, raising my eyebrows, asking if we are, and Liam says, "If we weren't happy, would our faces be this close together?" and this seems indisputable, and the joy crows, and I realize the researchers studying interspecies alarm calls left their conclusion incomplete. If we are able to distinguish the alarm calls of alligators and chickadees from their joyous calls then distress isn't the only thing that translates across species. So, too, does joy. And I think the joy approves of my silence, and I hope—a small, maybe shameful hope—that the silence doesn't ever end.

Over the next few days every hour that passes without a bomb threat or a SWAT team or a pizza delivery feels like victory. Eva texts me and Swaati with an update: the pause on navigation services has been extended for another month. I respond, Thanks. Swaati responds, Just over here waiting for the green light to ignore the bullshit and get back to work. Each morning, I reread hell0kitkat's posts. Liam says, "I don't understand why you're so interested in someone who's trying to ruin your life." I tell them Amalia asked me to find out who it was, and Liam says, "Like if-you-happen-to-know-let-me-know. Not like this. You're obsessed." Which is true. Each time I read the post about gender, it feels like my fingers brush the handle of a small, unobtrusive bucket in which the memory of our conversation lives. I might have asked the same question myself, before I found Liam and St. Cat, before the word genderqueer came to offer a stable, habitual comfort. Complacency, even, I think as I reread one morning while eating yogurt with our last frozen blueberries. For six years, I've used the same pronouns, the same word. It would have been harder, I think, if I'd waited as hell0kitkat did. And just like that, the handle of the bucket is within reach, and I remember. First, a metaphor—as if womanhood were glue that dried solid. From there I work back to the question she asked me on the call—"Doesn't it matter how long she spends trying to be a certain way?"—and I can see her. She's chewing her hair, a classic stim. The image is startling in its familiarity, like a photo of an old, nearly forgotten friend.

I text Eva. I haven't initiated communication with anyone for a week. But now I've remembered hell0kitkat's face. I've gone back through my emails and found her name—Gabriella Holt. My sleuthing won't be confirmed until the exposé comes out several months later, tracing Gabbi's relationship with Jennifer Flitok through social media posts and direct messages, linking Gabbi to the username hell0kitkat, to the Substack post and related Twitter scandals, negating the anonymity Gabbi had attempted to maintain. Still, I'm certain I'm right.

This is what I text Eva: I've figured it out, who she is.

Eva: you tell A?

Me: Not yet, I just figured it out. I should have known from the beginning.

Eva: they're pros. this is their whole job.

But Gabbi isn't a pro. Her posts make that much clear. She is awkward in my memory. Obvious. I should have known.

Me: It was clear what she was doing.

Eva: then why didn't you end the call?

That is what you're supposed to do. It's in the training guide. 1. Abort the call. 2. Alert security. 3. Alert management and communications. I could have helped St. Cat prepare for the article. I could have given them time to create a measured response, to be ready.

I think it's anxiety that keeps me on the call with Gabbi, a relentless desire to do a good job. I want to answer the questions she asks, which are real, I still think so. Whether there is such a thing as purity within the reasons one might have for gender. Whether one can ever track, completely and with certainty, cause and effect.

Me: I was stupid.

Eva: come on, its not your fault, its hers

But Gabbi, on the call, is also anxious, also trying to do a good job. What separates us? A thousand minor causes and their unpredictable effects, an accumulation so gradual, so inexorable and undeserved that the only word I have for it is luck.

I text Amalia, who thanks me. Nothing else for you to do, she sends. We'll take it from here.

But there is something else for me to do, and Liam has gone to work at a coffee shop, won't be back until midafternoon.

It's like making soap.

Testosterone powder, grapeseed oil, purified water, DermaBase. We don't have a double boiler, but it's easy to approximate one, stacking one pot inside another. I stand at the stove, stirring occasionally, watching the DermaBase soften. It doesn't look like much. It doesn't smell like much.

I add the water last, and it refuses, for a time, to mix with the rest. The recipe makes it seem easy, the water added little by little until you attain the right consistency. The water I add remains on the surface, a layer of water and a layer of gel beneath. I whisk it hard with a fork, which you aren't supposed to do. I rarely cook. I turn up the heat, let it simmer, which you also aren't supposed to do, but this helps, the agitation of the molecules allowing the gel and the water to mix. They need heat, which is to say, time. The recipe isn't for adults. It isn't possible to get the necessary amount of T through the skin of an adult without alcohol and DMSO, as in the commercial gels. This is a recipe designed for teens. I'm making it for Quentin. I pour the solution into the applicators. As the gel hardens, the joy flicks the applicators with a barbed tongue, and I think I was right all along. The joy wanted T.

The next few weeks are quiet. The emails are filtered directly into a folder I don't have to open. The joy no longer cowers when our neighbor comes by with cucumbers. It doesn't whine in warning when we make the decision to spend fifty precious dollars on a milk frother for Eva, who is married on a sweltering day on top of the mountain, as planned—we were so sweaty! sweatiest day of my life, she texts me after. The joy no longer dreads calls or text messages, ignores the frequent dancing of our phones, and so it gives us no warning, no intimation of tragedy, when Liam's phone and mine vibrate in synchrony one evening. We lift our screens to our faces in unison, and our low cries are also in unison. The text is from Quentin's roommate. Honeycub is dead.

Quentin, apparently, is beside himself, has put the body in the freezer and is now refusing to leave his room. The roommate hasn't seen him in more than twelve hours. There is no answer through his door. The roommate is worried. Liam says, "Isn't anyone in my life okay?"

We send one text each, then I send another, then Liam sends another, the two of us talking to each other in the group chat where Quentin should be also. Quentin is not there. We call, the phone ringing and ringing, clicking to voicemail.

The voicemail box hasn't been set up. "A child," Liam says. We call his roommate, who says the door to Quentin's room is locked. Quentin was coming out at intervals—the toaster and the coffee pot disappeared—but he hasn't emerged in maybe a day. Liam calls Quentin's mother, a last resort—Quentin is twelve hours from us and only five from her. "Can you check on him?" Liam asks. "Girl's grown," Quentin's mother says. "She's decided she was grown a few years ago now. If she's got herself into trouble what have I got to do with it?" Liam suggests we call campus police, ask for a wellness check, but I object. I won't do that to Quentin.

Neither of us mentions driving to Missouri. Neither of us says we have to leave right now. Neither of us mentions that there's no one in Missouri to send to check on him. Liam is busy translating. I am busy engaging the world as little as possible. In a causal story, this is the nexus. This is the decision that changes everything. If we don't go, we are still living in that cabin with our joy. If we both go, we are perhaps living in Missouri with Quentin, working on a vegetable farm. We could be. That most advanced of mental gymnastics, the conditional tense, the ability to project ourselves beyond small miracles into other worlds. But in the world in which we live, it is hardly a decision. Objects and events conspire around me, narrow my choices into a single choice. There is, first, my worry for Quentin, and my decision to prevent Liam calling the police, which makes Quentin's welfare slightly more my responsibility. There is, second, the testosterone, which has hardened in the applicators. I have been applying it myself each morning as Liam works at their translation. I experience no ill effects. I plan to bring it to Quentin. There is, third, my silence, which in the past has been broken by responsibility. There is, last, the joy. No longer a dragno reluctant to venture away from its paradise, the joy is restless in our small cabin, stalking from window to window, looking longingly at the horizon, ready to accompany me to Missouri.

We don't discuss the trip. Liam cannot go. Their translation is due in two days. They are planning to pull all-nighters, stopping only for bathroom breaks. I can go. When I emerge from our room with a backpack over my shoulder—headphones, cinnamon sticks, toothbrush, change of clothes—Liam only nods. The joy is already in the car, coiled in the back seat. I can't say why it wants to travel to Missouri. It is a dragon with a thousand stories to choose from. It might be vengeful as the dragon in *Beowulf*. It might be greedy like Smaug, seeking some treasure in the plains. It might be cunning and malevolent as Satan or, like Errour, just a woman who dares have appetite. It might be a shape-shifter like the dragons of Earthsea or a time-traveler like the dragons of Pern.

There are a few certainties, a few things all of these dragons have in common: protection, power. This thought sets a hard, bright coin in my chest. It's twelve hours to Quentin's apartment. Highway driving, the easiest kind. I can take it all at once, driving through the night, pausing only to nap at rest stops as needed. Time is of the essence. We are down to the wire. We must beat the clock. I imagine beating the clock with my fists until it shatters. With joy in the back seat, I am more than capable. I coast down the sandy drive, adjusting the rearview mirror. My only regret is leaving

Liam behind, joyless in the cabin. It doesn't occur to me that if I play the events backward in time, I am not taking the joy away from Liam but ferrying it to them.

I don't drive except in emergencies, but it always comes back—the dance of pressure on the pedal, checking the blind spot, the blinker. I can relax into long drives as I can relax into any pattern that is easy to see through to its finish. I don't consider, not in detail, what waits in Missouri. I don't consider my silence, not as an impediment. I believe, and Liam believes, that I am going to speak to Quentin, to help him. So I expect, when Quentin's roommate opens the door at dawn on the following day, to greet him normally and am surprised to find the words don't come. He doesn't seem to require them, and perhaps it is this generosity that allows me to maintain silence as he leads me to Quentin's door. I knock. There is a smell. It emanates from the door, its crevices. It disturbs me—something ill, something rotting—so after a third knock I use my credit card to open the latch. The latch is backward, insecure. It's a college apartment. Privacy is an illusion.

He isn't dead. The smell of rot comes not from the bed, where Quentin is stretched out—sleeping, maybe—but from the rat cage near the door. But he might have tried to die, Quentin. There is vomit on the floor, vomit on his lips. This, at least, is what I fear, the concern, the question he reads on my face as his eyes slide open, as he comes to at my rough shaking of his shoulder.

"Fuck," he says eventually. "Fuck. What are you doing here?"

I expect the words to return then, as they do sometimes in response to a direct question. But nothing comes. I make a sweeping motion with my hand—What's all this? What's happened? What have you done?

"I got drunk, okay. If you were a normal person, you'd recognize the signs. I got drunk, and now I have a fucking massive hangover and a random person waking me up at six in the morning, so I'm not in the best-ever mood."

I have never had more than a sip of champagne, have never experienced a buzz, so this confession alarms me nearly as much as a confession of suicidality. The two seem basically the same. Wasted, a desolate word. Blackout, what I've always sought when I've approached death. I look left and right, searching for the alcohol. Quentin laughs at my surveillance, or perhaps at my ineptitude.

"Yes. Drinking. I'm a college student. That's what I'm supposed to be doing. Leave me alone my god."

There is something Quentin needs. Liam would know what it is. Something that helps with a hangover. I offer my water, but Quentin doesn't want it. I offer my cinnamon sticks, which I keep on my person for the scent, which is capable of overpowering other scents, but Quentin doesn't want them either.

"I saw what they wrote about you," he says. "Did you ever know what you were talking about?" He is angry. I look at Quentin and say nothing. To Quentin my silence is invitation or provocation. I sense the rise, the snap of his fury. It gets him up to a sitting position. "Why did I trust you? Why did I ever trust you?"

And though I offer no rebuttal, though I do not insist to Quentin that no one correctly interpreted the Missouri law, that no one understood the implications of that clause until after the law was in effect, the injustice of his accusation is clarifying, opens a window that nothing else has opened, a window through which I can again understand the work I have done as fundamentally worthwhile. Quentin watches me. He is waiting. My words have not returned, though I sense they would if Quentin demanded them of me. He doesn't. He sighs, collapses back onto his bed.

Food? I sign to him, raising my eyebrows.

"Not hungry."

Water?

"You already asked about water."

Medicine?

"I'm fine."

Quentin curls up with his hands on opposite shoulders, hugging himself, blocking me out, a defensive gesture, but it is a sign, too. *Love.* He signs it again and again. *Love love love*, he signs. He has fallen, accidentally, into language. "I want parents," he says. We aren't, of course. We never have been his parents. I feel the word shatter as he says it, feel how far we are from parents. Alligator parents carry their young on their backs, and how have we carried Quentin? What have we sacrificed? I hear Liam say, "Sometimes I forget he's seventeen." A parent would never forget. We've been playacting, pretending, and maybe it would have worked if it were a little more normative—if we weren't trans, if Quentin weren't trans, if we weren't all queer. Maybe, with a slightly larger helping of heterosexuality, our pretense could have become something real, that's what I think, in Quentin's room, Quentin groaning on the bed, that there is no separating your own failures from the failures of the world, that this is the lesson Gabbi was trying to learn in front of me on that call, that the world can fuck you over in such a gentle, head-spin way that you can't differentiate it from fucking yourself over, or from fucking over someone else, even someone you love.

Sorry, I sign. Fist to my heart. There are other signs—*Sorry for your loss*, I might sign, or, *Sorry we weren't here when you needed us*. But Quentin knows only the most basic ones and is, besides, not looking at me. He is deliberately looking away. He blows air through his lips. He is making do. He wants me to know it. "Okay," he says. "You can figure out what the restrictions are, legally, on where you can bury a rat."

In Missouri, rats are supposed to be disposed of in biohazard bags dropped into a municipal trash receptacle, but pets can be buried fifty feet from any relevant property lines and three hundred feet from any bodies of water. The rat is in a plastic bag at the back of the freezer. I remember, now, this detail, which so alarmed the roommate but seems practical to me. The rat, being frozen, hasn't decayed and doesn't smell. I don't need my cinnamon sticks. We do not use a box. Quentin doesn't want one. We do not say any words, and Quentin seems not to mind. The hole we dig is deep, an attempt to ensure protection from desecration. Quentin wants Honeycub's body eaten only by microorganisms. The burial done, Quentin comes all at once into my arms. I squeeze him, offer what I'd want in his place. He is rigid. I can't tell if the touch is something he wants or something we are both bearing for the other. He says, "It's harder than I thought," and rage blossoms in me, the rage Liam and Eva and Amalia have felt, I feel it then, not toward Quentin, but toward the paltriness, the mundanity of this confession, this possibility of regret, which is supposed to be so terrifying, so monstrous it justifies Gabbi's actions and even Flitok's. Regret, that daily thing, which is common, a part of life, impossible to avoid unless one can predict not only the effects of medications, the complications of a medical procedure, but the entire future. Impossible—this is the word that summons my rage but only for an instant. On its heels comes fear for Quentin, an immediate, adjacent fear, that oldest elemental fear—the fear inherent in loving someone whose happiness I can't guarantee, so that instead of Gabbi I'm thinking about her daughter, and how slender a thing it is, happiness, too slender to support the weight of arguments. How slender a thing, joy, and the joy, which has followed us out to this place between two oak trees to bury a rat, beams, and I hold Quentin even a little tighter.

Afterward, in the colloquial sense, having gone to a nearby grocery store and filled Quentin's fridge, having cleaned the rotten vegetables from the corner of Honeycub's cage and set it on the street for someone to take, having hugged farewell, I am relieved. I start toward my car—if I leave now, I can make it home before midnight—but the joy doesn't follow. The joy pads away from me, away from Quentin's dorm, past a series of frat houses. The joy has already covered some distance. Panicked, I rush to catch up. The joy doesn't speed up as I run behind it, only continues to walk resolutely away from the car. Perhaps it knows something I don't about the drive ahead of us. Perhaps it's tired of me. Perhaps it just wants the chance to stretch its legs. I follow. We pass two students in black leggings, and I am momentarily perplexed by their nonchalance. No one—not the delivery person on their bike or the driver of the big rig waiting to make a left turn or the student locking up the campus bookstore—looks twice at the winged creature prowling the sidewalk, swinging its great, toothy head to track squirrels. The squirrels sense the joy, its murderous potential. They flee before it, making for the highest branches of whichever nearby tree. A man in a suit slaps his arm as the joy passes, the way you'd slap a mosquito, but it's impossible to know if the joy caused this, the joy that veers off the sidewalk occasionally to take long, appreciative sniffs of various early-fall flowers. The joy allows me to walk at its hip. It isn't, as I feared at first, attempting to escape me, but neither am I able to stop its wandering. I can only keep pace, walking just behind, avoiding its tail, which lashes with agitation or excitement each time a squirrel runs by. My phone vibrates: a text from Liam, asking how it went with Quentin. I'm not sure how it went, so I return my phone to my pocket without responding. With the joy beside me on the sunlit sidewalk, I start to think maybe it went okay, maybe I've done all right by Quentin, maybe I am all right, even good. I begin to enjoy it, the ridiculousness of walking my private joy past the library and the campus Lutheran church. The joy picks up the pace, and I jog to keep up, and even this is pleasant, the ease with which my body moves. Then the joy leaps, flapping its wings, and my pleasure evaporates. I cannot follow the joy into the sky. I cannot lose the joy. I break into a run, and the joy, perhaps sensing my sudden fear, pumps harder with its wings, gaining air and banking left across the street, momentarily out of sight. I must take a more difficult path across land. I dodge traffic. The joy reappears above the roof of a student apartment block, then disappears again. I try to save time by shimmying under the fence of a Church of Latter-day Saints, scraping my cheek against asphalt. My shirt catches and tears as I hurl myself away, racing across the churchyard after the joy, which is in sight again, above me, impossibly high. The joy veers left. I run through a park with a small cairn, past an elementary school, across a parking lot, catch a glimpse of the joy circling above a four-story garage, then it's gone again, and I run down a narrow side street to see the joy outside another church, perched in a small maple tree that is unaffected by its heft. The joy trills down at me. It pulses with happiness, its own. I lean against one of the church's four columns. The joy crouches above me, warm and protective. The trees are leafed out still, the sun visible through their shy crowns, and this shyness, the trees preferring not to touch, creates a fractal pattern overhead that repeats with a perfect amount of variation. Beautiful. I allow my legs to bend until I am sitting against the church's column, watching the joy above me. I feel the special glow that comes after movement, when the body catches up with itself. The column is warm, and the sidewalk is warm, and the warmth is welcome, and the contentment fades to a deep, sleepy peace. I am receding from something, like waves as the tide goes out. It's a sensation both involuntary and pleasant, like an effortless shit, a purging. I've helped Quentin. I've caught up to the joy. It's okay to sit, it's okay to rest for a while in the sun after accomplishing something difficult. Or maybe it isn't okay, not to sit the way I am sitting with my cheek scraped and my shirt torn, maybe sitting isn't the word for it precisely, I may be a little more crumpled than sitting implies, the angle of my neck may be slightly wrong, a posture that gives something away, so I shouldn't be surprised when the woman standing over me says, "Are you okay?"

My neck is cramped from staring up at the joy. I've been here long enough for my muscles to stiffen. Am I okay? There is Quentin, his accusations and his sweetness. There is the joy overhead, out of reach but not gone. There is my stillness against the column. I would explain all of this to the woman crouched beside me, but I realize now what I've purged, what I've left on the shore I'm retreating from, a shore so distant now it's barely visible—movement, speech. Neither is possible. Can't or won't?

"Are you all right? Do you need help?" With great effort I shake my head. This doesn't satisfy her. Her two questions are themselves at odds. I manage, with some effort, to put the thumb of my right hand against my chest and tap twice, signing *Fine*. I manage to make an *o* with my hand, a *k* with my hand. Neither of these impress her. She wants words, she wants spoken language. Not just any spoken language, she wants English. "Should I call someone?" she asks. "Do you need help? Are you okay?" The questions like this, compounded, impossible. The joy is disinterested, watching a squirrel some distance away. I try to ignore her, but she persists, asking, "Should I call someone?" She is entitled, now, to my answer, and this fills me with rage. You shouldn't be able to ask if someone is okay unless you speak many languages, enough that they can answer in whatever language they want and you will understand, and the thought fans my adrenaline, which only buries me deeper, so that if it had been possible, when she first approached, to push back toward the shore of human interaction, painful speech, it is impossible now. If you've never experienced this, I'm not sure I can make you understand how stiff a jaw can become, how great and sticky the tongue, so the whole mouth is cemented, a single object as incapable of movement as stone. It would take a hammer to shatter it open.

There are cards for this. On the front they say, My name is _________. I'm autistic. On the back they list an emergency contact—address and telephone. The cards are twenty-five dollars, which six months ago seems outrageous to me. Funds are always tight, but they are tighter then, stretching to accommodate the bill from the hospital and the separate bill from the psychologist, and I fail to foresee this moment, the card's inevitable usefulness, a failure that seems to me now to have its roots in arrogance, a sense that I wasn't so autistic, and my frustration with the woman becomes frustration with myself, and this buries me deeper still.

She says, "My daughter," and stops. I flick my eyes toward her face. There is, perhaps, some promise in this. She is no longer talking about my well-being, about making phone calls. "My daughter was on a sidewalk just like this one, and I keep thinking somebody might have stopped. Somebody might have stopped to ask her, 'You all right?' That might have changed something." She looks past me down the sidewalk for a moment, then she says, "Sometimes I think her death can make me a better person." A retrocausal construction, common in grief. I think of all the invented daughters—the stories told about them, the trouble they've caused. "The sort of person I used to be, I'd seen somebody out on the sidewalk like this, I'd have up and crossed the street, figured you were mixed up in something

I don't want to get mixed up in, but my daughter." Nine months ago, midwinter. They find her on the bench of the bus station. What she has in her bag is laced, the woman says, laced. She is stuck on the word, perhaps she can't help but associate it now with two disparate images—doilies and death. And the realization that comes then comes slowly, a crawl of dread. I didn't give it to Quentin, the applicator filled with T. It's in my backpack, the backpack that's currently crushed beneath me, and I feel, for the first time, real panic.

"You look like her," the woman says. For a moment I imagine this is Quentin's mother, unable to see Quentin as anything but a daughter. I imagine Gabbi telling Jennifer Flitok about her daughter, "She isn't trans." "She was such a happy baby," the woman says. The joy is bouncing a little, testing the branch, not looking at me. The woman shakes her sleeve back on her arm to check a wristwatch. "I do have an appointment I've got to get to, but maybe I get you what you need first."

I'm fine. That's all I need to say. Can't or won't. Can't or won't. Two words would set her walking, and I would be free of her, and you might be waiting, at this point, for me to make my escape, from the Latin *excappare*—to get out of one's cape, a disappearing act, leaving the cape behind, empty, a shed exoskeleton in your pursuer's hand. Perhaps you expect me to escape through the small miracle of speech, spoken language as a bridge to the counterfactual, to that other world where the woman and I exchange niceties and after a few minutes of lively conversation I send her off with gratitude, that other world where I return to Quentin and gift him the T, then the joy and I drive home in the car, which makes it most of the way before my front-right tire blows out, and I veer into the guardrail not fast, not a terrifying accident, I drive away with the spare on, but the front bumper and fender are damaged, which I can't do anything about. I can write that world. Liam and I replace the tire, leave the cabin in the fall, our belongings stacked in the back seat of the car, and the joy coiled around them, the joy that stays with us for several more years before fading during an afternoon rainstorm in some muggy, future July. It would take a large miracle for this world to become that one, a world of future joy, which isn't to say there's no joy ahead in this world, where the woman talks to me for a time, and times, and half a time, tells me about her daughter-in-law and her divorce, then mentions again that she could call for help. Is it likely to come down on St. Cat if I'm charged with possession? If I brought the T across state lines, does that make it a federal crime? Could Amalia get in trouble? Or Swaati? "You're sure complicating things, this day is sure getting complicated," the woman says, and I catapult myself into the future of this world, beyond this sidewalk, the woman, this city, the future where I return without the joy to Liam, who doesn't mention the joy's disappearance, is just glad I've returned, and we spend a week in the cabin, peaceful enough, a peace disrupted by an anonymous commenter posting an image of my face with a bullet wound through the forehead and fifteen bitcoin across my chest and another commenter replies, unironically? for that much, I'll do it, and at Amalia's behest we leave the cabin for a hotel, leave before the boar's head and intestines, which Trevor's aunt finds in the spring, a horror so generic it could be a threat or just the offal of a lazy hunter, and in a hotel comped by St. Cat I stand at the window, on the third floor, staring out at the rain, which is coming down hard, water pigbacked against water, and there is no joy, and we spend a week with Liam's parents, a week of plentiful food and few responsibilities, and there is no joy, and two weeks at a residency in Alabama are joyless, and a month in a friend's empty single-wide are joyless, and three days with Quentin in Illinois, where he's making do with a job at a video game store, his hormones covered by Medicaid, college "not something I'm thinking about right now," are filled with a care and concern that isn't joy, and our life is again a life of constant movement, though now the movement has a different, hunted quality, as my emails remind me daily, the filters siphoning off the worst into a folder I open only when I'm tempted to forget the threat, and then Amalia deletes my email, the entire archive disappears a few days before a records request from a state prosecutor. There isn't much in the way of records, just one list on a secure cloud storage site, and St. Cat, in a move Amalia decries as spineless, sends it immediately. The names on the list are nicknames, invented, but the phone numbers are real, the phone numbers of people Swaati has contacted and might need to contact again. I still think about this list, wonder sometimes who has seen it, how many times it's been copied, whether anyone has called those numbers and if so what they've said, and in the wake of the state investigation St. Cat shuts down the navigation services, no longer willing to take on the legal risk, so I don't know how the woman manages in Massachusetts, if she gets her genioplasty, if the boy with the new sneakers gets the blockers he needs, I don't know what happens to the rest, how many never access the care they need, if any die. To know this someone would have to pay attention, and no one pays attention. St. Cat apologizes formally, and the state drops the investigation, but St. Cat still folds in the winter when its government grants fail to renew. Amalia finds another job in the grants department of a nonprofit focused on abortion access, and Eva spends two years working at a vineyard, saving up for grad school, and Swaati disappears but not in a way that suggests tragedy, when I look them up there's often news about upcoming local art shows, and I spend three months getting interview after interview at public health organizations but never landing a job, I've lost some fundamental normativity, which causes the interviews to end with tepid discomfort, so I work at a local grocery store—all fluorescent lights and migraines—and I work at an environmental magazine where my boss tells me I'm the most productive employee they have and fires me in the next breath, and for four months I don't work, Liam supports us both, giving up translation to write copy for corporate blogs, work that makes them despair, which makes me despair, and we argue, and Eva and I talk regularly on the phone, say that Gabbi ruined our lives, but this isn't true, at least not permanently, it's too weighty a thing to offer Gabbi, the ability to ruin our lives. Eva goes back to grad school for her master's in social work, and I get a job at a small news organization, and though it pays next to nothing I'm still working there today, writing copy for a weekly column, a job that is fully asynchronous, so I rarely interact with anyone, and it isn't joy I feel, writing those articles, which shift over the months from recommendations for queer clubs in Boston to instructions for stockpiling medication to shrill warnings to get documents in order before the new year, but sometimes I do feel a certain satisfaction, and Liam and I find a room we can afford to rent and decide to live there for a year—which is to say, forever—and we hang a rope swing from the ceiling of our bedroom, and the swing helps ease even the worst of my meltdowns, so that one night Liam comes awake to find me swinging hard, kicking off the nearest wall, and says, "You're okay," and goes back to sleep, a new trust between us, which ushers in a long season not of joy but—sweeter still—of contentment, of harmony and peace, which Liam calls our honeymoon period come three years late, and in that time I write this book and dedicate it to my partner, who weathers my silences, for my escape was not through speech.

The woman takes out her phone. "I've got an appointment," she says. "I can get somebody over here who can help you before I go." Cannot or will not. Cannot or will not. Already the future is becoming concrete, taking on qualities commonly associated with the past tense, so that the officer came and greeted me and asked some questions and said, "Now, I know you don't have any drugs in that bag?" and I nodded to affirm that I didn't, and he said, "You do have drugs in the bag? That's the first time anyone's come right out and said they had drugs in their bag," and I was so befuddled by this exchange, a trap but perhaps not a deliberate one, that I handed over the bag when asked, and he drew out the stick of testosterone and said, "What's this?" and then listed possibilities—meth, cocaine—a trap, Liam told me later, a deliberate one, and the trap worked. I hurried to write the truth—which was surely less severe than those other things—on a note on my phone and show it to him, but the truth was not, legally, so different from those other things, led to a felony arrest, which resulted not in prison—I'm lucky; I'm white—but in a number of new expenses. Five hundred dollars for bond, two hundred fifty dollars to reclaim my car, which they towed, five thousand dollars for the lawyer who argued the charge down to a misdemeanor, though the felony arrest stays on my record, is expensive to expunge, makes the expunging impossible by making employment impossible, all of this solidifies before me, and if I give it everything, if I cleave myself from myself I can form the words. I'm fine, is all I need to say. Two words would set her walking. Can't or won't. Can't or won't. And whether I cannot or will not I do not. I do not speak, do not shatter myself to avoid that future, and then the joy dives from the tree, fierce and protective, a monstrous winged thing, and I am briefly afraid for the woman, briefly imagine an ending for her in fire, briefly desire that ending, but as it dives, the joy becomes liquid, flowing over the woman, then the joy becomes something less than liquid, something that is not phase state but photon. Light-like it floods through my body, a buoyant carrying sensation that brings me to my toes, my arms tense, fingers spread, every tendon of my body taut with joy, and I know cause and effect are unidirectional, defined by the arrow of time, but too I know, with certainty, that the joy begins here. It sears through me, taking shape from the matter of my cells, emerging from me full-bodied and grown. Excappare. To get out of one's cape. I am uncloaked, and the joy always begins here. Like a light that draws you forward through a forest, it has always been ahead of us. It always, first, barrels into me, tipping me into laughter, and the softness we experience in that earliest time, which we believe is the birth of the joy is in fact its waning, trailing edge, which reaches into the past. We have been haunted by the joy, by what was yet to come, the joy that soothes me now as I wait for the woman to call the police, but the woman doesn't call. She fiddles with her phone, takes it out, puts it back, asks me what she should do, tells me she's never been in this situation before, and then finally, a large miracle, she sets a pack of seaweed snacks and a water bottle on the ground beside me and walks away. I am alone on the sidewalk, and I gaze ahead into the past and think: Look! How joyous we will be.

NOTES

7 | "An impairment in . . . their attention" is quoted from "Is Autism Like a Magic Show That Won't End?" by Geoffrey Mohan, published in the *Los Angeles Times* on October 6, 2014.

8 | "Autism as a Disorder of Prediction," by Pawan Sinha et al., published in the *Proceedings of the National Academy of Sciences* 111, no. 42 (October 2014).

18 | *Etymologies*, by Isidore of Seville, translated by Ernest Brehaut in *An Encyclopedist of the Dark Ages: Isidore of Seville*, published by Columbia University Press in 1912; 16.14.7 (modified), as quoted in *The Penguin Book of Dragons*, edited by Scott Bruce, published by Penguin Books in 2021.

18 | Revelation 12:3–5, 12:14 (Authorized King James Version).

20 | "When researchers asked . . . future events" from "Time Perception and Autistic Spectrum Condition: A Systematic Review," by Martin Casassus et al., published in *Autism Research* 12, no. 10 (October 2019); and "'No Idea of Time': Parents Report Differences in Autistic Children's Behaviour Relating to Time in a Mixed-Methods Study," by Daniel Poole et al., published in *Autism* 25, no. 6 (April 2021).

39 | Lyrics from "Best for You and Me," by Helado Negro, from the album *Phasor*, released by Private Energy in 2024.

42 | "If an autistic person's . . . scissors" from interview of Lydia Brown, *Aftereffect*, "Episode 3: 'He Was Definitely a Handful,'" hosted by Audrey Quinn, produced by Only Human, WNYC Studios, aired on June 25, 2018.

44 | When characters are signing, American Sign Language grammar is

often used instead of English grammar, though this isn't the case in every instance, as Ro and Liam are still studying and learning ASL.

59 | "Fugue," by Lucie Delarue-Mardrus, in *Nos Secrètes Amours*, published by Les Isles Édition in 1951.

61 | "The Experience of Time and Its Disorders," by Thomas Fuchs, in *The Oxford Handbook of Phenomenological Psychopathology,* edited by G. Stanghellini et al., published by Oxford University Press in 2019.

61 | "autistic children . . . sequence them" from Casassus et al., "Time Perception and Autistic Spectrum Condition."

62 | Legend of St. Margaret of Antioch from *The Golden Legend: Selections*, by Jacobus de Voragine, translated by Christopher Stace, published by Penguin Books in 1998.

67 | "Time, whose . . . entropy" from *The Order of Time*, by Carlo Rovelli, translated by Erica Segre and Simon Carnell, published by Penguin Books in 2017.

68 | "I think of the study . . . will make" from "Decoding the Contents and Strength of Imagery Before Volitional Engagement," by Roger Koenig-Robert and Joel Pearson, published in *Scientifc Reports* 9 (March 2019).

69 | "Time is ignorance" quoted from Rovelli, *Order of Time*.

70 | Lyrics from "Evelene," by Quinn Christopherson, from the album *Write Your Name in Pink*, released by Play It Again Sam in 2022.

73 | *The History of Four-Footed Beasts and Serpents*, by Edward Topsell, reprinted by E. Cotes in 1658.

74 | "Little is known . . . whales" from "Social Signals and Behaviors of Adult Alligators and Crocodiles," by Leslie D. Garrick and Jeffrey W. Lang, published in *American Zoologist* 17, no. 1 (Winter 1977); and "Social Displays of the American Alligator (*Alligator mississippiensis*)," by Kent Vliet, published in *American Zoologist* 29, no. 3 (August 1989).

74 | *The Old French Crusade Cycle, Volume 5: Les Chétifs*, translated by Douglass Hamilton, edited by Geoffrey Myers, published by the University of Alabama Press in 1981.

81 | "my brain . . . minor sparks," from "Brain Time" by David Eagleman, in *What's Next?* edited by Max Brockman, published by Vintage in 2009.

82 | Lyrics from "Mary," by Big Thief, from the album *Capacity*, released by Saddle Creek Records in 2017.

82 | "it takes up to one-tenth . . . own lives" from "A Sparse Code for Natural Sound Context in Auditory Cortex," by Mateo López Espejo and Stephen V. David, published in *Current Research in Neurobiology* 6 (2024).

83 | "Philosophers . . . happened" from "Counterfactual Dependence and Time's Arrow," by David Lewis, published in *Noûs* 13, no. 4 (1979) and described in *Time and Causality Across the Sciences*, edited by Samantha Kleinberg, published by Cambridge University Press in 2019.

92 | Lines from "Love Letters," by Victoria Chang, from *Trees Witness Everything*, published by Copper Canyon Press in 2022.

93 | "I've since learned . . . so palpable" from Rovelli, *Order of Time.*

94 | "Ludwig Boltzmann . . . Adriatic," from Rovelli, *Order of Time.*

98 | From "The Dark Night of the Soul," by St. John of the Cross, translated by David Lewis, published by Thomas Baker in 1908.

100 | *Phaedrus*, by Plato, translated by Benjamin Jowett, published by Project Gutenberg in 2008.

111 | "I could cite . . . confusion of time" from several different studies, including "Sexual Violence and Suicide Risk Among LGBTQ+ Young People," by the Trevor Project, published in 2024; "School Restroom/Locker Room Restrictions and Sexual Assault Risk Among Transgender Youth," by Gabriel R. Murchison et al., published in *Pediatrics* 143, no. 6 (2019); "Youth Characteristics Associated with Sexual Violence Perpetration Among Transgender Boys and Girls, Cisgender Boys and Girls, and Nonbinary Youth," by Michele L. Ybarra et al., published in *JAMA Network Open* 5, no. 6 (2022); and others.

144 | "Most recently . . . nothing." The performance described here is based closely on a performance by the artist Sarah Gerats. Find her work on Instagram @sarahgerats.

187 | "There is a theory . . . cause and effect" from Rovelli, *Order of Time*.

187 | "apples grow where people drink cider" quoted from Rovelli, *Order of Time*.

191 | Lyrics from "Tides," a collaboration between Bonobo and Jamila Woods, from the album *Fragments*, released by Ninja Tune in 2022.

206 | "In the stories . . . rescues him" from Topsell, *History of Four-Footed Beasts and Serpents*.

222 | "In 1967 . . . nations." Statistics about Depo-Provera from "Black Women and the Development of International Reproductive Health Norms," by Judith Scully, in *Black Women and International Law: Deliberate Interactions, Movements and Actions*, edited by Jeremy I. Levitt, published by Cambridge University Press in 2015.

223 | "One in four . . . medically necessary" from "Past and Current United States Policies of Forced Sterilization," by Jacqueline Agtuca and Kelsey Turner, published in *Restoration Magazine* in November 2020.

226 | "Distress translates . . . elicit twenty" from "Humans Recognize Emotional Arousal in Vocalizations across All Classes of Terrestrial Vertebrates: Evidence for Acoustic Universals," by Piera Filippi et al., published in *Proceedings of the Royal Society B* 284 (July 2017); and "Hear Them Roar: A Comparison of Black-Capped Chickadee (*Poecile atricapillus*) and Human (*Homo sapiens*) Perception of Arousal in Vocalizations Across All Classes of Terrestrial Vertebrates," by Jenna V. Congdon et al., published in *Journal of Comparative Psychology* 133, no. 4 (November 2019).

228 | "One theory . . . threshold" from "A Neural Mechanism for Sensing and Reproducing a Time Interval," by Mehrdad Jazayeri and Michael N. Shadlen, published in *Current Biology* 25, no. 20 (October 2015).

237 | "Early explosives . . . opponents" from "Ming China as a Gunpowder Empire: Military Technology, Politics, and Fiscal Administration, 1350–1620," by Weicong Duan (PhD dissertation, Washington University in St. Louis, 2018); and *Thirty Great Inventions of China: From Millet Agriculture to Artemisinin*, edited by Jueming Hua and Lisheng Feng, published by Springer Singapore in 2020. Different versions of military manuals from the Ming Dynasty are referenced (the *Huolongjing*, the *Huolong shenqi zhenfa*, and others). Some scholars argue that some or all of these were

in fact compiled later or are fake. While several articles insist the weapon described was included in the *Huolongjing*, I was unable to verify this.

237 | "Animal linguist . . . snake" from "Alarm Calls Evoke a Visual Search Image of a Predator in Birds," by Toshitaka N. Suzuki, published in *Proceedings of the National Academy of Sciences* 115, no. 7 (January 2018); and "The Animals Are Talking. What Does It Mean?," by Sonia Shah, published in *The New York Times Magazine* on September 20, 2023.

241 | "The gene . . . time" from "TIMELESS Mutation Alters Phase Responsiveness and Causes Advanced Sleep Phase," by Philip Kurien et al., published in *Proceedings of the National Academy of Sciences* 116, no. 24 (June 2019).

242 | "It is Pope Gregory . . . Hellmouth" as translated by Scott Bruce from *Dialogorum libri quattuor*, by Gregory the Great, included in *Patrologiae Cursus Completus: Series Latina* 66 and 77, edited by J. P. Migne, published by Apud Editorem in Paris in 1859 and 1896, cited in Bruce, *Penguin Book of Dragons*.

243 | "We hear silence . . . continuous tone" from "The Perception of Silence," by Rui Zhe Goh et al., published in *Proceedings of the National Academy of Sciences* 120, no. 29 (July 2023).

246 | "show the hammer which hits the bell" quoted from *A Historical and Etymological Dictionary of American Sign Language*, by Emily Shaw and Yves Delaporte, published by Gallaudet University Press in 2015.

ACKNOWLEDGMENTS

With immense gratitude to Meredith Kaffel Simonoff for your fierce support and your exceptional ability to make my work both sharper and kinder, and to Jackson Howard for your precise and discerning edits and for the care and deliberateness with which you've brought this work into the world. I'm so thrilled to work with both of you. Eliza Rudalevige, thanks for your support across all axes and your excellent editing eye. And thanks to the rest of the team at MCD/FSG, especially Logan Hill, Janine Barlow, and Andrew Jacobs. Thanks to Charlotte Grimm for a great cover.

To the friends who read early versions of this book and helped me understand it more clearly—Charlie, 'Pemi, Swetha, Maya, Xueyi, Maryam, Daphne, Alessandra, and Itai—your brilliance amazes me, and my life is so much better for your company. Thank you. I love you.

KT, thank you for your generous notes about ASL.

This novel would never have been written without the support of numerous residencies and fellowships, including Hawthornden Castle, the Sitka Center for Art and Ecology, the Southern Studies Fellowship, and especially Black Mountain Institute, where I finished the first draft. Thank you for the invaluable gifts of shelter and time.

To Pawan Sinha, Margaret M. Kjelgaard, Tapan K. Gandhi, Kleovoulos Tsourides, Annie L. Cardinaux, Dimitrios

Pantazis, Sidney P. Diamond, and Richard M. Held, thank you for the magical world theory and "Autism as a Disorder of Prediction." Your article shifted my perspectives on time and causality and was a central inspiration for the novel.

To the many autistic authors to whose work *Mad Eden* is greatly indebted, particularly Anand Prahlad and Viktoria Lloyd-Barlow, your stories kept me company in a lonely time and did more to help me understand myself than any diagnosis.

Candy, thanks for the adventures.

Em, you read this book so many times it is surely partly yours, thanks for reminding me again and again how to write and live with joy.

To the people who continue to work toward health equity in an increasingly hostile country, risking life and livelihood, thank you.

A NOTE ABOUT THE AUTHOR

Morgan Thomas is the author of the story collection *Manywhere*, which was a finalist for the Pen/Robert W. Bingham Prize, the Los Angeles Times Art Seidenbaum Award for First Fiction, the Lambda Literary Award for Transgender Fiction, and the Publishing Triangle Edmund White Award for Debut Fiction. Their writing has appeared in *The Paris Review*, *The Atlantic*, *The Kenyon Review*, *American Short Fiction*, and other publications.